D1260789

Beautiful
Me

Natasha Jennings

BALBOA.
PRESS

A DIVISION OF HAY HOUSE

Balboa Press books may be ordered through booksellers or by contacting:

Balboa Press
A Division of Hay House
1663 Liberty Drive
Bloomington, IN 47403
www.balboapress.com
1 (877) 407-4847

Because of the dynamic nature of the Internet, any web addresses or
links contained in this book may have changed since publication and
may no longer be valid. The views expressed in this work are solely those
of the author and do not necessarily reflect the views of the publisher,
and the publisher hereby disclaims any responsibility for them.

The author of this book does not dispense medical advice or prescribe
the use of any technique as a form of treatment for physical, emotional,
or medical problems without the advice of a physician, either directly
or indirectly. The intent of the author is only to offer information
of a general nature to help you in your quest for emotional and
spiritual well-being. In the event you use any of the information in
this book for yourself, which is your constitutional right, the author
and the publisher assume no responsibility for your actions.

Any people depicted in stock imagery provided by Thinkstock are
models, and such images are being used for illustrative purposes only.
Certain stock imagery © Thinkstock.

Printed in the United States of America.

ISBN: 978-1-4525-1389-8 (sc)
ISBN: 978-1-4525-1390-4 (e)

Balboa Press rev. date: 06/26/2014

For all those that have
struggled with
food, weight and body image.
May you find your
beautiful me.

September 29

So I run to the door as fast as I can ... dragging my suitcase and handbag. 'You can't leave, Talia,' screeches some hideous looking witch who calls herself Amanda, 'you're committed under the Mental Health Act.'

'Like fuck I am,' I yell, grabbing the door handle and pulling with all my strength. The hideous witch ... big fucken nose; bet she had the wart removed ... and some other bitch grab my arms. I break free and swing my handbag, whacking the witch's big nose so hard she collapses ... blood everywhere.

The next thing I know people come running from all directions, the witch is screaming ... I am grabbed, dragged ... dragged and pulled like an escapee from jail. Where are the handcuffs? They shove me into a locked area they call timeout. Two assholes sit across from me, one reading magazines, the other attempting some kind of conversation with me.

'I understand you want to leave, but honey, you're not well.'

Honey! Like the fuck I'm her honey. Truth is I feel like spitting at her. If I had my handbag ... in fact if I had my suitcase and I could swing it ... fancy calling an anorexic honey. Dah! What fucken nursing school did she train at!? Oh yeah ... the one that specialises in assholes.

September 30

FUCK!

October 1

I'm scared diary. Scared.

This place is full to overflowing with mad and weird looking people. I saw this girl with a long auburn braid and a silver ring in her nose smash a guitar over a nurse's back. She was screaming and cursing and waving her arms like a complete and utter psycho. A male nurse had to direct the rest of us nutters out of the TV lounge and god knows what happened next but I could hear, 'Mother fuckers ... cunts,' and all sorts for some time. She freaked me out.

And diary some of them talk to themselves. Mumble and mutter to god knows who.

And there's this one young boy ... maybe fourteen, blond messy hair ... he can't talk at all. A nurse holds his hand so he can slowly walk. Bulging blue eyes staring straight ahead like there's nothing there. They barely blink. It's like he's gone and I don't know where.

This place scares the shit out of me and I just don't think I belong.

And I feel ... I feel so sorry for the mad-looking bastards. Makes me want to pace even faster. Walk. Move. Get away.

Disappear.

Later ... 2am or thereabout.

That's it ... I just want to keep moving. And moving and moving and moving ... never stop.

October 2

So I've been told that if I continue to lose weight ... lost 400g since arriving ... they are going to tube feed me. I said, 'Like fuck you are!'

'Sweetie, you are 31 kilos ...'

'Yeah 31, not 21.'

'Do you understand that every organ in your body is stressed? You are at risk of heart failure.'

'Whatever,' I laugh. 'I'm the fittest person in this place.'

'Reality check, you are very unwell. Your body is starving. Emaciated.'

It was at this stage I stood up and walked out of our, oh so boring, doctor's consultation. Of which of course I was followed by this fucken nurse. A nurse follows me constantly. Like a fucken black shadow ... a dark ghost haunting me, repeating over and over, 'Slow down, Talia. Walk slower. Slower. Sit down.'

'Sit down!'

I have to walk like a retarded snail and sit like an obese slug. I can't even stand watching TV or doing the craft activities. It's like I'm the only one that can see clearly, everyone around me has mist in their pupils and it's driving me fucken crazy.

PS ... I had a smile as wide as a dolphin when I was told I had lost weight.

October 3

Well now I have a fucken nurse on guard outside my room at night. Sitting there hour after hour. Minute after minute. When the hell am I supposed to work out now? I was up to sets of 100 sit ups and 30 press ups. This place is going to drive me cuckoo like every other nutcase here!

October 4

Had a visit from Mum and Grant this morning, she refused to bring me in the chewing gum that I asked her for. 'It's a laxative and the staff here said it's forbidden,' she says, filing her nails: Mum has nails like a film star.

'Mum,' I said, 'I ask you for one thing, one little thing and you can't even do that for me.'

'Talia, I would but I'm not allowed.'

'Whatever. You're the one who fucken signed me in here.'

Grant puts his hairy and hefty arm around Mum's scrawny shoulder and says, 'Don't speak to your Mum like that.'

'Don't tell me what to do … you're not my fucken father,' I glare. I mean … who the hell does he think he is … they've only been married five minutes. 'I'm outta here!' And I storm off with some dark fucken ghost shadow; name badge Julie; screeching, 'Slow down. Walk slower, Talia.'

'Talia!'

October 6

I'm down again. Another 200 grams. Relieved?

YES!!

October 7

The doctor said she wants to prescribe some drug, Lorazepam. She wants me to have it prior to each meal.

'If I wasn't forced to eat so much it wouldn't be a problem. And the food, it's not even the sort of food I eat. Bananas … I don't care how much potassium they contain, they taste like crap. And what's with the full cream milk, haven't you ever heard of heart disease? And yoghurt … full cream yoghurt. I thought this was a hospital! Like healthy and that. And butter, bloody hell … butter on my toast and a whole piece. I only ever eat half.'

And you know diary, she just looks at me through those black rimmed glasses, scratching her wrinkly forehead and smiles, 'Those are issues you need to take up with your dietitian.'

Like isn't she the doctor? Oh no not a real doctor, a fucken nutcase doctor!

Well I am not taking any Lorazepam or any antidepressant. What would she know? … she doesn't even have the intelligence to know what's good for your heart.

October 8

It's 2am … the nurse is there, some slitty-eyed Asian bitch … sprawled out in that navy blue armchair … like a vicious Asian crocodile about to bite if I so much as climb out of bed (not even sure if crocodiles live in Asia but you know what I mean). I so want to exercise diary, I want to move and move and move and move again. And again. I don't feel well. I don't feel well inside.

Sick.

October 8

Well I say fuck the lot of them! If I don't want to eat, why the hell should I?! I'm sick of arguing every day, every meal.

I say, 'Can I just take the ham out the sandwich?'

'No.'

'What if I just eat half?'

'No.'

'Maybe if I just take the cheese out then.'

'No.'

'If we made another one that had no butter. Really I don't like butter.'

'No.'

'Can I swap for an apple or even a banana? And I hate bananas but I'll try really hard today … I'll try my best to eat it.'

'No.'

Well as you can imagine I'm so frustrated by now that I inform the unsociable and rather unpleasant bitch of a nurse, Taylor: who should visit one by the state of the clothes she's wearing, 'I am not drinking that juice … it's full of sugar.' Diabetes as with heart disease is promoted in this place!

'Talia,' she says; and I thought she only knew one word! … 'the juice is on your meal plan.'

'I'm not drinking it, I'll have water instead.'

'What say you just eat the sandwich and worry about the juice later?'

'I don't like ham.'

'I know.'

'I don't like cheese.'

'I know.'

'I don't like butter.'

'Yeah,' and she's beginning to yawn, pulling at a strand of her black hair, 'I know.'

'Did you have a late night?' I ask, smiling.

'Just eat Talia. Should I ask Julie over there to get a damp cold flannel? You're sweating.'

'Maybe if they turned the heating down it wouldn't be so damn hot!'

'Flannel?'

'Please.'

'Julie,' she calls out, 'will you fetch a cold flannel for Talia?'

'Sure,' says Julie, walking briskly towards the linen cupboards.

'I know,' I say, wiping my brow, 'what if ... what if I leave the sandwich and just drink the juice?'

'No.'

Well fuck no and fuck Taylor who should go on some makeover TV programme to sort out her ridiculous dress sense. Yellow and red just don't go ... what is she? On fire.

And Julie, well Julie she can go suck that wet flannel ... either that or I'll shove it down her fucken throat.

Every day diary, I have to defend my right to eat or not eat. Every day I have to argue with some bitch or bastard of a nurse and I'm over it.

Over and fucken out.

I say to them all ... fuck the fuck off. Go on just fuck off and eat it yourself. Yeah that's it diary, that's exactly what I say, actually I yell it at the top of my voice,

'YOU EAT IT!'

October 9

I just had a dream … a nightmare, my palms are sweaty but I feel cold. I'm shivering and I can't breathe.

I'm too scared to tell you what I dreamed … too ashamed. I think this place is making me psychotic like the other poor bastards in here. Maybe that's it … maybe you go home more fucked up than when you first arrived.

That slitty-eyed crocodile is back again in the armchair outside my room. I wish she would pull up her chair next to my bed … I'm too scared to sleep. I'm so scared diary … I'm scared of food.

October 10

Yesterday I had my weigh in. I drank as much water as I could but I still had lost weight. Another 200 grams.

First thing in the morning the black ghost marches me off to the surgery room. I'm not allowed to even get dressed. I have to walk down the corridor in my blue floral pajamas … totally undignified! Then she takes my blood pressure, pulse and temperature … fuck knows why … some other lady in a white lab coat takes my blood … something to do with electrolytes … then finally I have to stand on these white electronic scales.

'Another 200grams,' she mutters, sighing heavily … with the size of that sigh you'd think I'd done something really bad like robbery … 'Talia … let us help you. You're …'

'I'm what?' I ask.

'Doesn't matter.'

'Yes it does what?'

She bites her lip, puts her hand on my shoulder, 'You are so thin and getting thinner. You're ... your blood pressure is low, too low. Something has to change, Talia. You need to start working with us. The medical team ... we are going to have a meeting this afternoon, you can't go on losing weight.'

'Yeah I can.'

'No you can't,' she says, shaking her head and rubbing the back of her neck. 'No you cannot.'

I don't believe, Julie, my morning dark shadow. Fuck her.

Fat bitch.

October 10

Just had a run in with Amanda. She caught me hiding my muesli bar up the sleeve of my jersey. And the cheese in my socks. Shit ... I'm usually so careful, I think they were questioning why I was still losing weight ... watching me like a fucken hawk.

Now not only will I have a nurse sitting opposite me ... supporting me to eat ... their words not mine! ... but now they'll have an oversize magnifying glass in each hand ... studying my every move.

SHIT.

I ended up throwing it … well actually them, the cheese and muesli bar that is, on the floor and storming off to my bedroom. Of course Amanda followed behind, red faced and fuming. Man, I'm not a violent person … but I so felt like turning around and charging at her like a bull. Maybe it was that red face … provoking the bull in me. 'Talia,' she screeches, 'Talia … you need to eat your afternoon tea.'

'Not hungry,' I inform her. 'Piss off.'

'It's not about being hungry. You know that.' She looked so frustrated and pissed off; despite pretending to be calm… I had to laugh. I think that pissed her off even more. Which of course made me laugh even more.

She reminds me of my Mum. Leggy, blond, exasperated and thick.

October 11

Had that dream again. Diary please don't tell anyone … I'm whispering as I write this … I dreamed that I was swimming in a sea of food. Donuts and cream buns and custard and milky-bar chocolate. The food was everywhere, all over me, swimming towards me like schools of fish. And I was the shark, engulfing it all like I was starved.

Oh diary … this place is making me go mad. It's making me hungry … and I … I …I can't.

Susie the night nurse; she reminds me of a child she's so small; heard me shaking and asked what was wrong. I told her I was cold and needed a blanket. She got me one and laid it on top of me, real gentle like. She said, 'Warm enough? If not I'll get Simon to get a hot water bottle.'

'Please,' I said.

The hot water bottle was so nice to cuddle until I began to panic thinking it was fish and chips, wrapped up in newspaper like when I was a kid. And I'd cuddle the packet and sniff in that smell. That yummy fish and chip smell ... diary ... I am going mad.

I threw it out of the bed, told little Susie I was warm. But diary I was shaking.

Shaking inside and out.

October 12

Diary ... can I tell you a secret ... sometimes, sometimes I run my hands over my pelvis, my ribs, my collar bones ... they remind me of judder bars. I know I am thin. There are moments when I feel like an old, old woman ... dying.

Dying of cancer or Aids or something. Dissolving into the earth like dirt in rain.

Diary ... I feel weak, tired and unwell. Sick in every cell of my skinny, repulsive body.

But diary, I like it ... I like the feeling I am disappearing.

Safe.

October 13

Another dream, another nightmare … food trying to eat its way into me. The shark was being eaten by the schools of fish. I got out of bed; started running on the spot. 'Talia, Talia, no,' echoes a voice in the darkness.

She turns on the light and I don't give a shit I just keep on running. Faster and faster and faster and faster. 'Talia,' she says, 'please stop. Stop it now.'

She grabs me, grabs me by the arms and says, 'No, Talia, no.'

I feel all dizzy and spinny and feel my heart heaving through my chest like a hurricane. It's the slitty-eyed crocodile. She sits me back on the bed and says, 'What's going on?'

'I just … I dun know … needed to go for a run.'

'You are shaking.'

'No I'm hot,' I tell her, I feel like there is a fire in my lungs.

'Did you have a bad dream? I heard you calling out.'

'No,' I tell her. 'Can you get out my room … please? I want to go back to sleep.'

She goes back to her armchair and I snuggle in my bed with my head under the blankets. I started to imagine strangling myself with the sheets. I wonder how hard that would be.

October 14

Down again … 200 grams. Another frowning, grumpy bitch nurse … treating me like a disappointing daughter, which is maybe appropriate, as having a daughter locked up in a lunatic asylum has to be pretty disappointing!

October 15

Had a visit from Anna and Maggie. They brought me some magazines and purple grapes. I can't believe they were my friends … that we used to hang out and go to the mall and stuff. Seems so long ago. Like a story I read as a child. I'm not sure I like them anymore, not sure I like anyone … least of all me. Wonder why they wanted to visit me? … fucked up me!

October 16

Lost another 100 grams which makes me 30.1 … I know it sounds low but …

Anyhow … apparently they had a big meeting about me today. Mum was allowed to go but not me. How rude is that. I'm fed fucken up with this shit hole and their constant harassment of my rights. I don't even have the right to go to the bathroom alone. I feel like running away, oh but wait, I'm not allowed to run and the fucken doors are locked.

Later … Diary today, please don't tell anyone but … I feel thin. Incredibly thin and weak … tired. So so tired.

I am a grain of black coarse sand in the ocean.

A dot.

October 19

I was escorted to a room down the end of the ward by not only one nurse but two. I should've known then. When I entered the room there was another two nurses and my psychiatrist. She was sitting there looking at papers and files over her black-rimmed glasses.

'Talia,' she says, 'the team has made a decision that you are to be tube-fed. I know that scares you but we believe it is the best possible option for your care at the moment. When you have gained weight and are willing to work with us, instead of against us … we will introduce a meal plan again.'

I run for the door. No one runs after me … it's locked.

Diary … it was the worse day ever. I was like an insect caught in a web. Five blood sucking spiders about to suck out what life in me I had left.

'Please, no,' I pleaded. 'I'll eat. I promise.'

'No Talia,' she replies. 'You can't make that promise. You are too sick.'

'I'm not. I'm not.' I can feel my insides begin to cook, fry. I wipe the sweat from my forehead. I turn to Julie. 'Please.'

Julie smiles and says, 'We just want you well. Let us make you well.'

So much of the rest is a blur. A horrible blur.

I know I screamed at the top of my lungs. I kicked, I hit … I scratched. I yelled out, 'Please don't make me fat. I don't want to be fat. Please.' Which is true because I don't want to be, most people don't do they.

They pinned me to the ground, a nurse holding my legs, my arms, even my head … I was rolled over, pants pulled down. Given an injection in the bottom. Oh diary I screamed and begged and pleaded. But I received no mercy … no kindness.

Eventually the injection made me feel like I was sinking into the carpet. Floating like clouds. And diary I was so tired. So exhausted … it was like I was a wilting weed. Nothing left.

Then while each limb was held; I actually don't think they needed to anymore; Julie inserted a tube through my nostril all the way down into my stomach. It was not long later that I was fed something called Ensure, followed by warm water.

The tube is taped to the bridge of my nose and cheek and hung over my ear. I must look pathetic. I've pulled it out once … but diary … I don't have any fight left. I'm tired. Very very tired. And I don't feel well inside. Fragile … like tears are leaking from every pore in my body.

Every weary cell.

Tears … and I don't cry … haven't for years.

October 23

They won't let me see my weight any more, said it causes me too much anxiety. A paper towel is placed over the top. But I know the weight is climbing. I can feel it. I can feel myself expanding. How could it not with all that Ensure they are pouring into my stomach. Overnight I am connected to some machine that looks like an intravenous drip … it drips Ensure all night, through my nostril and into my swelling belly. Sometimes the machine beeps and the nurse in the armchair outside my room comes in and releases an air bubble or puts up more Ensure. It is … I am … maybe I could wrap that tube around my throat and pull it till I'm blue.

October 24

Not much to say … spent the day staring at magazines and the cream of my bedroom walls. Listening to my iPod at times. I'm not allowed to attend any activities, not allowed to hardly move … truth is that suits me just fine. Maybe that Lorazepam has … I'm tired.

That's all, tired.

October 25

Bed rest is boring and long and long and so fucken long.

October 27

I had the most awful dream. I was laying there, nothing or no one holding me down … but I couldn't move. Couldn't move a single limb. Fingertips were softly touching my face and lips and I couldn't move … couldn't brush them away.

I woke up, got out of bed … turned the light on. It still felt dark. It's morning and it still feels dark.

Later …

I ripped out the tube today. Julie entered my room pushing that small silver trolley containing all the equipment for feeding: syringe, litmus paper, water and stuff. And I just looked at it … looked at her, down at her green sneakers, back at the Ensure on the trolley, into her green eyes, at her small hands, at her engagement ring; ruby not diamond … deep deep red … red. Shake my head and just reach across to the side of my face and pull. Tug … tug and pull until the tube came all the way out of my nostril.

And it felt good … good good good.

'Talia … why did you … we just have to put it back in again,' says Julie. 'You know that.'

'I know,' I say, nodding my head and closing my eyes. 'I know.'

She sits down next to me on my bed and says, 'Then why did you pull it out? You've been so good with it all lately. Did something happen?'

'No,' I say. 'I'm only good because I have no choice. No rights.'

'We just want to get you well.'

I look at her, look real hard and say, 'Sometimes I don't want to be well.'

'Why? Don't you miss your friends, your family … your twin brothers, don't you miss your studies and sport. I hear you were a talented footballer.'

'No … sometimes I guess. I just don't want to be fat.'

She takes my hand in hers and says, 'I promise Talia, no one here will make you fat, just well, just healthy. Like you used to be.'

'But I felt fat. Ugly.'

'You are very thin, Talia, tell me do you still feel fat?'

'I do,' I say, nodding my head. 'Obese and ugly.'

'So that's the journey … to learn to feel beautiful in your own skin, in your own beautiful and soon to be healthy body. And when you are well enough a therapist will work with you to achieve that. But right now … that tube needs to go back in. Do I need nurses to hold you or can I just put it back in?'

'What's the litmus paper for?' I ask later.

'That, Talia, is to ensure it's the stomach the tube is in and not your lungs. So we use this syringe and draw back stomach contents and then test the contents on the litmus paper. Like this.'

We both watch as the litmus paper turns pink.

'Good stomach acid you have.'

'Julie … do you think I can get well?'

'Of course … really well,' she smiles.

'I'm not sure I can. Not sure I … just not sure.'

'Hold on to hope and hope … it will hold on to you,' she says, looking up from the Ensure she is organising for my feed. 'I say that and I dearly believe it. Hope Talia, hope holds on tight … it reaches out if you reach towards it. It will meet you so much more than halfway.'

I think diary, if I ever get well and … if I ever have a daughter, I'll call her Hope.

October 29

I've been thinking about what Julie said, about feeling beautiful in my own skin. Beautiful? Does anyone really feel like that? Is that possible? The thought makes me feel all squirmy and uncomfortable. Not sure why … just does. I really want to ask her if she feels beautiful, even comfortable in her body. But I … well seems like a … just I don't want to embarrass her … she's kinda full-figured, big bust and that. She's not as much as a bitch as I first thought … she's even kinda nice. But beautiful … what is beautiful … I don't know. That's a foreign word to me.

You know I was good at football … I stopped playing when I was sixteen. I stopped playing because I was so uncomfortable in the uniform. Shorts. Blue shorts with a thin white strip and all I could think about was how big my thighs must look. How repulsive. I couldn't concentrate on chasing the ball when all I could think about was how fat everyone must think I looked.

The thing is ... all my muscles have dissolved ... I know my legs are little, thin even, but I still feel incredibly fat. I still wouldn't want to play ... wouldn't want all eyes observing their oversized ugliness. I wonder if anyone looks at their own legs and thinks, gosh you're gorgeous. What beautiful legs.

Somehow ... that seems insane.

November 2

Same old ... tube feeds, bed rest ... getting fatter each day. Trying real hard not to think about it ... I think that's why I've not been writing much. Trying to pretend it's not happening. But I know ... I can feel my skin expanding. Part of me wants to scream ... another part ... she's holding on to hope.

November 4

I'm eighteen today. Eighteen and locked up ... cuckoo and fucked.

Later ...

Mum and Grant bought Mac and Sol to visit today. I was so embarrassed and ashamed ... sitting there with the tube taped to the side of my face and draped over my ear like some kind of sicko. It was so lovely to see my little brothers ... they looked so blond and cute and squeezy and smoochy ... but I so hadn't wanted them to see me in hospital. I had told Mum not to bring them in until I said so ... she didn't listen. I guess that doesn't surprise me.

They wrapped their little arms around me and kissed me on each cheek. 'Happy birthday,' they squealed.

I felt all uncomfortable but I pretended to be fine … didn't want to upset them.

They each gave me a present. A cereal box with a painting folded up inside. Well actually, Mac's was neatly folded and Sol's kinda just screwed up. That made me laugh … so typical of their funny little personalities. The cereal boxes were wrapped in newspaper … Mac's neat and tidy, Sol's messy and so him.

'What beautiful paintings, I love rainbows and suns,' I said, smiling, 'I'll hang them in my room.'

Mum gave me a new cell phone; silver Nokia; my old one broke ages ago. Well that's what I told her. I just kinda stopped using it. Didn't feel much like texting or that anymore. Still don't. Grant and the boys also made a carrot cake with cream cheese icing. That used to be my favorite. They sung happy birthday which was nice but kinda awkward. Kinda embarrassing. Then Mum and I sat and watched the twins and Grant eat the cake like it was their last meal.

'Yum,' says Mac, licking his fingers.

'Yummy,' says Sol, smearing white icing all over his face.

'Delicious,' says Grant, with his mouth full. 'We made great cake boys. Have a piece, Kim.'

'No thanks,' says Mum. 'Watching my … not hungry.' I don't think I've ever seen Mum eat cake … ever.

November 5

Got a big surprise today. Maggie and Anna turned up for my birthday. Brought me perfume and nail polish.

Anna's like, 'Wanted to come yesterday but couldn't borrow Mum's car. God I need my own wheels.'

'You've cut your hair ... it looks real pretty ... a short bob,' I say, running my fingers through my own dark mess.

'Don't you just love the color?' smiles Maggie 'What's it called, Anna?'

'Iced chocolate,' grins Anna. 'It's like this really cool mousse dye. You don't have to wet your hair first or anything.'

'We could get you some, Talia. Bring it in and do your hair for you if you're allowed,' says Maggie. 'Makes it look all glossy and shiny and that.'

'Oh ... thanks,' I say, 'but I don't think the nurses would let me. Might get all over the tube and stuff. Or even in it.'

Truth is diary ... I've never dyed my hair and it feels a bit freaky to let Maggie and Anna ... the nurses probably wouldn't let me anyhow, although Maggie's like, 'Can't they just take it out or something?'

'Take it out or something,' I repeat like a stupid parrot, 'ar no ... I don't think so.'

'Oh ok then ... give us your toes then and we'll paint your toenails,' Maggie says, pulling up her golden brown hair into a pony.

And with that she jumps up out of her chair, kneels at my feet, removes my blue socks and proceeds to paint my toenails crimson. Very embarrassing but cool.

Oh and diary ... I do like the color.

November 7

On the way to the visitor's room to see Mum, I saw this new girl. Maybe fifteen or sixteen, actually she looked so hideously thin it was hard to tell. Angry brown eyes looking out from this skeletal face. Blond hair that could seriously do with a cut ... hairdryer? ... perhaps. She had the pace of an Olympian walker with nurse Kendall following ... chasing behind, 'Slow down, Lila,' says Kendall. 'Lila ... slow down!'

I haven't had a black shadow or dark ghost following behind me for some time now. Probably about the time I decided that it was Me, that was the black, dark shadow ghost and the nurses, they were more like annoying white lights ... one or two even white angels. The funny thing was ... I missed them at first. Now I just get checked every fifteen minutes or so. Although a nurse usually hangs out with me for about half an hour after a feed.

It was Julie that hung out today. She's a bit of a white angel. Anyway I said to her, 'Did I look as thin as that new girl, Lila, when I first came in.'

She laughed, 'Talia, you still do.'

'I still do. Really?'

'Yeah, really.'

'Oh.'

November 9

So I had a meeting with my psychiatrist today, only just found out her name, it's Arleen Adelaide. Although, I discovered, she prefers Doctor Adelaide ... after I called her Arleen. I went so red but personally I think she's being a bit pretentious ... don't you? I guess they train hard for the title but still!

Anyhow, she's like, 'We think, the nurses and I that is, that you are doing really well and it is time to remove the tube and reintroduce a meal plan. How do you feel about that, happy?'

'Oh ...' I mutter.

'You can go back to the original meal plan you had or work on a new one with the dietitian. What would you prefer?'

'Oh ...' I say, 'um um.'

'Well you think about it then and consult the nursing staff. Or Taylor over there,' pointing in the direction of Taylor sitting in a chair next to me. 'She's your nurse for the day isn't she?'

'That's why I'm here,' smiles Taylor, looking awful in that pink and white polka-dotted cardigan. Still she's nice most the time.

'Oh ok,' I say, starting to analyse the surroundings. The pot plant in the corner, a peace lily I think, the stripy blinds ... different shades of blue and the palm outside blowing against the window.

I feel this sudden dislike for Doctor Arleen with her wrinkly face and small china blue eyes highlighted by her black framed glasses. She's a bit like Taylor and needs a major makeover.

I stand up, 'If that's all ...I'll be off.' I open the door and look back at the Doctor ... she could definitely do with a haircut! ... smile and say, 'Thanks, Arleen.'

November 10

Its 2 am ... had that yuck dream where I can't move. It's like I'm frozen in time ... like those people made of candle wax, those stars in museums. I've seen pictures in magazines. They look like the star but are lacking life in their eyes and expressions. I guess a bit like being dead and embalmed.

Dead.

I wish a nurse would walk past, just so I know I'm not alone. Diary ... I feel so alone. Alone and starving for something but I don't know what. Like there's no one or nothing to hold on to and like I'm falling. Falling through the very earth that supports my feet. Have you ever felt like that?

I wish ... I wish sometimes I could just disappear. Dissolve.

Be unseen ... unheard.

Untouched.

Diary … does that mean I'm fucked?

November 11

Julie arrives first thing this morning, bright and cheery, raving on about the beautiful day, pushing that silver trolley. I've hardly had time to wake up and she's like, 'Let's get that tube out shall we.'

I'm like, 'Is your hair naturally that red or do you dye it?'

'Umm … oh it's all natural.' She looks puzzled.

'Nice color,' I say.

'I use to hate it when I was your age but yeah now I love it. Right ready then?'

'What about the wave … is that blow dried, is it actually real curly like a lot of red heads and you straighten it?'

'Talia is there a … it's all natural, the wave, the color. What about yours, it's amazingly dark,' she says, pulling up a chair and sitting down.

I lay back down on my bed and say, 'It's dark … like my father's.'

'When's the last time you saw him?'

'Don't know … can't recall. My hair use to be the same length as yours … I had it cut just before I came to hospital.

It was so dry … like pigs hair. Seem to be moulting like a dog too.'

'You suit short hair,' she smiles. 'Highlights those big dark eyes and lashes.'

'I bet you say that to all your nutty patients.'

'Talia … you are very pretty.'

'So it's a nice day outside,' I say, feeling awkward. I'm not sure I like being called pretty.

Julie leans forward and says, 'Are you worried about the tube coming out? Are you worried about eating food?'

'I just think,' I say, sitting back up, 'that I should meet with my dietitian to discuss a few things.'

'You met her yesterday.'

'Yeah I know … I have a few more questions. Can I just have the Ensure this morning and meet with her today sometime?'

'I'll have to see if she's available,' Julie sighs. 'You're scared aren't you?'

'It's just I'm use to the tube now … and 1200 to 1500 calories a day seems so much.'

'The Ensure you've been having has as much calories.'

'I know,' I sigh heavily. 'But I don't have to … just I don't know.'

'You don't have to what?' asks Julie, running her fingers through her hair.

'I don't have to …'

'Yeah?'

'Chew.'

'You don't have to chew and swallow the food. Is that right?'

I lower my head and wriggle my toes, 'Yeah.'

'Oh … ok,' she smiles. 'What say we give you the Ensure now, I'll have to go get some first and then I'll page the dietitian? Ok?'

'Ok.'

November 12

The dietitian wasn't available yesterday … I'm meeting her today at 10 am. So the tubes still in and the Ensures still going down.

Diary … I am scared. I never thought I'd confess to such weirdness but I wish the tube could stay in forever. Eating food is like being a baby and learning how to walk. I can't even crawl … in fact I don't think I can even roll over.

I might need to talk to Doctor Arleen about upping the Lorazepam or putting me down. The latter sounds attractive!

November 14

I've been too screwed to even write … too fucked in the head and fucked off at every bastard that exists. In fact I still feel that way!

November 15

I said to the dietitian that day I met her, you know a few days ago, 'Why the full cream milk? Isn't it full of saturated fat?'

The funny thing is she is super tiny and super trim and super fit looking. Short dark hair like me. Only … gorgeous face.

'You need the calories. And you need the fat.'

Well fuck her I do not need the fat! 'Why?' I ask, tapping my feet.

'Talia … fat in our diets is actually a necessary thing. Our brains are made up of saturated fat … ever heard of a foggy brain?'

Yeah I have one. 'No.'

'A foggy brain can be due to a diet with insufficient fat. And the linings in our intestines … saturated fat. The thing is it's all about moderation. A little bit of some things and a lot of others like fruit and veg.'

'But four servings of full cream dairy seems so excessive.'

'Talia … four servings of calcium-rich dairy products is exactly what your body needs.'

'I bet you don't eat full cream.'

'Sometimes I do ... I prefer the goodness and taste of full cream yoghurts but tend to stick with trim milk. On occasion I eat ice cream. Talia ... the thing is I'm healthy ... I'm at a healthy weight. I eat a nutritious and yummy diet. I love to eat but I listen to when I'm full and what my body needs.'

'Do you work out,' I ask, looking at her muscular calves. 'You look like you do.'

'I love exercise ... I swim, do Pilates and go to the gym. Love going on long walks and looking at the surroundings. We all need exercise, for our bodies and our minds. And when you are well, exercise will be great for you too. But Talia, I know when to rest ... I know when to relax ... I listen to my body.'

'Do you think ...?'

'Yeah?'

'Do you think I could ever be like that? Be able to listen to my body?'

'Talia,' she says, leaning forward and smiling warmly, 'I know you can.'

What do you reckon diary? That would be a miracle wouldn't it? Listening to my body feels about as foreign as Spanish.

November 16

So I'm back to arguing and debating, chewing my food about a thousand times before swallowing. But diary I am swallowing. I am trying and no one here gets how fucken stressed I am. Maybe except Lila, who's still being chased about by her dark fucken shadow. And who still looks like a skeleton on roller skates. I'm sure I'm twice her size by now. I fucken feel like I am. Everything's getting tighter ... I'll need a new wardrobe soon. My thighs are looking like clumps of lard and I feel like running on the spot a million trillion times. But I don't. I just keep on eating like a good little girl and drinking that full cream milk, waiting for all that saturated fat to find its way to my brain ... so it can let the sun shine and clear up all that fog.

November 17

Here's my meal plan ... you tell me if you don't think that's too much food!

Breakfast

1 piece toast (buttered, jam or honey, vegemite etc)

Half cup cereal with half a cup full cream milk

250mls pure juice

Morning Tea

250mls full cream milk or juice

2 biscuits or 2 cheese crackers or 1 muesli bar

Lunch

2 bread with butter

A protein filling (ham, cheese, humus, chicken, egg)

A salad filling (tomato, lettuce, cucumber etc)

250mls pure Juice

Afternoon tea

1 full fat yoghurt

250mls full cream milk or pure juice

Dinner

Small trayline meal with the dessert (not just jelly option, has to be ice cream, sponge and custard, apple crumble and cream etc)

Supper

Hot chocolate or Milo made with full cream milk

2 cheese crackers or 2 biscuits or 1 muesli bar

I mean seriously and honestly … not just because I have some apparent food disorder, don't you think that's a lot of food to eat in one measly day. That would feed my Mum for a week! And I'm supposed to chew and swallow it all like some fucken cow … in fact even when I regurgitate I'm still expected to swallow. And what with all the food … I need at least four stomachs to digest it.

November 18

So I had another meeting with my super fit and super trim dietitian. Her name's India, man I love that name. So not only is she super trim and super fit but she has this exotic name to prance around in. She assures me once I'm at a healthy weight … but who gets to determine that? … I will be placed on a maintenance plan. And she says smiling, 'You'll be able to increase your activity and introduce a little bit of exercise.'

God … I can't wait.

All this chewing is going to wear down my teeth! Ever seen a cow with no teeth?

November 19

Got Julie to arrange another meeting with India, the super trim, but says she eats, dietitian. She can't come until tomorrow. I was thinking diary, if I ever get well … I wonder … would it be too weird if I became a dietitian or nutritionist? Well it is an interest … of sorts. I wonder if they are forgiving of girls with histories of being locked in a mental asylum for food disorders at wherever it is one studies nutrition. Something to ponder. Food for thought! … ha that made me laugh and there's not much to laugh about these days … maybe I should be a comedian. Now that is funny.

November 20

India says, 'A healthy weight is determined by your BMI … has to be at least 18 or 19, which is still very slim, Talia.'

'So I won't be fat?'

'You won't be fat.'

'Promise?

She leans forward uncrossing her legs, 'Talia … I promise.'

'I like your broach, dragonflies are cool.'

'Thanks.'

November 21

So I'm trying real hard to just eat without too much debate … trying to believe and trust that they know what they're doing. That they won't make me fat.

Remember that young blond boy that couldn't move and had a blank stare. Saw him today shooting hoops with one of the male nurses. He was laughing and moving about like a little white Globetrotter. I felt all overcome to see him look so normal. I wonder if he looks at me and thinks I look like a freak. Because I look at Lila and think, shit what a horror. His name is Ryan and he was something called catatonic. He had meth or some drug and his body said fuck and reacted like an uncharged robot.

So maybe diary, just maybe there's hope for me and the white lights and angels and India the super fit and super trim dietitian and even Arleen with her china blue beady eyes, looking at my file through her black rimmed glasses know what they're doing … I hope so diary, I do hope.

November 22

Same old … eat, eat, eat.

Chew, chew, chew.

And finally … swallow.

November 23

I managed to lift up the paper towel with my toe today … I was 34.9 kilos. I so thought I'd be at least 40. I don't think Julie noticed, if she did she never said anything. She said my pulse and blood pressure is better, which I guess is good. She certainly seem to think so she's like, 'Oh Talia, that's fabulous. We are all so proud of you … you have been working so hard.'

I managed to smile but honestly I felt all kinda yuck.

November 24

Mum came in with Aunty Maxine. They bought me some magazines and a new deodorant. I asked Mum if she could bring the boys in soon. She's like, 'Sol has the chicken pox … probably Mac soon. As soon as they are well I'll bring them in.'

'Oh is Sol okay?' I felt so awful diary … I miss him and all his mess so much it hurts.

'He's fine … just grizzly and itchy, very itchy. Mac will be the one … far less tolerance for feeling unwell.'

Oh diary I should be at home, making sure they are ok. I am such a selfish screwed up bitch to still be locked up and not being a good and reliable sister.

Aunty Maxine says, 'Can you remember having chicken pox, Talia?'

'Ar … not sure,' I reply.

'It was Christmas and you and Mum and your Dad came to ours. I'll always remember you,' she laughs, 'wearing a Snow White dress up with your face absolutely covered with spots. I have a photo at home. I'll bring it in if you like.'

'Ok,' I say, 'I'll show Sol and Mac.'

'How old was she Kim? Five?'

'Four … she was four,' says Mum, looking up from one of the magazines she brought in for me. 'Clay wasn't around for Talia's fifth Christmas.

Clay … so the last time I saw him I must have been four.

November 25

A month until Christmas, I wonder if I'll be home by then.
It will be hard what with all the food and chocolates and
fruitcake and Christmas pudding ... too much food makes
me anxious. Makes me want to retreat and not eat ... but I
need to think of Sol and Mac. Not just myself for once. I'll
need to speak to Doctor Arleen ... see if I can be discharged
by then.

November 26

Arleen, oops I mean Doctor Adelaide, snobby bitch, says
'Discharge ... no.'

'Why?' I ask, feeling like throwing my shoe at her. And
diary, I'm wearing my favorite All-stars, Converse. Grant
bought them back from London last year. I even gave him
a sorta hug.

'Talia ... if you keep gaining weight and appearing settled
we'll look at day leave. Maybe even overnight leave.'

'But ... I thought by a month I'd be well enough and weigh
enough, have a high enough BMI and stuff. It's Christmas
... my brothers and stuff.'

'Talia I understand but...'

'I bet you'll be at home.'

'Yes I will be and Talia like I said ... keep doing what you're
doing and you can go home for the day or even overnight

leave. Sweetie, Christmas, although lovely, can be a very stressful time for people.'

'What ... you mean anorexics?'

'Yes ... but not just anorexics, people in general. Families.'

I'm not sure if she was saying something specific about my family or all families but diary I'm still in shock at her calling me, sweetie. Sweetie, Doctor Arleen Adelaide ... she really let her side down today. Perhaps she had a bag of lollies for morning tea.

November 26

If I hadn't of wasted so much time mucking around, arguing and fighting with the staff, hiding and smuggling food ... smearing it under the table, on my clothes and stuff ... I might've been able to go home by Christmas. I look at Lila with her tube taped across her nose and cheek and think, stupid girl. Did I tell you another one arrived, another skinny starved female, wild and pissed off like the entire universe has it against her.

The staff must get so tired of all the chasing and following and debates. Her name is Norma, she's eighteen and apparently she's been here before. God I hope and I pray, I pray and I hope, I never return.

I get well ... stay that way.

November 27

I've been looking at the magazines Mum brought in the other day. Title, Stars Without Make-up ... title, Summer Bikini Special ... title, Who's Gained Weight and Who Hasn't ... title, How To Lose 10 Kilos In 4 Weeks.

I tried to just put them aside ... hide them under my pillow but they called me like a candle in the dark. So instead ... I sat fixated, reading every word: that shows how far I've come, I can actually concentrate enough to read! Studying the pictures, oohing and ahhing at the stars with and without makeup. Enjoying the sight of pimples and wrinkles and cellulite. How cruel am I!

Feeling overwhelmed and fat at the sight of perfect star bodies in tiny bikinis. Flat stomachs and trim thighs and overflowing cleavage.

And what star has gained or lost weight this week. Pictures of before and after. And there I am admiring the slim ... frowning at the extra kilos. Searching through with vengeance the following article for weight loss techniques. 10 kilos in 4 weeks ... fabulous!

And now Diary, I'm looking down at my thighs feeling the jeans rub against them. Feeling the waist band grip and tighten around my stomach. And I feel tired.

Tired and fat.

November 28

Its 1: 38 am ... had a bad dream ... can't remember the details. Or maybe I just don't want to. Anyhow I woke up scared and trembling and feeling unwell inside. I'm looking around my small room like there's someone hiding under my bed or in my wardrobe like I used to when I was a kid. I'd wake up screaming and Mum would stand at the side of my bed and say, 'Talia just think of something nice ... something you like ... like a lollipop.'

And I'd look around my room in the darkness, trying real hard to imagine the taste of a lollipop, one of those really big ones with all different colors; they look a bit like a rainbow. Mum would never buy me one no matter how much I begged. She only ever bought me one of those tiny ones, the size of a 20 cent coin. Eventually I'd fall asleep ... wake up to hop-scotch and skipping and handstands and cartwheels and school and drawing and coloring-in. Wake up terrified the following night ... like I was the only person ... the only child in the whole world.

Alone.

November 30

I wrote this today. Don't know what it means but who cares.

ugly

she lay on her side

in bed

buried beneath

pink and white

gingham sheets

and

a purple and white

duvet.

a black cat

climbed in

a closed window

brushed its tail

against her head

like new shoes

on a table

a weeping mirror

smashed.

'don't tremble

little one,' shouts

the furry black gorilla

from inside

the toy box.

'beauty loved

the beast ...

he was ugly.'

December 1

Anna and Maggie visited today. Maggie's like, 'You're looking really good, Talia. So much better.'

'You are,' grins Anna.

I kinda half smile ... do they mean fat?

'We were really worried, especially when you had that tube and stuff,' says Maggie.

'Yeah,' agrees Anna.

'What about you guys, what's been happening?' I ask.

'Exams,' they both say and laugh.

'Exams,' I echo, 'oh yeah ... I forgot.'

'So glad they're finished,' sighs Maggie.

'Me too,' smiles Anna.

'So what now?' I ask.

'Work more hours at McDonald's,' says Maggie, 'and then off to Teacher's College. Don't you remember, Talia ... I was always going to be a teacher.'

'Oh yeah,' I say. 'I do now ... what about you Anna?'

'Work too ... Dad said I can have more hours at his work, cleaning, clerical and stuff and then University.'

'What are you going to study?'

'Law ... don't you remember I wanted to do law?'

'Umm ... yeah, I do now.' But I didn't and I don't.

Where have I been diary, what far away and fucked up planet? I forgot about exams and dreams and stuff. Forgot.

December 3

Eat, chew, swallow. Sometimes regurgitate ... swallow. I'm trying my absolute hardest ... even though sometimes I just want to give up and disappear.

I can't believe I have wasted my final year at school ... if I had known that starting that diet to lose 5 kilos would have ended like this ... I. Fuck.

Diary, do you think I can ever be normal? Truth is I'm not sure I've ever felt normal. At least not for as long as I can remember.

I have a meeting with India tomorrow. Want to ask her how you become a dietitian and stuff.

PS ... that blond boy who was catatonic went home today ... Ryan. He looked so well and I felt so happy for him. So did the staff ... hugging him goodbye. It was nice. I even went up to him and said, 'See ya ... goodluck!'

He gave me a big grin and high fived me. I laughed.

December 4

I felt all uncomfortable asking India about training to be a dietitian. Embarrassed.

But I muttered my way through and she was so positive and encouraging that I relaxed eventually. She said, 'Oh Talia, that sounds a great goal to set yourself.'

'You think,' I say.

'Oh yes,' she beams. 'We need goals … something to work towards.'

'Yeah,' I agree.

'So tell me what subjects were you doing at school? You really need biology and chemistry. Health, food and nutrition are useful and perhaps physical education.'

'I did chemistry and biology and physics. And statistics and English. I really hated physics … struggled.'

'Oh that's perfect,' she smiles. 'You can drop the physics, don't need it … maybe pick up health or something you just enjoy. So does that mean all going well you plan to go back to school and finish your last year?'

'Yeah … I really want to be a dietitian or something like that.'

'Oh Talia, that's awesome, I'm so excited for you. You realise that means university. You need a Bachelor of Science or a Bachelor of Consumer and Applied Science, majoring in Human Nutrition and Food Service Management. And then you do a Post-graduate Diploma in Dietetics.'

'So that's a lot of study.'

'It sure is but chances of getting are job are extremely high as there are a shortage of trained people.'

'Oh,' I say, 'well that's good then.'

'I'm so excited,' smiles India, rubbing her hands together.

'You don't think ... well I've had anorexia and I mean ... been admitted and stuff.'

'Get well and stay well and Talia ... you'll be the most highly qualified dietitian around.'

'But ...'

'No buts ... a mental illness is just like any other illness ... well it can be. You get sick, you get help, treatment, perhaps therapy, you get well. You move on and take with you all you've experienced and learnt to become the best possible you. And perhaps that best possible you can help others ... but first and foremost Talia that best possible you has to continue to help you. To take good care of you.'

I like that idea diary, becoming the best possible you. I like it even more than the idea of becoming a dietitian. I hope I can.

December 5

I think diary, I've come a long way. I'm eating everything on my meal plan ... drinking all that full cream milk. Maybe the fog in my brain is beginning to lift: maybe even a little blue sky is beginning to beam. Oh sure there's a few, ok several, dark clouds. There's someone in me that just wants to scream, she's in a panic, feels repulsive and wants to disappear. Diary ... she even wants to die.

But here I am ... I'm getting better. I look at those two anorexic girls and I don't want to be one.

December 7

Mum and Grant finally brought the twins in. It was so nice. Mac did get chicken pox and was very miserable. The spots got infected on his bottom so he had to go on antibiotics. They both still have scars on their face. Mac has one near his dimple on his chin. Funny how he has a dimple and Sol doesn't.

They were so happy to see me ... I wonder if I was free with affection when I was their age. They kiss and wrap their little arms around me like it's the most natural thing in the world.

Sol's like, 'Tala,' all smiles and a runny nose.

And Mac's like, 'We missed Tala, coming home soon?'

They both had done more paintings and drawings ... funny there was a painting that was entirely blue. And I thought a blue sky maybe like my brain. I hung that one up straight away: near the side of my bed so I can wake up and look at it.

'I love this blue one,' I said, 'who did this.'

'I did,' they both said.

'It looks like a lovely blue sky,' I smile.

'It's a blue sea,' says Sol.

'It's a blue river,' says Mac.

No … it's a blue sky.

December 8

So I'm allowed to start attending some groups: craft activities and stuff. Although Julie's like, 'But Talia the condition is you must be sitting down. No standing ok.'

'Ok.' I do think I can manage that.

Truth is I do want to get well … I do want to go home. That girl with the long auburn braid went home today … the one that hit Melanie with a guitar. Her eyes … they still look a bit far away to me. Or perhaps it's just she still freaks me out! I wonder how Melanie puts the incident aside and smiles and interacts freely. Perhaps she's terrified inside … I mean most people act don't they. I guess nurses are no different. Mind you when you think about it I kicked and scratched and hit out at several nurses. Fuck. In fact I really hit Amanda hard … she hasn't had much to do with me since so perhaps I freak the fuck out of her. That seems weird that I could be perceived as scary … most of the time it's me that feels terrified.

Perhaps I have a gene defect! The one that determines fear … yeah that makes perfect sense. I've been fearful for as long as I can remember.

December 9

I know this seems kind of bizarre but I really don't like being in the same room as Lila and Norma. It's not so bad with Lila: she's being tube feed and on bed rest and stuff but Norma … I'm expected to eat in the same room at the same time and I really don't like it. It's like she has some contagious disease like leprosy and I'd prefer if she'd take her disease and go live on some quarantine island.

I'm trying my best to eat and I can hear her saying, 'What's with the strawberry yoghurt … I hate strawberry.'

'Ok,' says Brian, 'I'll get an apricot, that's what's left in the fridge.'

'Apricot,' screeches Norma, 'that's worse.'

'Well strawberry it is,' says Brian.

And I look down at my raspberry … sigh and wonder if I should offer it to her. This is her second admission … I really want to ask Julie if I can eat somewhere else. But I … I don't.

'She can have my raspberry one,' I say.

'No Talia,' says Julie, 'it's yours. Raspberry is your favorite.'

'Oh it's ok,' I say.

'No,' says Julie again.

So then I have to eat it feeling bad. It's soft and smooth but it feels like swallowing hay.

December 10

It was fun at crafts ... we made candles. I made a crimson one shaped like a heart. It was whole and perfect looking. Wouldn't it be great if I could take out my heart and put that one back.

PS ... I only had to be told to sit down twice!

December 11

She's really beginning to agitate me ... that Norma. I wish she'd dye her hair mousy brown because that bleached blond look so stands out. Is it bad that I have thoughts of injecting her with leprosy so they will quarantine her?

She's like, 'I'm not eating anymore,' tipping the remainder of her cereal on the floor.

Brian, he looked pissed off but bit his tongue. I know what he was thinking. Just fucken eat it!

Next thing, she's up running on the spot with legs like an emu. Running and running and running and freaking me out. Brian jumps up, looks at Julie ... says, 'Norma, sit down!' But she just keeps on running like she's sprinting for her life. Julie jumps up ... Brian and Julie grab her by the arms ... I'm not sure how, she was moving so fast!

Norma's breathing like she's about to give birth, 'I'm not eating it!' she cries.

I sit there stirring my cornflakes and looking at my glass of juice ... hoping like hell that Norma's wrong and that it's not poison.

Julie and Brian escort Norma away, hopefully to that island. I'm left sitting there with my cereal, juice and toast smeared with butter thinking ... if I was quick I could tip it in the rubbish. I just stand up when Shanti this new nurse says, 'Have you finished?'

'No,' I say.

'Well ... sit down then ... I'll replace Julie.'

She sits down opposite me with a cup of coffee and two pieces of toast with jam and says, 'You don't mind if I eat do you ... I'm starving?'

'No.'

So Shanti and I sit at our table and eat. It was almost nice.

December 11

Shanti is my nurse today. She's Indian or something similar. So pretty ... enormous brown eyes, shoulder length shiny black hair, lovely teeth ... brown skin. I look so white and sickly next to her. I would definitely call her beautiful. I wonder if she feels beautiful. If she looks in the mirror and thinks, yeah, looking good. Does she feel blessed to have such an exquisite face?

She's new to mental health … I guess I'm the easiest of the anorexics. I like how she eats with me instead of just staring with radar eyes.

'I love cheese and onion,' she smiles, chewing and swallowing her toasted sandwich. 'Do you?'

'Umm …' I say.

'Yum … I have a mint for after,' she laughs. 'Don't want to smell.'

'I use to like cheese toasties.'

'Maybe you could have one tomorrow for lunch.'

'Oh … it's not on my meal plan.'

'Two pieces bread right, cheese for protein … only difference … cooked.'

'Umm … I usually stick to what's on the plan.'

'Ok … beautiful day,' she smiles, looking outside.

'I guess so,' I reply.

'We should take our lunch and sit outside. Want to.'

'Umm … I usually eat here but ok.'

So we pick up our lunch and sit outside at a barbeque table in the courtyard, just outside the dining area. It's like eating at a café and I don't have to hear Norma moaning.

December 12

'Can I talk to you?' says Shanti.

'Ok,' I say, puzzled.

'Let's sit on the sofa,' she says, pointing to the green sofa at the end of the sleeping quarters.

We sit down and I feel all nervous wondering what I've done.

'Did I make you anxious yesterday … taking you outside for lunch?' she asks. 'I'm really sorry if I did. I didn't want to make things any harder for you.'

'Umm no … it was ok … nice.'

'Really,' she sighs. 'I have been told that it could've made you anxious … you seem relaxed.'

'Well,' I say, 'maybe a couple of weeks ago, the littlest change could've set me off. But I'm doing better and it was … I liked it actually. And I might even try a cheese toastie but soon ok. Like in a few days.'

'Ok,' she smiles. 'So I can tell the rest of the team you're ok with eating outside sometimes. It can be written in your nursing notes.'

'Yeah,' I nod, smiling. 'Outside will be good sometimes.'

Truth is … outside will be awesome if it gets me away from seeing those emu legs sprinting.

And … I could probably do with some vitamin D.

December 13

Alarms were ringing and nurses and doctors came running from all directions ... a nurse running pushing a big silver trolley. We all knew something was going down ... diary this girl, Gloria ... she was only sixteen ... she hung herself in her bedroom. Everyone was supposed to be in groups and she quietly slipped away and hung herself ... I'm not sure what she used; a sheet perhaps ... anyhow despite all those running doctors and nurses she's dead.

She was solemn looking or perhaps in retrospect, sad ... pretty honey brown hair always in a high pony and amazing green eyes with thick liner ... she always wore these pink Doc Martins which I had been envious of. Actually I said to her once, 'Where did you get those Doc Martins?' Those amazing green eyes gave me this, fuck off bitch, look and that was it. The end of any more conversations. And now that's the end of her.

Just like that.

I wonder if she felt like me ... like there's someone inside that is so terrified, so alone ... so confused and fucked up ... death ... it's welcoming ... it's familiar. Living ... that's the hard part. Sometimes just taking a breath hurts.

Diary ... I could just ... sometimes I feel the urge so strong to just leap from a cliff, swallow masses of pills, drown myself in the bath ... this little person in me ... she ... just wants to die. Disappear. In a way ... she already has.

I wonder if sad and solemn Gloria ... felt like that.

December 15

So now it's the staff that look pretty sad and solemn. I wonder if someone gets held accountable, which would be so horrific wouldn't it. I wonder if from wherever she is now she's glad she did it. Glad it was successful. If she's smiling and finally can relate to her name which I think means glorious. I wonder if ... how her parents feel. She might not even have any now that I think about it ... never saw her go to the visitor's lounge much. Not like me who's there every other day ... sitting with Mum while she flicks through magazines or files her nails.

I wonder what it is like to die ... if God is there all kind and loving or menacing and judgmental. And if you commit suicide ... do you still get to go to heaven? To be honest diary when I have seriously considered suicide it's the fear I'll be sent to hell that stops me. And I guess I don't want my brothers to have to know ... but then sometimes what good am I anyway?

Diary ... killing myself ... the thought enters my head most days. It's like brushing your teeth or having a wee ... it's ordinary ... just a thought, sometimes fleeting, sometimes like concrete.

Are those thoughts normal do you think?

December 16

Two hospital chaplains visited the ward today offering to counsel any staff or us patients over Gloria's death. I really wanted to ask if they thought Gloria would get to go to heaven ... but nah, I didn't. They also said a blessing or prayer or something like that in Gloria's room. Which I thought was nice ... you hear of ghosts and stuff after suicides don't you. I'll feel more relaxed now when I walk past her room. I keep expecting piercing green eyes or a pink Doc Martin to clonk me on the head.

December 17

I've just realized its eight days until Christmas. I have no present for Mac or Sol and don't know if I'm allowed to go home. Diary I'm going right now to ask Julie if I can talk to Doctor Arleen. Surely with the size I am now they'll let me go ... I mean I can hardly do up my jeans.

December 18

I was so nervous walking to her office, Julie following behind: funny it's been ages since I've heard, 'Slow down, Talia ... Talia.'

I turned around and smiled, 'Sorry.'

Doctor Adelaide is like, 'Hi Talia ... take a seat ... Talia, sit down dear.'

There I go again ... I wasn't aware I was standing ... must be because I'm stressed.

'So,' she smiles, 'I understand you'd like leave to go shopping and have overnight leave for Christmas.'

'Please,' I say, standing back up. 'I want to get my brothers a present ... and stuff.'

'Talia,' Julie nudges, 'sit down.'

'Oh sorry,' I say, sitting back down. 'You said,' looking towards Doctor Adelaide, 'if I kept gaining weight and my blood pressure went up, which I'm sure it has ... I'm not dizzy anymore, that I could go.'

'What I'd like to do is say yes to going shopping with a nurse,' she says, frowning and folding her arms, 'and discuss with the other staff overnight leave.'

'But you said,' I say, 'I could go.'

'I'm not saying you can't, I'm just saying I want to discuss it with those that look after you every day. And then Talia, we need to discuss it with Mum and Grant,'

I sigh heavily, 'What's Grant got to do with it?'

'He's your Mum's husband. Do you not like him,' she asks, looking at me curiously.

'He's alright,' I say. 'A dork sometimes.'

'What do you mean a dork?' she asks, biting her thumb.

'I don't know ... he tucks his t-shirts into his jeans.'

'Oh I see,' she smiles, 'and that makes him a dork,'

'Yeah.'

'Look, Talia ... shopping tomorrow and we will get back to you in the next day or two about Christmas. Ok?'

'Ok,' I say. 'Not like I have any choice.'

I was so tempted to say, "Bye Arleen," as I walked through the open door.

Bitch.

December 19

Its Gloria's funeral today … I know this sounds extremely selfish but I'm so pissed off. I can't go shopping as the ward is short staffed. And what staff we have are mostly casuals. So it's, 'I'm sorry, Talia, not today.'

I'm fighting the urge to walk like I'm trying to keep up with a 100 metre sprinter and I so feel like tipping my muesli all over the floor … but I know if I do I'll blow any chance I had of being home for Christmas.

I guess the fact that Gloria's body is being placed 10 feet below the ground to rot and be eaten by insects and here I am with a sour face just shows how much of a bitch I am. If I was her I'd come back to haunt me.

December 20

I'm so nervous about going shopping that eating breakfast is going to be like swallowing mud. Actually I had a friend that liked the taste of dirt … something to do with a zinc deficiency. Somehow I doubt I'd be deficient in anything with all the food I've been eating … so yes … eating breakfast is going to be like swallowing mud. And that full cream milk … like beer. I hate the taste and repulsive smell of beer.

December 21

Going shopping was weird and at times diary I so wanted to say to Julie, "Can we go back."

But I didn't.

It's the first time I've been out and even being in a car was unfamiliar. The plaza was quiet which I was grateful for. Diary, got those fat feelings or are they thoughts? You know like everyone's looking at how repulsive and fat I look. My thighs … kept checking my reflection in the glass of the shops. I must be the vainest bitch alive.

And then we walked past this ice cream shop. Secret … I love ice cream. I tell everyone I hate it but I love ice cream. Any flavors … all flavors. Sometimes I have this thought that if you put me on an island of ice cream, I'd eat the whole lot and have nowhere to live. I'd swim around the ocean desperately searching for another ice cream island. Yeah ok … I'm fucken mad, ever heard of an anorexic that fantasises about ice cream?

I couldn't stop staring at the people leaving the counter with their cones piled to overflowing and licking the ice cream with wide smiles. Julie's like, 'Do you like ice cream?'

'No,' I snap back.

We sat down at a nearby café and I had a cup of tea, English breakfast, Julie had a trim latte. Yes I definitely heard her say trim. Mind you she had a big raspberry muffin with white icing. Fortunately muffins are not ice cream ... though another secret, I like icing.

I bought Mac and Sol transformer robot things and a book each. Mum, I got some pink nail polish and a pretty file with little pink sparkly looking diamonds. She will like that. Grant ... black socks. Two pairs.

On the way home, Julie said, 'We've got a bit of time, would you like to go for a bit of a drive?'

'No thanks,' I said. 'But thank you.'

Truth is I was glad to get back to my little bedroom and eat dinner not long later in the dining room, even though Norma was there.

December 22

Dreamed last night about being ice cream ... started eating myself beginning with the inside of my wrists. Reminded me of those psycho girls here ... cuts like railway tracks all up their arms. Looks disgusting.

Told you I was fucken mad.

December 23

Guess what ... going home for day leave. Doctor Adelaide's like, 'How would day leave be, Talia?'

'Oh really,' I smile. Felt like jumping out my chair and wrapping my arms around her and diary, you know, that is so not me.

'Yes really,' she smiles. 'Talia you have worked so hard and the team here … they acknowledge how far you have come. And all going well, we will have to start giving you more leave, more outings. How does that sound?'

'Good, I'm just glad I get to see Mac and Sol and stuff. I'm not sure what's happening, where Christmas will be held.'

'Your Mum says at your home. Now as far as eating goes, breakfast here and then morning tea and lunch your Mum will assist you with. You'll take a copy of your meal plan. But it is Christmas Talia, you could try and join the family meal. Mum has said she'll be cooking a turkey, salads and roast veges.'

'I'm not sure,' I say. 'Think I'll just stick to a sandwich, maybe a turkey and salad sandwich.'

'Sounds good, Talia,' she says nodding.

'Yeah,' I smile back.

'Well then … Merry Christmas Talia, hope you have a really nice day.'

'Yeah you too … and Merry Christmas.'

I'm such a bitch diary, wanted to say, "Merry Christmas to you too, Arleen."

December 24

It's Christmas Eve and I've just wrapped my presents in lovely Santa Claus paper; he looks so jolly and plump and kind. And guess what? … I had a cheese toasted sandwich for lunch and sat outside with Shanti absorbing vitamin D. Which I understand according to Shanti, will boost my immunity and help me absorb all that calcium I just ate. 'Scotland has the highest rates of multiple sclerosis,' she says, in between swallowing her juice. 'And how much sun do they have?'

So diary … I should be just about glowing with good health.

PS … not sure what multiple sclerosis is, are you?

December 25

Merry Christmas to you diary! Had breakfast … just waiting to be picked up. We all got little gifts this morning from the staff or ward or whatever. I got a lovely pen with butterflies and hearts and girly things. It writes bright pink which is pretty cool. And I got a cute little pink notepad to go with it. I thought that was really sweet.

Speak soon.

December 28

How was Christmas? … Fucken merry.

December 29

Back on fifteen minute observations. Caught doing sit ups in my room. Don't know why … I mean I'm still eating everything on my meal plan. Well most things. Hid my biscuits up my sleeve yesterday. Julie said, 'Are you not hot in that top? It's such a warm day for long sleeves.'

'No,' I said. 'I like it.'

'It is a lovely color … I love deep purple.'

'Got it for Christmas. From Mum.'

'So Talia,' she says, leaning forward, 'how was Christmas, I haven't seen you since?'

'How was yours … did you go away?'

'Lovely thanks and no, just at home … a nice quiet break. And yours … did Sol and Mac like their presents.'

I smile. 'Yeah they did … they were so cute and excited and got so many toys and it was so much fun watching them.'

'And Mum, she liked her nail polish?' says Julie, sipping her tea. 'And Grant his black socks?'

'Yeah … I guess.'

'And what else did you get?'

'Oh clothes mostly … this top, couple of books … haven't read in ages. Use to read all the time. And stuff,' I say, looking down at my juice. My biscuits.

'What did you get?' I ask. 'Anything nice.'

I nod and smile as Julie tells me about the presents she got ... while quietly putting the biscuits piece by piece up my sleeve. Chewing on saliva and air. First decent feed I've had in ages.

December 30

Do you think perhaps I suffer from a mood disorder, grumpy bitch syndrome or just bitch?

December 31

Diary ... Christmas was good. I just ... maybe it was all that food. Puddings. Ice cream. Yes ice cream which Sol and Mac gobbled down like little piglets. Maybe it was ... yeah too much food does make me anxious. And Aunty Maxine, she gives me a box of chocolates: is that a joke? ... and that photo. That photo of me with chicken pox, wearing a Snow White dress up. It's emerald blue with a big white collar and a yellow apron and I look hideous. I should've been wearing the wicked stepmother's outfit ... I mean ... I am so vain I'm anorexic.

The chocolates and photo were wrapped up together like best pals. They actually feel like they are ... pals that hate me. She even put the photo in a white frame, like I'd want to put it on my dresser. And she's like, 'Look Sol and Mac ... see Talia with chicken pox. She was so gorgeous with that long dark hair.'

And I just look at her as she grabs the photo out my hands and feel like grabbing it back and throwing it across the room. I catch a glimpse of myself in the mirror on the wall, partially hidden by the Christmas tree branches and see my short hair. Told you I was more like the wicked step mother, who's really a witch ... evil and things.

Mirror mirror who's the fairest of them all

Not you ... you short haired vain bitch.

January 1

Happy fucken new year.

January 2

Maybe I'm premenstrual. I mean I'm fat enough ... surely my period could return.

January 3

So I've been thinking of joining Gloria in feeling glorious wherever she is. Least I hope she is. I hope she's singing with forgiving angels that embrace fucked up fuckers like us with kindness.

January 4

Doctor Arleen Adelaide's like, 'In preparation for discharge the team want you to have more day leave, outings with staff and perhaps Mum could stay over in the family room. You could prepare your meals together and so on.'

'Oh,' I sigh, looking around the room. 'Is that your kids?' pointing at the photo on the desk. Three teenagers in a gold frame, smiling like the world is just great.

'Yes,' she smiles.

'I bet you don't have to doctor them. Prescribe medications to put that smile on their face.'

'No,' she says, 'they have been very fortunate and so have I.'

'Good,' I say. 'That's good.'

Good … good.

Diary, right there and then I so wanted to kneel at Doctor Arleen's feet and place my head in her lap. In her grey slacks. She would run her fingers through my hair and tenderly stroke the side of my face … and I … I would cry. Just a little.

Soft wet tears.

And I don't even like her.

She just seemed calm and restful … like a park bench looking out to a beautiful view.

I so need a place to rest.

January 6

In group today we had to say something positive about ourselves … just one thing. Everyone in the group looked around blankly, some like me going red and twitchy. All except this guy Jason who's like, 'Yo wass up? ... ya only need one look at me to see I'm all that and some more. I reckon if I took a trip to Hollywood ... I'd be snapped up just like that.' And he stands up waving his arms and gesturing like some L.A. gangster. His pinky and pointing finger in the air.

'I reckon I'm like gonna be famous when I get outta here,' he beams, smiling so wide his cheeks look like they could burst. ''Cause man ... I'm like the black Eminen. I love Eminen. Hey hoe,' his voice booms in a hip hop tone, 'how'd ya blow? Pack it on babe. Take ya to my cave. I'm ya man. Get it up, get it up, cos I can. Yo,'

'Jason,' says Mick, the psychologist coordinating the group, 'thanks that was awesome. But you can sit down now.'

But Jason, he keeps on singing, 'My name is Jay, Jay from the Bay. Smoke it ... I said smoke it. Sniff it ... it's so good it's illicit.'

Mick and Taylor say together, 'Jason, sit down now, please.'

'So my name is Jay, Jay from the Bay,' he continues to boom and dance like he belongs in some video clip; he can move! 'Will ya, I said will ya? Roll with Jay, Jay in the hay. I'm so hot, we should smoke some pot. Yo. I said smoke it. Toke it. Sniff it. It's so fine, it's illicit.'

Mick stands up and taps Jason on the shoulder, 'Jason, thanks bro ... sit down now though.'

Jason looks Mick up and down, 'Ya know I should take you shopping. Ditch that brown suit ... the tie ... wanna look hot like me.' Hot in a white singlet, muscles galore and black and red basketball shorts.

'Yeah thanks Jason, Taylor perhaps Jason could do with some time in the music room. That be cool Jason?'

'Call me Jay,' he sings, 'Jay from the Bay.'

'Music room Jay?' says Taylor, placing her arm in his.

'Be cool,' he says, 'been learnin' drummin since I got here.'

'Yeah I know,' smiles Taylor, escorting Jay from the room.

'I reckon I might be good enough to take on Tommy Lee or ...' His voice dies out as the door closes.

I look around the room at all the red faced twitchers who don't know fuck what they are good at and wish Jason was back spreading whatever he had with a sneeze.

January 8

See that Jason around ... he is good looking ... very. Hot as he calls it. I was thinking maybe I should take up sniffing or smoking whatever it is he sniffs and smokes. He was in the TV lounge this evening, dancing around and when one of the other patients asked him to be quiet, he's like, 'Don't panic, I'm just manic. Don't panic, I'm manic. Yo.'

Then he turns to me, sitting in the corner of the room, 'Yo girl ... Wass up? Don't look so sad. It's all good. All fucken good.'

I smile but feel like a snail retreating back into its shell.

'Cause I'm feeling so fucken good. Things are finally going my way,' he says, looking right at me, 'I'm not actually a mental just manic. Which is all fucken good. Why you so sad?'

'Not,' I say, standing up and walking towards the door.

'Yo,' he beams after me. 'Yo girl ... take ya to my cave.'

Cave ... shell, I'm already in one thanks.

January 9

Does that mean manic depressive? And how do I get some?

January 10

Had an outing with five other patients to the beach. I sat with Julie in the very back of the van and chatted. She's such a nice person ... I started to think beautiful, even though she's kinda plump, I guess you could say voluptuous. Her boobs burst through her jade t-shirt like melons and ... shit I'd be so self conscious but she just seems oblivious. Some girls pay good money to have boobs like that but me ... I'd rather strap mine down. Not sure why ... just this feeling I don't want to be seen. Anyhow, I noticed how pretty she was, all that lovely red hair and clear green eyes with lots of black mascara. She's a bit freckly but most of all ... it's her smile. Such a tender smile.

I wanted to rest my head on her shoulder, close my eyes and just breathe in her warmth. Her tenderness. Diary, does that make me a lesbian?

'Talia,' she says, 'you have done so well and here you are going out again … do you still plan to go back to school?'

'Yeah,' I say.

'Still want to be a nutritionist?'

'Yeah, do you think I'll be out for the new term?'

'That's the plan, Talia,' she smiles. 'Get you home for the start of the new year. Get you back to school.'

'It's nice to be out,' I say, 'but you know what I think I'll miss some of you.'

'We'll miss you too, but we'll be and are so happy to see you looking so well. To be getting on with your life.'

Diary … I do feel physically well … strong … like my bones are supported which they are I guess in flesh. I know that means I'm fatter but I'm trying to think healthy. Strong. I still wouldn't want melons bursting through my t-shirt, or lumpy hips … but she is beautiful. Especially when she smiles.

January 12

I don't think I am lesbian after all … Shanti and I sat outside eating our lunch watching Jay from the Bay shooting hoops with Max, one of the Health Care Assistants. Jay from the Bay stripped his top off; tied it around his head like some Arab. Though … so not Arab like with all this exposed chocolate flesh … I could hardly take my eyes off them … him. Tattooed biceps and triceps and pectorals that bulged with every athletic move. Max was like, 'Put your shirt on bro.'

'Yeah nah,' laughs Jason … bouncing the ball.

'We'll have to go inside if you don't put your shirt on,' says Max.

'It's all good,' laughs Jason, shooting a perfect hoop.

Max reaches up, grabs the white shirt from Jason's head, 'Put it on bro.'

Jason runs off laughing, 'Catch me.'

Max looks around the courtyard … at Shanti and I … I wana say, "We don't mind his bare and gorgeous flesh." But I don't … I just give him this innocent look … like I'm eight not eighteen.

So it turns out … Jay from the Bay is definitely hot and I'm definitely not gay!

January 13

Julie's like, 'So … it's time Talia that you start preparing your own food and I'll just sit here and watch.'

'Ok,' I say, picking up the muesli container and pouring it into a bowl.

I look at Julie sitting at the table, smiling; boobs like two big bombs about to blow up her blue shirt and I want to throw the white porcelain bowl at her.

Give me the remote. "You fucken do it," I'd say, pushing the button.

I guess I'm just one fucked up fucker. Some kind of bomb solider in disguise.

I ate the muesli, drank the juice ... but I ... I ... where's the rest of my squad?

Allies?

January 17

Lila's got her tube out and Norma has one in and Jason's still rapping and dancing, did a head spin during the ward morning meeting. And me ... still eating, preparing my own food and still not gay.

January 18

'How do you feel about weekend leave, Talia?' asks Arleen Adelaide. 'I've talked to the team and Mum and Grant and everyone feels positive about it. School starts in just over two weeks.'

FUCK.

'Yeah great,' I smile and nod. Fucken marvellous.

'Talia, we really are so pleased with your progress and you look wonderful.'

Ok now my leg is twitching and I feel sick and I get this feeling like I'm gonna burst into tears. Which diary, as you know is absolutely weird. 'Umm ... so I'm ready for discharge?' I ask.

'Getting there, Talia. Would love you to be able to start back at school. But not before you're ready. Let's see how weekend leave goes.'

Diary ... I know I'm fat, well healthy, still thin says Julie and India. Gonna start on a maintenance meal plan next week. But am I ready to eat all that food on my own. Am I ready ... to close my eyes and have bad dreams without a nurse offering me a hot water bottle. Sometimes diary I'm just so tired ... I wish I had a place to rest my fucked up head.

January 20

Jason says, 'Talia, wanna shoot some hoops.'

I look up from my book, 1984, George Orwell, and mutter, 'What?' Even though I knew exactly what he said.

He plops his body down next to mine, leans his head on my shoulder and says, 'Shoot some hoops with me.'

Well what was I supposed to say, well actually I prefer to sit here watching you and your muscles play ball? 'Sure,' I say.

So diary, we shot hoops and I had so much fun and hardly even thought about being ugly or fat. It was both fortunate and unfortunate he didn't remove his top ... but since he was wearing a singlet I still had an interesting view. Learning lots of anatomy and physiology ... at least about muscles ... perhaps hormones too. He made me laugh till I felt like I could burst and I surprised myself at how strong I felt. He's so free and funny and I wish I could be more like that.

PS ... Weekend leave tomorrow. Might ask Grant if we can buy a basketball hoop so I can practice.

January 21

So I'm freaking about leaving hospital ... is that weird? Went on another day trip to the mall and stuff and sometimes I get these feelings like I just want to retreat, like a snail into his shell. Have to stop myself looking at my reflection ... every glass window yells at me, 'Fat bitch.'

Diary, dear diary, how did I ever end up so obsessed with my body? How did I end up feeling like I want to disappear ... like I want to be so small that no one will see me.

Another thing happened today ... blood in my knickers.

Deep red ... blood.

January 22

Gotta pull myself together and stop being so obsessive, so that's it ... I am determined to get well, remain well, eat all my dinner like a good little girl and get over whatever it is I need to get over. This is a setback in my life not a forever sentence. I look at Norma, tube down her nose, so thin if I sneezed next to her she'd fall over and I ... that cannot be me.

Weekend leave tomorrow, Julie's like, 'So excited Talia.' And she puts her arm over my shoulder and we walk like that to the dining room and she sits down and hardly watches me prepare my breakfast. She sips her coffee and says, 'I need that ... had a late night, went to the movies.'

'What you see?' I ask, buttering my toast.

'Avengers. Not my pick but it was actually really good. Do you like movies Talia?'

'Yeah ... I like movies but not scary or violent. Julie ... do girls actually die of anorexia, like dead?'

'Oh,' she says, looking up and smiling gently. 'Surely you realise that anorexia ... I think I read recently that it has a 6% mortality rate.'

'How, how do you die,' I ask, sitting down opposite her with my breakfast.

'Cardiac arrest mostly ... related to electrolyte imbalance.'

'Do all girls come back like Norma ... can you just have one episode and get well.'

'I think something like 20% remain chronically ill.'

'I don't want to be that 20%.'

'You don't have to Talia, you don't have to be.'

January 23

So here I am, lying on my bed, in my very own bedroom writing to you my dearest friend and surprise surprise I feel kinda good. Almost happy.

Sol and Mac greeted me like I was wearing a crown. A great big diamond cluster crown. Little children can make you feel so special can't they. I wonder was I ever warm and embracing. Or have I always had icicles in my heart. Grant tries to hug me and I squirm inside like filthy mud … obviously Sol and Mac don't get their huggable arms from Grant since he's not their father. I must have inherited Mum's stiff unloving body since I can't remember her ever touching me with affection. Fuck … why am I rambling on about shit that doesn't matter. I'm here, I'm well or at least wellish … and I'm gonna stay that way.

Aunty Maxine says, 'Talia, what did you think of the picture I gave you for Christmas? You never said.'

'What picture? 'I say, without looking up from the wooden block house I am building with the boys.

'The photo,' she laughs. 'The photo of you with chicken pox and wearing that Snow White dress.'

'Oo … I had bad chicken pox, my face is covered.'

'Oh you were covered alright, never seen spots like it. Talia,' she says uncrossing her legs, straightening her navy blue dress and leaning towards me, 'but wasn't your hair lovely.

So long and dark … shiny. Talia are you going to grow it back. You looked so pretty.'

'I like it short.' When is this bitch going home?

'I guess you have the face to carry it off but now that you're well you could grow it.'

Well diary I didn't even answer I just got up and walked out the room leaving the boys crying, 'Talia.'

And fuck … ten minutes later there she is, so like my mother only 20 kilos heavier standing in my doorway. Yeah she even opened the fucken door without knocking. 'Talia,' she smiles, fuck she's like a hyena, all sneaky and creepy, 'do you still have that Snow White dress? I thought I could give it to little Lola, she loves dress up.'

'I'm fucken eighteen,' I glare, 'I wore it when I was four. Do you think I'd still have it?'

'Well,' she snarls, 'you were so thin you'd probably still have fit it.'

I just glare back like I'm the fucken hyena about to pounce and you know what she laughs. Walks out my room laughing and I thought for a second I was the hyena!

Were… what does she mean were?!

Later …

Ok now I'm obsessing … about what? Were, fucken were. 'You were so thin …'

Thought about sticking my fingers down my throat and bringing up dinner which I struggled to eat. And there she goes again, talking with food in her mouth, 'Kim whatever happened to Talia's Snow White dress?'

'Oh,' frowns Mum, 'I think ... did it get ripped or torn ... actually what do you remember Talia?'

Diary, everyone turns their head and looks towards me, mouths full of spaghetti bolognaise and I snap, 'I was four ... I can't remember.'

Fuck ... can't wait to get back to hospital.

January 24

Julie's like smiling and grinning on my return, 'Talia,' she beams, 'how did it go?'

I wanna collapse in to her melon chest and ... and ... well actually cry. Secret ... I wish Julie was my Mum or my Dad or both or just someone I could tell the truth to. But I go, 'Yeah, great, sucks to be back in this place.'

And then I see Norma being pushed in a wheelchair towards the nurse's clinic. I look at Julie, back at Norma and I don't know where the fuck I belong. Here with skinny fucked up girls getting thinner, about to cardiac arrest or at home where I don't know what the fuck is going on. But shit diary ... don't wanna be a Norma. Don't want to have a heart attack from starvation ... that seems fucken ridiculous.

'Julie,' I say, 'what's with the wheel chair?'

'Norma's dizzy and really needs to stay off her feet.'

'Oh,' I say. 'Hope she gets better soon.' Lie again ... because what I really wanted to say was: "I was dizzy ... how come no one pushed me in a wheelchair?!"

Bitch.

January 25

I promise Diary, I'm trying to be a recovering anorexic ... not a skinny retard with ostrich legs sticking out from a wheel chair, tube down her nose, taped to the side of her face but when I see her being pushed attentively by the nurses I feel this whimper inside. This little cry that says: I need taking care of too. I need a place to rest my head ... where I can speak the truth. Which sounds absolutely ridiculous ... what truth?

Sometimes I just feel so tired ... so small.

Lost.

January 26

Been shooting lots of hoops which I gotta say is absolute fun. Jason just makes me laugh and laugh ... he's come down a bit from his manic episode but he's still grinning and bouncing round like a beach ball. He's struts like some L.A. gangster, gesturing with his pinky and pointing finger in the air. 'Could do with a toke,' he beams, 'smoke it, toke it. They reckon I gotta give it up cause I'm manic. And

I'm like, yo … don't panic, I'm not manic. And if I am, it's fucken awesome!'

Diary … he is awesome.

January 27

And when you think about it, can Norma shoot hoops with awesome and in his own words, 'HOT', Jason? No. Can I? Absolutely yes.

Can she even win, beat him, ok he's flying high but still. No. She can hardly fucken walk let alone bounce around huffing and puffing in fun.

And is she starting school in about ten days, about to be discharged at forty-six kilos to begin a fantastic new chapter in life, going to become a dietitian, no. Am I? … absolutely fucken yes.

Grant is picking me up tomorrow and taking me to school to discuss subjects and so on for this year and I'm excited.

Later …

I wonder if everyone knows I've been admitted to a psychiatric hospital … not exactly the best resume. Julie says, 'Talia, mental illness is nothing to be ashamed of … it's just an illness like any other, like diabetes or pneumonia or whatever.'

'You think,' I say, frowning.

'I know,' she smiles, placing her hand on my arm. 'And anyone that judges, well they are no real friend anyway.'

'But a mental asylum,' I say, looking at the ground.

'Just another hospital ward for youth actually, Talia.'

'With mental problems.'

'Yeah, with mental illness. But like I said, nothing to be ashamed of. And Talia, I've seen friends visit you.'

'My good friends are off to university. Teacher's College and Law. But me ... I'm repeating the year.'

'Yeah I know that ... but the point is, real friends won't judge you for having been ill, real friends stick around and care.'

Trouble is Diary ... my real friends won't be there.

January 28

So Grant picks me up and on the way driving to school he says, 'I'm real pleased you're being discharged in two days. Your Mum's been cleaning your room ... fresh sheets on your bed. And Sol and Mac, excited.'

'Yeah,' I say, looking at the oncoming traffic.

'I just hope,' he says, rubbing the back of his hairy fucken neck, 'for your mother's sake you stay well.'

'Yeah.'

'It's taken a lot out of her, your illness. It's not all about you, Talia.'

'Yeah.'

'And Sol and Mac, not easy for them either. But my biggest concern is the stress on your Mum.'

Yeah. Yeah. Deary fucked up asshole yeah.

Anyway … I'm signed up doing: English, Biology, Chemistry, Health and Statistics. The Guidance Counsellor was really helpful and funny with a big grin and even bigger teeth, Mr Simms. He was wearing this blue shirt that said, "Wasn't me!" and I said, 'Wasn't you what?'

He laughed, 'My wife bought me this … wasn't me.'

I grinned and laughed.

I didn't see any students I know but as Julie says, I have nothing to be ashamed of.

Well … apart from causing my mother undue stress.

January 29

So I met with India today. She's still super trim and super fit looking with muscular strong calves. And she's still super positive about my future. 'I'm excited,' she grins. 'Excited and so proud of you.'

'I'm forty-six kilos,' I say.

'I know. You look fantastic. You've worked so hard.'

'Yeah …'

'And how are you finding the maintenance food plan.'

'Well,' I laugh, 'trim milk was a bit of an adjustment. I was used to that creamy full milk flavor.'

'Ar funny,' she grins.

And for a wee moment I thought I was gonna burst into tears. Gonna miss India. She's super inspiring and she looks amazing and she swears sometimes she eats cake and ice cream. 'Banana cake with lemon icing and I love French vanilla ice cream.'

'Really?' I say, sighing.

'Really,' she giggles, 'and what flavour ice cream do you like?'

'Ar … I don't like ice cream,' I say. Still can't admit the truth … fuck knows why. Feels all too scary. Like if I admit I like it I'll never be able to stop eating it … and what then … fat. And diary, I still don't want to be fat.

January 29

Sitting in my room, sun pouring in, thinking about closing the window it's so damn hot … no air conditioning in this place. Home.

Funny though, hospital feels more like home. The nurses and fucked up patients, India and even Doctor Arleen Adelaide, stuck up bitch … I miss them and I've only been home two hours. I miss them more than I missed Sol and Mac or anyone when I was in hospital. Truth is in this world … I feel so alone. I wish I could go shoot hoops with Jay, Jay from the Bay. Probably never see him again … he's from way up north. I wonder what he's like when he's well ... still extraordinarily hot I guess. At least to look at!

I think I'll console myself by saying when he's not manic; he's dull and boring ... hardly ever laughs. Sounds like I'm describing me. Diary ... he hugged me when I left, never felt so held by anyone. Like I fitted into his arms ... fitted into his body. He said, 'Whose gonna shoot hoops with me now?'

I smiled.

'Keep eating, you skinny pull through,' he says, kissing my cheek.

'I will,' I say, blushing like the crimson on my toe nails.

'Promise, young Talia.'

'Promise.'

So I made a promise ... I had more hugs that day than I've had in my entire eighteen years and you know what ... I could actually hug back. More, 'I'm so proud of you,' and 'You've worked so hard.'

No wonder the mental asylum feels like home.

January 30

So what next? Eat. Stick to my maintenance food plan. Eat. And ignore those fat thoughts and I'm yuck feelings. 'You can do it,' Julie said.

I can!

February 1

Had a visit from Maggie which was way cool. We went to the mall and ate sushi, like we used to. I had tuna, Maggie had salmon. Diet coke. We looked at clothes and stuff. Maggie bought red skinny jeans and make-up. She wanted to buy me something but I was like, 'No way.'

She's like, 'Yes. It's my money, let me shout you that t-shirt with Elmo on it. You keep picking it up.'

'No,' I say, 'let's go,' placing the t-shirt back down on the table and dragging her off.

Later she says, 'I just need to go toilet, wait here and I'll be back.'

And when she comes back she hands me a blue plastic bag with the Elmo t-shirt inside and says, 'Here.'

'Maggie,' I blush.

'Well you couldn't work this summer, could you?'

'No,' I nod.

'Come on,' she says, 'we'll miss the bus.'

So I'm wearing my Elmo t-shirt and I love it. It's white with an enormous red Elmo face grinning. Sol and Mac like it too … had this fleeting thought that I should've got the Cookie Monster t-shirt instead.

February 2

Have to meet my therapist or counsellor or whatever tomorrow. Personally I think the best therapy for me would be, shooting hoops with Jason. Having a laugh and working up a sweat. A hug at the end of it would be very therapeutic.

February 3

Seriously, why do I need therapy or counselling when I have you?

I'm eating, have a B.M.I. of 18 or close to it, doing just great. Ok ... still a little obsessed with being and feeling fat but what teenage girl isn't? Maggie drank diet coke and had sushi rather than a Big Mac. I bet if she was a boy, she'd have real coke, full of sugar and stuff and two Big Macs. Probably fries too. In fact, not just teenage girls, adult women too. Look at Mum, skinny long legged pull through. If she didn't have legs she'd look like an eel wearing a blond wig.

February 4

So my counsellor is some white haired, dreadlocked Rastafarian. Skin like coffee and gorgeous teeth, whiter than her trousers. Mostly she did the talking ... what the fuck do I have to say. I don't remember much of what she said ... I was entertained by the surroundings. The cream walls and charcoal carpet, bluey grey curtains surrounding the one window in the room. A pot plant in the corner, some kinda palm or maybe a fern, a wooden bookcase full of counselling and psychology type books. Several on eating disorders. A crystal hanging from the window... it made lovely rainbows around the room. I liked that.

She had other crystals too, a pink one the size of a mug sitting on the window sill and three deep black ones, placed opposite each other in the room so that they formed a triangle. I've heard about crystal quacks ... they think crystals have special powers or something. So now I'm thinking what's her qualifications ... is it her that needs therapy. Probably!

The only question I remember her asking was, 'If you were your Mum, what would you say to you? What would you want to hear?'

Well fuck me ... what would I say. I shrugged and said, 'Dunno.'

But diary, truth ... the truth is that question made me feel like running out the room. Escaping to a familiar world ... I need to diet. I need to be slim.

February 5

School tomorrow and I wish Jason was here so we could hang out and have a laugh.

February 6

How was school you ask? Ok I guess. Felt fat in my uniform ... it used to hang on me. I've had to remind myself all day that I was underweight and actually unwell then. But those fat feelings kept on screaming and I struggled to eat lunch. Just my apple. Actually just a bite of my apple. Was everyone looking at me thinking there's that anorexic freak? … don't know but sure felt like it. Maybe Mum was right and I should've started at a new school. She always thinks she's right, don't know how Grant puts up with her orders … but maybe this time she really was.

Mum.

The answer to the white haired Rastafarian's question would be, 'I love you.'

Just like that … I love you.

February 7

Keep thinking about that bloody question. And why all I want to hear is, 'I love you.' And how hearing that makes me feel and then I decide no I don't want to hear that because then I feel like crying, crying an enormous lake full of tears. Tears and tears … wet soggy tears. Like torrential rain and I don't know why … just do. What's inside me diary that feels so sad and lost and afraid? Like … please don't ever tell anyone … I just … there's this little person … this little me … she wants … she wants to be held in my mother's arms and soothed. Only my mother has no arms.

She's a fucken double amputee. An eel.

And I think about that Rastafarian hag and wonder why she's asking such stupid questions that make me want to search the latest magazine for weight loss ideas.

February 8

Well I survived the short week at school and it's the weekend already. Mum wants me to go to a Zumba class at the gym. 'You'll love it,' she says. 'You love to dance.' Like fuck, when have I ever loved dancing.

'Plus,' she says, drinking her smoothie, 'now you're a healthy weight ... well you want to stay that way don't you.'

'What?' I say.

'Well let's just say you look fantastic and that's great.'

'Oh.'

'Well ... everyone needs exercise. Easy to get fat without some movement.'

'Arh ha.'

'Your case worker did say you are allowed to exercise and well ... I just thought it might be fun and Zumba is supposed to be great for the waist line and hips and abs.'

'Ok,' I say, 'I'll go with you.' Just between you and me I like that idea of it being great for your abs and hips and waist. Yay.

Later...

So we went and guess what Mum was right again ...I do love to dance. It was fun fun fun and though I felt like an uncoordinated octopus ... I haven't smiled so much since hanging out with hot Jason. So Mum was right and I will definitely go again.

February 9

Guess what ... took Sol and Mac to the park and we all had an ice cream. All. Yes that means me too. I know I should be telling you about what fun we had on the swings and stuff which we did ... but I had an ice-cream ... a vanilla, single cone ice-cream and it was delicious and yum and diary, are you not exceedingly proud of me. I did chuck the cone to the birds ... a little seagull with a big squawking squawk flew away with it ... lunch and dinner perhaps! And ok so the single scoop will replace my lunch and perhaps dinner ... but I am only little like the little seagull with the big squawk.

Only so much we can digest.

February 10

Hung out with Maggie and Anna, we watched DVD's and drank diet coke and ate light popcorn and laughed talking about the old days. Maggie's like, 'Remember when I had braces and the wire got caught in my cheek?'

'Oh yeah,' I laugh, 'Luke must've felt so bad for knocking you with his elbow, especially with you screaming the cafeteria down.'

'You threw your sausage roll at him,' laughs Anna, 'tomato sauce and all.'

'Oh yeah, I did. It really hurt,' frowns Maggie, 'have you seen him lately, he's looking fine.'

'I know,' says Anna, 'mighty fine. He was so chubby and awkward and now he's smokin'. Doesn't he go out with Jodie?'

'Jodie … really she was such a bitch,' says Maggie.

'Oh Jodie Burns … yeah she was such a bitch, always remember that day she pulled up the skirt of Chrissy, that kinda handicap girl,' I say, 'and everyone stood round laughing and then Jodie called her tree trunk legs.'

'And then Chrissy tried to run away and that mean bitch held her skirt so she couldn't,' said Anna. 'You were so brave Talia when you told Jodie to leave her alone.'

'Chrissy was crying,' I say.

'God, what does smokin' hot Luke see in her?' says Maggie.

'She is beautiful,' I say, 'and slim. And she always looks so groomed, gorgeous make up, long blond hair.'

'You sound like you have a crush,' laughs Maggie.

'No,' I say, shaking my head, 'just saying, she is beautiful. And I guess that's what Luke sees.'

'Talia,' says Anna, 'you sticking up for Chrissy … now that's beautiful. You sat down with her on the bank after everyone left, me included, what did you say to her?'

'Told her not to worry, that Jodie was a mean bitch.'

'See mean bitch,' smiles Anna.

'Still gorgeous,' I say.

'Mean. Bitch,' says Maggie.

Mean. Bitch. But still incredibly beautiful which let's face it, is why smokin' Luke is at her side.

February 10

And when you think about it, the reason Jodie is at Luke's side is because he's beautiful. If he looked like he used to, plump and awkward, would she have her hand in his ... I don't think so. That is reality, is it not?

February 11

Have that Rastafarian quack after school today. Seriously thinking about not going, don't see the point. Last time I left wanting to lose weight and feeling argh! ... so what the fuck is all that about. The only trouble is if I don't go she'll inform my caseworker who will track me down like a drug dog at the airport.

Later...

So I went and blah, blah, blah.

BLAH!

Later ... again

Guess what the Rasta's name is ... you never will ... Grace.

Grace.

Can you believe it? A dreadlocked fifty or perhaps sixty year old called Grace. All I could think about was how people say grace before eating and how here I am sitting opposite her looking at her dimple on her chin, considering the fact that the name Grace is ridiculous for a therapist working with eating disorders.

And furthermore, she's thin!

February 12

I was sitting on the bank eating my sandwich when Chrissy came and sat next to me. Diary I'm ashamed to say that I became all self conscious. My sandwich ended up back in my lunch box.

She sat with her legs folded, gobbling down a hotdog like she was a Labrador and chatting to me as if I was her best friend. Which when you think about it aren't Labradors like a man's best friend. She's like, 'Are you going to the school dance?'

'Ur no,' I say, scratching my nose and wriggling my toes.

'Oh I am,' she grins, licking sauce off her hand.

'That's nice.'

'My foster Mum bought me a pink dress. Baby pink and it's got frills and she says I'm gonna look beautiful.'

'I'm sure you will,' softening at the mention of foster Mum. 'I bet you'll look real pretty. I think pink is your color.'

And she giggles like she's just a little kid, 'That's what my foster Mum says.'

'What's her name?' I ask.

'Pinky,' she beams, 'I call her Pinky cos she's pink.'

'Oh I meant … that's a perfect name for a dress. Just perfect.'

'Want chippies?' she asks, handing me the packet.

Salt and vinegar… yum. 'Um no thanks, they aren't on my meal … I mean I don't like chippies, but thanks Chrissy. Look I better go … gotta go to the toilet before class.'

'Ok,' she smiles, stuffing an enormous chippie in her mouth.

I stand up … look down at her … she has the most gorgeous eyelashes with yes Labrador brown eyes. 'You know what … you really will look pretty in your pink dress.' She's chunky, tree trunk thighs but wow, I had never noticed what lovely warm eyes. And not a lick of mascara.

'That's what my foster Mum says,' she says.

'I know,' I say, beginning to walk down the slope of the bank. 'So when is the dance?'

'August.'

'August,' I wave and walk towards my class with a big smile on my face.

February 13

Diary ... I feel really awful and like a mean bitch but I sat inside the library during lunch just in case Chrissy sniffed me out. She's a sweet girl but I don't want everyone thinking the only friend I have is in their words, 'a retard'.

I gazed up from my homework to look out the window and I saw her shoving down a hotdog arm in arm with another, 'retard', Stacey. Stacey wiped tomato sauce from Chrissy's chin and retard me felt a wave of jealousy. I missed those Labrador eyes and enthusiasm for pink frilly dresses and diary so fucked up am I that even as I write this I feel like I'm gonna burst into tears. What the fuck is that about?

February 14

Can't believe that Maggie and Anna leave for university this weekend. If I hadn't got screwed in the head would I be going too? Truth is I don't know ... I would've felt worried to leave Sol and Mac which is ironic considering I left them anyway. It's not that Mum is bad or nasty ... though sometimes her tongue fires venom, in fact eel? ... she's more like a cobra. A rattlesnake ... especially with all those bangles she wears! It's more that she's not there, doesn't listen, doesn't see. And like I said since she's eel like, sometimes snake and has no arms she can't touch. Oh my god ... she is snake. I read a book the other day that said ... snakes are practically blind, mostly deaf and leave their babies to fend for themselves.

Fuck !

Later …

I feel really bad for writing that stuff about my Mum. I mean she didn't just walk away like my Dad … even though I'm glad he did. And sometimes I sit and watch her with Sol and Mac and she seems like she has arms.

They sit on her knee or next to her and she doesn't shove them away or give them a get out of my space vibe.

She doesn't wrap her arms around them like I see some Mum's do but she doesn't pull away. Which is nice isn't it? She reads them a book and kisses them goodnight as she tucks them in. I stood at the doorway about an hour ago and watched her kiss them both on the forehead and say, 'Goodnight my sweeties … love you both.'

February 15

I've been feeling oh so fucken fat today. Maybe if I just lost a little weight I'd feel lighter and free. And maybe even beautiful.

Don't want to go back to looking like Norma with emu legs but just …

February 16

Party at Edwards's house for all those going to university. Maggie's like, 'You have to come.'

'Nah,' I say.

'Oh Talia, please.'

'I'm not going to university remember. And I have nothing to wear and everyone just hangs out drinking beer and smoking pot.'

'Talia, please.'

'Nah.'

'Heaps of people there aren't going to university. Mason, April, Hilary, Lucia. Oh and Cian, I just heard he's got a plumbing apprenticeship.'

'Oh really … what's Hilary and April doing, I was sure they'd be going?'

'Hilary is working at McDonald's, just for a year to save money for uni and stuff. And April, she's going to Polytech to study Design or something.'

'Really,' I say.

'Yeah really. So you aren't the only one not going to uni and you have loads to wear and beer, I'll put a peg on your nose.'

'Maggie,' I say, 'I haven't seen anyone from that crowd since I was sick and it's just kinda embarrassing.'

'Oh Talia,' she pleads, 'look how fantastic you are now. And what bloody teenage girl doesn't get screwed up at one time or other over being fat or feeling fat or whatever.'

'Do they?' I ask.

'Do they,' laughs Maggie. 'They might not end up in hospital but everyone I know, every girl I know worries about how she looks and if she's slim enough or too fat in the thighs or too small in the bust and then when you get to our Mums' age it's wrinkles and grey hair and fat tummies from having babies.'

'You think?'

'Talia,' she says. 'My Mum wants to get collagen or botox or her frown lines but I think she's gorgeous.'

'Your Mum seems so together and confident. She's a Principal.'

'Well she is in a way I guess ... but I don't know ... we all seem fucked up about how we look.'

'How'd you get so wise?'

'Reading, thinking, seeing you so sick ... I guess ... when Liam dumped me I convinced myself that it was because I wasn't pretty enough, or slim enough especially when he hooked up with Macy ... she's so pretty and petite. And I really loved him.'

'You're pretty. And slim.'

'Talia, thanks ... she's tiny and I'm athletic and muscular.'

'Yeah,' I agree, 'still slim.'

And Diary, then she's like, 'I still love him,' tears falling.

And I don't know what to do or say so I'm like, 'I'll come to the party.'

'Oh great,' she laughs and cries all at once.

February 17

So I'm wearing my purple skinnies … ironic, why, you guessed it, I feel so fat. And this black lace top which Anna lent me; still not sure it's me. Grant's like, 'You look nice Talia, good to see you going out.'

Mum looks up and starts flicking her nails. And you know what; I had this flash of grabbing her hand and poking her in the eye with her long pink nail. What the fuck is wrong with me? Nervous? You'd think I was heading out the door to get a Brazilian wax.

February 18

So I get to the party, Anna's Dad dropped us off and I'm so nervous that by the end of the drive I'm convinced my thighs have expanded by four inches. I wish desperately I hadn't worn skinny jeans and get this mental fucked up feeling of wanting to tear them off. But standing there in my knickers; oh god even fatter.

Maggie puts her hand on my shoulder and says, 'Ok? You look gorgeous.'

'Thanks,' I say. But gorgeous … I knew I shouldn't have worn so much make-up and maybe the lace shirt is too racy. Oh fuck diary where's my shell when I need it.

'And are you ok, Maggie? Liam and his tiny teddy might be here,' says Anna, reapplying her lipstick.

'Hopefully,' Maggie sighs, 'they didn't come.'

'We'll be here for you,' I say.

'Come on then let's go in,' says Anna and Maggie together and we all laugh.

The place is buzzing with music and chatter and laughter when we get inside and diary though I wished desperately I was a tortoise with an amazing shell on my back to retreat in, I gradually began to relax because everyone was so nice. People high fived me and said stuff like, 'Great to see you,' and 'You look awesome Talia,' and 'Wow Talia, cool.'

I danced with Anna and Maggie and we laughed and sang and waved our arms in the air to cool songs and I felt almost normal … if there is such a thing. But then as people got drunker and smellier and slurier I wanted to go home. But I had to wait for Anna and Maggie because we were all going together, staying at Anna's house, so I found an armchair and sat myself down and just watched everyone. And there in the corner were Liam and Macy pashing and groping each other; shit she is petite. Maggie's like a race horse next to her. And she has the most gorgeous red hair, all wavy and red.

Anna leans on the arm of my chair. 'Maggie's upset, she's outside, I've texted Dad … he's on his way. You ready?'

Poor Maggie.

She sobbed herself to sleep; must be true when they say love hurts.

February 19

I feel so lost and ... I don't know what ... sad? Maggie, Anna and I had our last evening together. They both leave tomorrow for University. Did I tell you Maggie changed her mind about Teacher's college?

Anyhow, Maggie's like, still sobbing, 'I know we only went out for six weeks but I read somewhere once it's not the length of time, it's the moments you share.'

'Is it?' I say.

'Yeah,' she nods, 'the way someone made you feel.'

'How'd he make you feel?' I ask.

'Like we fit ... together.'

'Oh,' I say. I felt like that with Jason.

And I don't mean sex ... no, like when he put his arms around me and I'd just melt into his body. And he'd kiss me gently on the forehead and I'd just feel so loved I guess.

'Did you sleep with him?' I ask, leaning forward.

'No, maybe I should've,' says Maggie, wiping the tears from her cheeks. 'Does oral sex count?'

'Umm ... not sure,' I say, blushing with images of Maggie umm ... on the end of Liam's ... thing ... sucking like an ice cream.

'Look Maggie,' says Anna, moving closer to Maggie and taking her hand, 'I think you need a reality check. And I hate to be the one to reinforce this but he broke up with you. You might have felt something but Maggie he didn't.'

'But maybe … he's just scared because he felt it too.'

Diary he didn't look scared last night!

'And maybe … you just need to give up on that dream,' says Anna.

'But he used to look at me,' says Maggie, 'with such, I don't know … tenderness. And he said, "I'm so into you, Maggie.".'

'And now he's looking at Macy with such tenderness. And he's so into her. I'm sorry Maggie it's true,' says Anna. 'Maggie, remember that DVD, *'He's just not that into you'*?'

'Oh yeah,' I say, 'if a guy wants to be with you he'll make it happen.'

'But,' weeps Maggie.

'No,' says Anna, 'no buts. And Maggie, he's with someone else.'

Maggie begins to smile through her tears, 'If he wanted me, he'd be with me. He chose her … didn't he.'

'He chose her,' replies Anna. 'He chose her.'

February 20

Can't believe my friends have gone and I'm still here hanging out in the library doing my homework because the only person that wants to associate with me is a retard. And I'm such a bitch! And fuck I have that Rastafarian tomorrow which is just fucken fantastic. I mean why do I need a therapist when I have you?

February 21

Grace the Rastafarian is a widow and has two daughters … I found that out today. She used to be in a band; a singer and can play the keyboard and piano. I must admit I was impressed. She retrained as a counsellor when her husband died twelve years ago. I so wanted to ask how he died but didn't want to make her sad or uncomfortable. Anyhow I did talk a little today, I'm like, 'My best mates have left for university.'

'And how does that make you feel?' she asks.

'Happy.'

'Happy? Why happy?'

'Um … because my mates are following their dreams and going to become something which is cool.'

'True,' she says. 'And what's your dream?'

'You'll probably laugh but I want to be a dietitian,' I say, going red in the face.

She smiles and nods, 'Why do you think I'm going to laugh, I think that if that's your dream … then fantastic.'

'Oh … well … cause I'm fucked up round my body and food and stuff.'

'You don't have to be forever,' she smiles. And I notice her teeth which are dazzling white and wonder if she's had them whitened.

'Grace … do you like your name?' I ask.

'Actually,' she smiles, 'I love it. It means graceful, lovely and thanks. I'm not sure I'm graceful or lovely but what beautiful words. And the word thanks, I love being thankful.'

'Ar,' I say, 'I thought it was a bit weird you being called Grace.'

'Why?'

'The whole idea of giving thanks for food.'

And she laughs.

February 22

But am I really happy? What do you think? I'm such a selfish bitch I wish Maggie and Anna were both still here. Following their dreams, like fuck … I want them here, hanging out with me. Making me laugh and helping me to feel normal even though I know it's not true.

I really feel for Maggie she's so hung up on Liam. Liam … he's so put his hook into her. He was pashing that Macy like no one else was there. Personally I think they looked gross.

Is it possible to still like someone but be all over someone else? What the fuck would I know about love or lust?

I haven't told you but I fantasise about Jason. Most days. We'd live happily ever after; not married, I so don't believe in that! ... but happily ever after larking around, shooting hoops in our backyard. He'd make me laugh every day, laugh and laugh till my tummy hurt. That's so what I want, just to laugh. Just to be able to collapse into his gorgeous chest, sweat and all, laughing at his crazy antics. Course ... he's probably not so funny when he's well. Imagine that, I'd be giving him sugar pills saying, "Here honey, take your Lithium."

And he'd be singing and dancing around, "Oh Talia, let me take you to my cave, get it up, get it up cause I can."

Well actually, I'm not too sure about the getting up business ... but being held in his tattooed muscular arms ... I think ... I did like that diary.

I so did.

February 23

Yeah that's me, in love with some manic, crazy but so hot guy who is probably covered from head to toe in hickies from all the girls he's had hanging off him.

Oh God ... I'm worse than Maggie.

February 24

Mr Sullivan, the physical education teacher; a gaunt looking marathon runner ... apparently he's run over forty marathons and he's what? … fortyish; chased me up the slope to my next classroom, 'Talia, you're looking really well. You fit?'

'Not really,' I say, 'only exercise I been doing is Zumba classes with my Mum.' And walking and situps and pressups and squats.

'My wife does that, she loves it,' he says. 'I'm hoping you'll play footy this year.'

'Umm … I … not sure,' I say, kicking the ground.

'Think about it,' he nods, 'you're a real talent. Wish my son could kick a ball like you.' And he laughs. 'He plays hockey.'

'Oh,' I smile.

'Just think about it, Talia. Love to have you on the team.'

'I'll think about it,' I say.

Thought about in the following two seconds.

Nah.

February 25

Mind you playing footy might give me something to do in the weekends. There's only so much playing with Sol and Mac I can take. And homework … if I read any more Shakespeare I'll start talking old English.

I said to Grant and Mum, 'Can we get a basketball hoop? Please.'

'Why?' says Mum, sipping her coffee.

'So I can shoot hoops,' I say, biting my toast.

'Talia,' says Mum, 'I can't see butter on that toast. Is there butter on that toast? It's part of your daily plan. Grant is she getting thin?'

'Um,' he says, looking me up and down; creeping me out. 'It's hard to tell in that nightie.'

Fuck … I'm outta here. And I was. Leaving my unbuttered toast on the plate.

February 26

Mum's been checking my meal plan, 'Are you eating your protein as part of that sandwich?'I lift up the bread to reveal a slice of ham.

'Good,' she says.

The thing is if she starts freaking out because I don't put butter on my toast she'll freak me out and then I'll struggle to eat my toast. And then I'll be just like her. 'You don't even have toast, let alone butter,' I said. 'One large coffee and that's it.'

'I haven't eaten breakfast in twenty years,' she said, raising her eyebrows and looking up …duh!

'Then don't go on to me,' I say.

'Excuse me,' she glares, 'who was it that spent months in hospital so thin she could've been in a museum … in the skeleton department.'

'I wasn't that thin,' I say, putting my sandwich down. I wasn't was I?

'Talia,' she says, tears welling up in her green eyes, 'if you get sick again, I just don't think my nerves could take it.'

'You mean you'd lose your babysitter.'

'No,' she says, 'do you think Grant is going to want to hang around with my daughter in a mental hospital again. He's been so great but you and your problems ... they could drive him away. And I just don't think I could take being left again.'

I look at my Mum ... feel like crying myself, she looks so small and childlike and I don't know where to run. But one thing is for sure, that ham sandwich is ... it tastes like sour milk.

February 27

She's standing outside the shower this morning; can't believe I didn't lock the door!

Fortunately I'm wrapped in a towel and there she is ... hair in curlers, definitely not so pretty without make-up, hands on her hips.

'What?' I glare.

'Nothing,' she says and walks out.

What the fuck!

February 28

I'm sitting in the library, rereading my essay for English, when I hear this, 'Hi, Talia.'

I know that voice ... look up to see those lovely Labrador brown eyes and a grin so wide I had to smile back. 'Sit down,' I say.

'Oo, I can't,' says Chrissy, 'meeting Stacey, we gonna go get lunch at the cafeteria and Stacey's got the latest Girl magazine.'

'Ar fun,' I say.

'You like the Girl magazine?' she asks.

'Sure,' I say. Never read it.

'Wanna come ... Stacey says you aren't nice but I told her you are.'

'Thanks Chrissy,' I say, 'but I really want to finish this essay for English.'

'Ok,' she laughs, 'we don't do big essays like that in our class.'

'Oh you're lucky,' I smile.

'Better go,' she waves.

She's gonna tell Stacey I'm nice. How nice am I? Chrissy's good enough for conversation in the library but too simple to be seen around school with.

And two of them ... shit.

February 29

I left a message on Grace's answer phone to say I won't be in today, that I was sick. Considering I have a mental illness, it's kinda true.

February 29

I feel really bad about lying to Grace … just feel, fuck I don't know. Talking is the last thing I want, well talking about stuff that's inside I guess. I mean how can I talk to Grace when I don't even know what it is that I feel.

Still, I feel guilty.

Keep thinking those thoughts that if I just lost a few kilos I'd feel a whole lot better. My clothes would be looser and I'd feel calmer and more in control and like nothing else really mattered. Just being slim.

That's all that matters, being slim.

March 1

I've been studying my meal plan like I used to study weight loss books and celebrity magazines hoping the plan will permeate into my psyche. Like I used to hope those rib bearing stars with their weight loss tips would permeate into my body.

Saturate me with their thinness.

Oh fuck … as if.

I keep hearing Julie say, 'Twenty percent become chronic.'

Chronic.

March 2

Guess what? I come home from the park with Sol and Mac to find Grant putting up a basketball hoop over the garage. It's black and white with this blue and white net and soo cool, 'What you doing?' I say.

'What's it look like,' he grins, reminding me of this big grizzly bear that's just caught a salmon.

I stand staring while he attaches it; imaging Jason and I larking around, him saying, "How'd someone so small get so good?"

And I'd say, "How'd someone so big get so bad?"

Then he'd throw the ball at me laughing.

'Talia,' says Grant, climbing down from the ladder, 'we need to go back to the sports shop.'

'Why?' I ask.

'I forgot a ball,' he laughs.

'Oh,' I smile.

'I'll just go grab the keys, your Mum's at the hairdressers so we have to take the boys.'

And so we all went to the sport shop and Grant bought me the most expensive ball in the shop just because Sol and

Mac loved the color. Its navy blue and white, not just plain old orange and according to Sol and Mac that made it the best one.

I didn't like to say so … but I thought so too.

March 3

Grant's been shooting hoops with me. Sol and Mac running around under our feet until Grant set out their wooden train set by us. I couldn't help thinking, what does he see in my Mum?

And …three kids, different fathers, one a fucked up anorexic … actually a recovering anorexic and two three year olds that drive me crazy and I love them.

March 4

I have Grace on Thursday and as much as I don't want to … I will go. The thought of lying again, yeah, not great.

Been shooting hoops 'with Jason' and it's so much fun. Is it possible to miss someone that you never really had a relationship with?

I miss him.

Miss his laugh and his smile and his beautiful arms and shoulders and his brown eyes that seemed to look right in me.

Or maybe I just miss … miss someone. Someone that's not in my life and never has been, someone that makes me feel like it's ok to be me. Ok to be in my skin.

March 6

I've just reread yesterday's entry and I've just concluded that I must be fucken mad. Shooting hoops with Jason! What am I?…psychotic! Obviously in a mental asylum too long.

And.

And … how come it takes a mentally ill, flying higher than a fucken big bird to make me feel like it's ok to be me. Ok to be in my skin.

As if in reality he'd give a shit!

I bet when his wings have been clipped and he's back on the ground he wouldn't even remember my name.

March 7

I hardly sit down when Grace is like, 'Talia, I know coming here is difficult for you but it's better you come and we talk about the weather or whatever than you not come at all. In fact if it's a day you really don't want to come … I'd rather you came and we just sat in silence.'

'Wouldn't that be wasting your time?' I say, blushing.

'Sometimes saying nothing is saying everything,' she says.

'Hah?' I say, confused.

'Well,' she smiles, 'if you come in here and sit in silence … it tells me that something is in fact so hard to talk about that you don't know how. It tells me that perhaps you don't trust me enough to talk, yet. And it tells me … that that's what you do, you shut down instead of opening up. That's probably what you've done your entire life.'

'Oh,' I say.

'I could go on … you see, everyone has a story and when that story is stuck inside … stuck in the body, illness will eventually result.'

'Like anorexia?'

'Like anorexia, bulimia, compulsive overeating, any addiction really.'

'And what about cancer?' I ask.

'Cancer … there's a lot of research to say that cancer has a lot to do with repressed rage, repressed bitterness. I guess, Talia, all I'm saying is behind every illness is a story and more often than not it's a story that hasn't been shared. Often not even to ourselves.'

'Really,' I say, intrigued.

'Really,' she smiles, sipping from her glass of water. 'That's what counselling is … telling that story. And sometimes we communicate in silence … as we have always done.'

I nod and sip from my glass of water.

'And sometimes I communicate in silence. I just listen … be,' she says.

Well diary ... I think about that and am torn between wanting to talk nonstop about anything and everything and taking a deep breath and not saying a word. I go with the latter.

March 8

I'm crossing the road when I see this enormous girl. When I say enormous, well actually it's a kind way of saying fat.

Very, very fat.

I'm talking hippo. An overweight one.

She had short curly brown hair, kinda unkempt. And these fat hands like lard that were obviously so heavy they seem to drag her whole body down. Oh diary, she looked so sad and my heart – which most the time I'm convinced I don't have one – felt like her hands.

Heavy and big.

Even now thinking about her... I have tears in my eyes.

Diary ... is she just like me ... only fat? Is she trying to disappear into food and layers that surround her? Layers and layers of protection. Layers and layers of fat. I wonder what her story is?

Sad.

Has to be sad.

And what is my story?

Why do I feel the need to disappear also? Only I disappear into nothingness, into thin air. Not eating is my overeating. What then is my story?

Sad?

Am I sad?

All I know for sure is … I wanted to wrap my arms around that fat girl with curly brown hair, tell her I cared. Tuck her into a warm bed, kiss her gently on the forehead and tell her she was safe … now. I'd sit by her all night, guarding her like I was her lioness. And then she'd wake up a healthy weight knowing she was heard and protected.

March 9

Wrap my arms around her! … Jesus, she's so hippo like they wouldn't even go halfway. And who the hell do I think I am … Mother fucken Theresa?!

March 10

Mum and Grant had a night out so as soon as the boys went to bed I went too. Not much else to do. Two am after one of those bad dreams where I can't move, I wander into the kitchen to get a glass of water and Jesus fucken Christ … Mum's squealing like she's in some erotic movie. Legs in the air, still wearing her high heels and there's Grant's ass, pounding between her. On the fucken carpet right in front of the TV.

A live porn DV fucken D.

So there you have it … now I know what he sees in her. I remember Anna telling me and Maggie how she overheard her Mum and friends talking after a few glasses of wine. Anna's like, 'Alison, Mum's mate said, "Men are simple creatures, all they need is sex and food."

'"Yep, Max gets so grumpy if he's not getting it," says Mia, you know, Cameron's Mum. And then my Mum … my prudish, headmaster Mum, giggles, "Yep, all they really care about are tits, ass and a vagina and in my experience sometimes they'll even bypass the first two and just get straight to the vagina."'

Well … now I know it's true.

March 11

Had to bypass … gross that just reminded me of bypassing tits and ass … getting straight to vaginas. Fucken delightful! Guess it would be if I was a man or teenage boy or some long legged porn queen. Then again porn queens probably like a little more tit and ass action … a lick and squeeze … oh fuck … can I live somewhere else?

I so could not sit at the breakfast table and eat my toast; Grant sitting opposite me with this ridiculous smile. Stuffing his face with toasted muesli, milk dribbling down his chin. Anna's Mum's friend is right, men are such simple creatures.

And where was the squealing porn star, 'The oo oo oo Grant' and 'Ah ah AH!' In fucken bed recovering.

March 12

Couldn't concentrate in class.

Kept having images of Mum's red stilettos dangling from her feet ... Grant pounding in between her legs like a jackhammer at a construction site.

Mr Reiding, my English teacher is like, 'Talia, can I speak to you after class, please.'

I look up at him and nod.

'Thanks,' he says.

And then I can't concentrate because I keep thinking I've failed my Shakespeare essay and right now that's more than I can take. I've never failed anything, unless you count last year when I ended up in a mental asylum and dropped out entirely.

The bell goes for lunch and everyone wanders out. I stay seated at my desk and look around the room, out the window at the rain.

'Over here,' says Mr Reiding, tugging at his beard and pointing to a seat next to his desk.

I take another glance at the rain, wish I was running through it catching drops on my tongue because boy do I feel thirsty.

'Talia, you coming?' Mr Reiding asks.

I wander over, sit myself down and say, 'Yes?'

He smiles. Lines form all around his tired brown eyes, in his cheeks and I couldn't help but smile back. 'You look tired,' I say.

'That's an English teacher's vocation,' he says, looking through piles of paper on his desk. 'Ar here it is.'

'You're the head of department, aren't you?' I ask, changing the subject.

'I am.'

'That means you're extra busy.'

'True,' he says, tugging at that beard again.

'You wanna take it easy,' I say, 'relax, read a book. You must love reading.'

'I do love reading but sadly the only chance I get to read is in the school holidays. And then I read and read, lie on the couch and read till I fall asleep.'

'Cool,' I smile.

'But during the term,' he says, rubbing his rumbling tummy and looking down at it, 'must be hungry,' he smiles.

Standing up I say, 'You eat and we'll talk another time.'

'No, no,' he says. 'I'm fine,' picking up some papers on his desk. 'This,' he says, 'is astounding work and I could not have produced a better essay myself. And I wanted to personally congratulate you.'

'Oh,' I say, sighing heavily and placing my hand on my chest.

'You must have worked really hard; your use of quotation is excellent.'

'You don't think it reads better than it is because you're so tired?'

'Talia,' he says, in a tone so gentle I could weep, 'these bags are a permanent fixture … but they don't affect my ability to recognise excellence. This essay on Othello, it really is top class. Soak that in,' he smiles.

'Ar sorry, I'm sorry Mr Reiding … I … thanks.'

His tummy rumbles like the sound of an earthquake.

We look at each other and laugh.

March 13

So, wow wow wow … does that mean I'm clever? It must do because Mr lovely Reiding said so and he's highly qualified with a Masters in English Literature or so I heard. I wish I had someone to share my fantastic news with. I'm like, 'Sol guess what?'

'Uh,' he says, picking up a dragon figurine.

'Mr Reiding,' … too late he's off, flapping his arms like dragon wings.

'Mac,' I say.

He's eyes are glued to the TV.

'Mac … Mac.'

Still glued. I consider turning it off but feel too mean.

Mum's in the kitchen drinking coffee and flicking through a magazine and Grant, now he might be interested but he's at work. Perhaps I'll tell him later … he must have a degree of sorts being an Engineer. As I said … what was it he saw in my uneducated mother … oh shit that's right!

Don't remind me.

March 13

Today with Grace I rambled on about this and that … I don't want her thinking I have some kind of difficult story to share. Even though sharing anything is kinda difficult.

I'm like, 'Still raining.'

'I love the sound on my corrugated iron roof,' she says.

'Why?'

'Hmmm … makes me want to snuggle up in a blanket and listen to the drops. It's relaxing.' And diary, she looks relaxed just talking about it.

'I like walking in the rain,' I say.

'Yeah,' she smiles, 'why?'

'It's nice.'

'Nice … how.'

And I sit back and can almost feel the rain hitting my face. 'It's fresh and wet and it makes me feel … feel. I don't know.'

'How does it make you feel, Talia?' she asks, smiling.

'I don't know,' hanging my head.

'Think of one word that describes how walking in the rain makes you feel.'

'Umm …' I say.

'Perhaps have a sip of water that might help.'

I take a gulp, in fact drink the entire glass, 'Wet,' I say, 'wet.'

'Wet,' she echoes and laughs.

March 14

Diary, I don't think I'm a literary genius after all. I think it's just that I'm like Othello. Easily manipulated and jealous. I'm sitting in English, listening to the rain fall on the roof when I overhear Mr Reiding say, 'Renee, that's great work. Excellent.'

Fucken excellent.

Fucken Renee.

And I'm so full of jealousy I want to cry and scream all at once. 'Bitch,' I mutter, biting my lip and clenching my fists. I'm not sure who I'm jealous of. Pretty Renee with her sleek black hair and Katy Perry eyes or Mr Reiding tugging at his beard.

And not only am I jealous but murderous as well. I have these thoughts of wanting to knock both their heads together.

Bang fucken bang.

Told you I was like Othello.

March 15

Do you ever think I'll grow up and not be such a nasty jealous murderous bitch? The thing is ... I'm not like Othello in that I don't have an evil and cruel Iago taunting me. I'm just jealous and murderous all by myself. In fact maybe that's the problem. I'm more like Iago, evil and cruel ... only it's me I taunt.

Haunt.

Later ...

So I'm crossing the road and bloody hell, there she is.

Hippo girl.

Dragging her fat legs and feet like they weigh the ton that they do! She's tugging at her green jersey, pulling it away from her belly but there's no disguising all that lard.

Oh diary, she haunts me with her hanging head. It's like sadness surrounds her ... seeps from her ... like the falling rain. And with her curly brown hair damp ... she looks even more unkempt.

I wish I could spin a cocoon around her. Wrap her up in warmth and kindness. And then ... well then when she felt safe enough, cared for enough ... she'd transform into a butterfly. Open her amazing wings and leave all that fat behind.

March 15

I think from now on, I'll take another route home from school. I can't sew or knit let alone spin cocoons.

March 16

Grant's like, 'Gumboots on boys, it's finally stopped raining, let's get outside.'

Mum looks up from her coffee, 'Grant it'll be so damp and wet, they'll get all muddy.'

'Kim,' frowns Grant, 'they've been inside for days ... let them have some fresh air.'

'Well you do the washing,' she says. What was it he saw in her?

Grant opens the back door and the boys run outside and I follow. The sun is sneaking a glance behind grey clouds.

I watch Sol and Mac run up and down, down and up the grass just for the joy of running. Even Mac doesn't seem bothered by flecks of water on his jeans. He has always loved running. As soon as he could toddle, he ran. And ran and ran. Sol likes to run too but not for as long. He soon sits in the damp sandpit pushing diggers and trucks, making, 'Brem brem,' noises.

I say, 'Sol ... wanna make a volcano?'

'Yeah,' he grins.

'You start building one in the sand and I'll run inside and get the vinegar and baking soda. Ok?' I smile.

'Ok,' he says, already shaping the sand like a volcano.

'Now,' I say, several minutes later, 'tip this baking soda in the crater and then the vinegar.'

I yell, 'Mac, come watch this.' He looks over then continues to run. 'It's an eruption,' I yell.

Sol's eyes are open so wide I think they might explode too.

Diary, he looks over at me and says, 'Talia, you're beautiful.'

I smile.

He takes my face in his little dirty hands with his little dirty knuckles and little dirty finger nails and gently kisses my cheek.

And I'm molten rock, flowing down our volcano. 'You're beautiful too,' I say, sighing deeply. 'And Mac,' I say loudly, turning towards Mac still running, 'you're beautiful too.'

'What?' he yells, in between breaths.

'You're beautiful,' I yell back.

'No I'm not,' he says, hands on his hips, 'I'm handsome.'

'Oh,' I laugh, 'you are.'

March 19

So guess what? I'm in English thinking about the word beautiful. I look it up in the dictionary and here it is … beautiful : very pleasing to the senses. Another definition … beautiful : having beauty, pleasing to the eye or ear or mind or taste.

And so there I was in English with this big wow look on my face. The mind … the ear … I am truly wowed. Mr Reiding pulls up a seat next to mine and says, 'Talia, the work you've done on the Sylvia Plath essay is excellent.'

'She's … interesting,' I say. What I really wanted to say was … she's fucked in the head like me.

'She is interesting and a brilliant poet. I bet you could write brilliant poetry too if you tried.' He smiles.

'Ar …' I say, 'I don't think so.'

'Talia,' he says, touching his beard and face, 'I bet you could … you could try sometime.'

He precedes to hand me my draft essay pointing out any comments that he has made. As he walks away he turns back and says, 'Excellent stuff.'

I look at him sitting at his desk, rubbing his tired lined eyes, gently touching his brown beard with flecks of ginger and grey and conclude, with the help of the dictionary, he is a beautiful man.

March 20

I think I may have made a friend. I haven't told you but I still hang out in the library most days, not so much to hide from Chrissy and Stacey, in fact they pop in now and then. All giggles and smiles and stories about what they have been doing. Stacey's like, 'I'm going out with Jona, his Dad is friends with my Dad, they fish together.'

'He kissed her,' giggles Chrissy.

'Really?' I smile.

'He's got big lips,' grins Stacey.

'And did you like it?' I ask, looking at her tiny lips wondering if they got lost.

'I love it,' grins Stacey, twisting a strand of her brown wavy hair in her finger.

'Especially when he puts his tongue in your mouth, aye Stacey,' laughs Chrissy.

Stacey giggles and whispers, 'He put his fingers up my fanny.'

'Oh,' I say softly, nodding.

'And what about his dick?' says a wide eyed Chrissy.

'Shh,' says Stacey. 'He wants to but I said I'll just try your fingers first.'

'That's a good idea,' I say. 'And did you like it …?'

'I wanted to wash first,' she whispers, 'but Jona said, "Don't worry," but I did feel worried.'

'And you know about contraception?' I ask.

'Mum got me the injection,' says Stacey, pointing to her bottom. 'It hurt.'

'I got it too,' says Chrissy. 'But no boy likes me.'

'With eyes like yours and your lovely smile and laugh,' I say, 'I'm sure they will.'

Chrissy smiles, cupping her boobs, 'Stacey says they'll love my boobies.'

'Well … they will,' says Stacey, 'Jona loves mine and yours are all … all … bigger.'

And I look at them both and nod, 'Most of all you know …,' all serious like, 'a boy will love you because … because you're a beautiful person that makes him feel warm inside.'

'No he won't,' laughs Chrissy and Stacey.

I look at my black shoes …they could do with a clean.

'We better go get our lunch now,' says Stacey, 'I'm hungry.'

'Bye, Talia,' they say, arm in arm walking away.

'Bye,' I say, biting my lip and blushing.

Diary … is it true? Will a boy love a girl because she warms his heart not just his groins?

Except … what does that mean for Mum and Grant?

And … oh fuck I'm confused.

Later … I apologise … I went off on such a tangent: I'm so confused; I didn't tell you about my new friend, Elli. I'm so tired right now but I'll fill you in tomorrow.

March 21

I was sitting on my bed looking at my meal plans; thinking how well I was doing … yes it's true. A positive vibe was radiating from this body.

This mind!

When I get a call from Maggie; apart from the odd text we haven't spoken since she left for Varsity. She's like, 'Hey Talia, how you going, you well?'

'Yeah good,' I say.

'Good? Really?'

'Yeah good,' I repeat, starting to feel annoyed. 'What about you, Varsity ok?'

'Talia,' she says, 'I wanted to tell you something amazing that happened but then I thought that I was selfish especially if you've been having a hard time.'

'I like amazing,' I say, 'tell me.'

'Well it's kinda naughty too,' she says.

'Naughty,' I say, intrigued, 'tell me.' I love the idea that someone other than myself is bad. I guess that reflects how bad I am.

'Well, me and these girls went out clubbing, we all got plastered. I was so drunk. Anyhow I hooked up with this guy I'd seen around Varsity, Scott. Tall ... which of course I need, athletic ... which I like, blue eyes and dark hair ooh and a ring in his nose.'

'A ring in his nose,' I say, 'that's not your type, is it?'

'Loads of guys seem to have nose rings or studs at Varsity and it kinda grows on you.'

'Oh,' I say.

'And tattoos ... a sleeve. Yummy forearms.'

'And tattoos,' I say, 'wow your taste has changed.'

'Anyhow we went back to his flat and I was drunk I can't really remember the sex but ... now here's the amazing part. We got up, I showered, because I felt like crap, had coffee and toast, was gonna leave, kinda all awkward and he's like, "Come back to bed," and he takes my hand, leads me to his bedroom. I was tired and starting thinking of Liam, then I thought what the fuck. He goes down on me and Talia ... wow, I had an orgasm.'

'You what?' I say, blushing.

'Orgasm, come, went off ... like a rocket.'

'Really,' I murmur, wanting to hang up.

'Talia, I wasn't sure what was happening at first.'

'Yeah,' I say, tapping my toes and looking out the window.

'I said, "I think I just came." And he looks up with this grin and my body felt all weak and then I just burst into laughter.'

'Uh ha,' nodding. And why exactly are you telling me this?

Surely Stacey's news was enough!

'I said to Scott, "where did you learn to do that?"'

'And he's like, "I googled it."'

'"You googled it," I said.

'"Yeah, how to go down on a girl," he said. Then we just cracked up laughing.'

'So what's it like?' I ask, more out of politeness ... at least I think.

'What, coming?'

'Yeah.'

'Um ... really hard to describe. Like all this amazing, intense, really intense sensation that just like builds up and builds up and keeps building up, then release. A wow feeling of release and your legs feel all weak and you wanna lie back and go "Arrrrrrr."'

'Weak,' I say, 'your legs feel weak.'

'In a great way,' she reassures.

'So Liam, your over him, are you going to see Scott again?

'Liam,' she says softly, 'I'm trying to listen to what you guys said. That he's just not into me. But truth is ... the orgasm was amazing, great, so want to do it again but when I got home I cried. I'll always love him, even though I'm, well, he doesn't love me.'

'And Scott?'

'Scott ... not sure, see what happens I guess.'

'What's he studying?'

'Music ... something to do with music and film and scriptwriting and stuff I think. But definitely music.'

'That's cool,' I say, genuinely enthused, 'Wish I had learnt an instrument. What does he play?'

'Not sure,' she giggles, 'how to make your vagina sing.'

March 22

How to make your vagina sing!

According to Maggie, every girl needs a Scott, at least once. I'm not so sure. The thought of going weak and dizzy and letting some guy put his tongue down there is ... well it just doesn't seem normal. And I'm with Stacey, do you wash first? Fortunately for Scott, Maggie had showered.

Diary ... I've never even kissed a guy. I know that's rare at eighteen. Anna lost her virginity at fifteen. Maggie, seventeen, I think.

And me ... I love music but I'm not sure I want it between my legs.

March 23

So I'm sitting with Grace looking at the pink stone she has on the window, wondering if her husband made music between her legs. 'Grace,' I say, 'do you think …?'

'Yes,' she says, leaning forward.

'Do you think …' I frown. 'What's that pink stone on the window sill, it's pretty?' Just can't bring myself to ask such a stupid question as, "Do you think sex is normal, good even?"

'It's a rose quartz.'

'A what?'

'Rose quartz. The love stone.'

'A love stone,' I say. Yeah right!

'Crystals like the rose quartz come from within the earth … are part of the earth and send out vibrations. The rose quartz vibrates love and compassion. A gentle stone.'

'Gentle,' I repeat. How the fuck can a stone be gentle?

'And even if you don't believe that,' she smiles, 'it's lovely to look at.'

'You like pink?' I say.

'Love pink,' she says, 'though I love all colors, what about you Talia do you love pink?

'Umm,' I say, 'not sure, I guess that rose quartz is pretty.' But shit, would I want to wear it like a three year old … I don't think so.

'Do you wear pink?' I ask, gazing at her white baggy trousers, ropey sandals and white shirt with a woven colorful vest.

'Sure,' she smiles, 'why not … depends on my mood.'

'Pink seems like a color for little girls,' I say, gazing at her necklace. 'Is that a crystal too?'

'Uh ha, 'she nods, placing the crystal in her hand, 'its clear quartz, given to me by my husband.'

'And what does it do?'

'A clear quartz is known as the 'master healer'. It balances and revitalizes the whole being … physical, mental, emotional, and spiritual.'

'So I should wear one,' I laugh, 'the biggest one my neck could carry.'

She laughs too. 'The crystal hanging in the window, that's clear quartz too.'

'I like,' I say, looking up at it dangling from what looks like fishing wire, 'how when the sun shines on it rainbows reflect about the room.'

'You love rainbows?' she smiles.

'When I was little … I used to … I used to live at the end of a rainbow,' I say softly.

'You lived at the end of a rainbow,' she says, leaning forward.

'Well … I used to love drawing them. All my pictures had rainbows and that's …' lowering my head.

'That's ... that's what Talia,' she gently says.

And I don't know why ... but a tear drop touched my lip and my throat hurt.

'Talia,' she says, 'all your pictures had rainbows and that's ...'

'That was my home ... at the end of a rainbow ... in a pot of gold,' I say, standing up. 'Are we finished yet?'

'Would you like a glass of water,' she asks.

I nod.

'Sit back down and I'll refill your glass.'

So I do ... wishing I could grab that crystal from around her neck, silver chain and all, and wrap it around mine.

'And what are the black stones for?' I ask, putting down my empty glass and wiping my mouth.

'They're obsidian, formed by rapidly cooling volcanic lava,' she says, 'extremely dense.'

'What do they do?' looking about at three placed opposite each other, either side of the room.

'They absorb any negativity,' she says, 'purifying the atmosphere.'

'So ...' I say.

'So?' she repeats.

'I need to eat one.'

And we laugh.

Not long later when I walk out the door to leave, I turn back and say, 'Grace, you did say you had children didn't you?'

'Two,' she nods, 'two girls.'

'They're not adopted?'

'No,' she smiles. 'Not adopted.'

'Ok … bye,' I say, waving. And that confirmed that … she along with everyone else in the universe has definitely had sex.

March 24

I've been rambling on and on about so much other stuff … well I still haven't told you about Elli. My friend.

We, my dearest diary, are going to hang out today. I'm meeting her at the mall in approximately two hours and twenty three minutes!

She's a library dweller like me. Nose in a book, scratching her head and chewing the end of her pen. She moved here this year and like me … is somewhat lost.

But diary … the weird thing is she's what you'd call a Barbie. All this blond hair she scoops up in a bun when she studies. Then when that task is complete she unravels it like something out of a TV ad. Even removes her glasses. And there she is, Barbie, long legs and all.

You'd so expect her to have friends hanging off every arm. And boys. Definitely boys. There's no way Barbie's a virgin!

But Elli ... she could be ... she's, I don't know ... maybe there's no mirrors in her house. Or perhaps she needs glasses for more than just reading.

March 25

Elli's like, 'So cool to see you, I'd be hanging about, nose in my books, even though I've finished my homework.'

'Yeah,' I smile, 'me too.'

We hang out ... spend most of our time in book shops. She loves all the pretty and quirky and funky journals like me.

'Look at this one,' she says, 'I love dogs. Especially puppies. So cute.'

'I like this one,' I say, picking up a replica of you diary.

'Rainbows,' she grins.

'Yeah,' I say, placing it back on the shelf, 'should we go get a coffee ... now.'

'I'm starving,' she says. Does she know ... anorexia and stuff?

'Me too,' I say. 'Me too.'

So we eat ... she has McDonald's would you believe! A Big Mac ... no not the salad and ... a chocolate milkshake ... large.

'You're healthy,' she says, looking at my tuna sushi and diet coke.

'Um … I like sushi.'

'I tried to like it … but umm … a Big Mac fills the gap,' wiping sauce from her mouth.

I sit gazing at this Barbie … this strange alien Barbie and feel like I'm gonna burst into tears. I watch her suck her milkshake saying, 'Yum, McDonald's make the best milkshakes.' And I so want to say, "What planet did you say you came from?"

March 26

I'm so happy happy happy to have a friend even though just between you and me I wish she wasn't quite so gorgeous. If she kept her hair up in that bun it would help …oh and the glasses, black rimmed and all. As soon as she performs that TV ad and shakes her head … fuck there she is, queen of all the Barbies. And I kinda shrink into my seat until I have visions of a Big Mac being stuffed into her gob and I smile. She's like, 'Talia, what you smiling at?'

And I burst into laughter cause I know I'm crazy but happy too.

'We'll get kicked out of the library,' she says, 'oh well,' and she laughs too.

March 27

Elli came to mine after school today and we played B ball and it was fun. Yay. Fun. I think she's Sporty Barbie because she's not bad. Mind you her legs are exceedingly longer than mine.

She's like, 'Any food, Talia, I'm so hungry?'

'Oh …ok,' I say.

'I hope you don't mind me asking,' she says, walking with me inside, 'it's just I always eat when I get home from school, even if it's an apple.'

'Umm …what do we have,' I say, opening the pantry, 'muesli bars, chippies that Sol and Mac eat, umm what about rice crackers and hummus and carrot sticks, that's what Mum and I eat.'

Mum walks in the kitchen and smiles at the Barbie … I know, wishing she was her daughter. 'And who is this?' looking Elli up and down.

'Elli … this is Elli,' I say, pouring two glasses of water.

'Gosh what lovely hair you have,' she says, 'doesn't she, Talia? Stunning.'

'Yeah,' I murmur, wishing I was water being sucked into the sink.

Mum pulls out a plate with chocolate cake and begins cutting it, 'Sol and Mac's afternoon tea,' she smiles.

'Oo … can I have a piece? Love chocolate cake' grins the gorgeous Alien.

Mum just about chokes on the air she's breathing. 'Of course you can,' I say, cutting her a huge slice. 'There's cream in the fridge, Grant loves whipped cream with cake.'

'Yum,' says Elli, 'please.'

Elli eats her cake with a fork dipping each piece in the cream before putting it into her full lipped mouth, saying every now and then, 'This is delicious,' or 'Yumm.'

Mum and I sit on the bar stools opposite Elli studying her alien ways. And I don't know why but I have to escape to the bathroom … tears are trying to escape from my eyes. I put them back in prison and come back smiling to an empty room. Elli's empty plate … except for a tiny slither of cream and cake. I so want to taste it but I just can't and have to run back to the bathroom to put handcuffs back on those tears.

March 27

Grant comes back from a run; actually he calls it a 'jog' and collapses like a falling pine on to the carpet. 'Why isn't it getting any easier?' he says, wiping sweat from his brow.

Sol climbs on Grant's chest and rides him like he's a pony, 'Get off Grant,' says Mum, 'he's all sweaty.'

Sol looks at Mum, back at Grant and continues to ride his pony. I look on and smile.

'Wanna ride too, Mac?' says Grant.

'No,' says Mac and runs off pretending he's Spiderman in his Spiderman suit.

'I know why it's not getting any easier,' says Mum, 'that tummy, it's too big.'

Grant gently removes his rider, stands up, lifts up his green singlet and sticks out his hairy stomach, looking pregnant. 'This cost a lot of money to get this big,' he says, 'anyhow Kim, you love it.'

Mum looks all coy and leans her head to the side, half smiles and bites her lip, 'I do.'

Grant grabs her hand, places it on his belly and moves her hand in a gentle rubbing motion.

'You stink,' laughs Mum, 'go have a shower, but first let me wash my hands.'

March 28

I looked across at Grant this evening, legs sprawled out across the couch, remote in his hand, a banana in the other and felt this urge to pick up a pillow and throw it at him. His stomach full looking … you wouldn't say necessarily fat … just full, thick. I mean he is a thick set man. Like a bear I guess.

And it's true … Mum does seem to love it. His fullness and all.

And I think … I remember when I started my first diet and I was losing weight and she'd praise me.

She gave me praise.

'Talia,' she said, 'you look fantastic.' And 'Talia, that top looks really good on you,' and 'Talia, gosh you look like a model.'

And Talia … fucken Talia.

And how come Grant gets to be thick round the middle and she still likes him. 'You love it,' he said.

'I do.'

I do.

March 29

I said to Grace, 'I heard these girls talking at school about the diet they were on, how you only eat protein and veges and this girl, Kariana; I think that's her name; she's like, "I lost two kilos in the first week." And she was beaming like she won prom queen.'

'And how did that make you feel?' Grace asked.

'Don't know … I just looked at those girls and thought will you end up like me?'

'Well,' says Grace, 'I was reading an article recently that said … those that go on a diet are seven to eight times more likely to develop an eating disorder than those who do not diet.'

'Uh ha,' I say. 'But my friends went on the same diet with me ... Maggie and Anna and they didn't get ... didn't get sick.'

'An eating disorder is so so complex, Talia,' smiles Grace, 'has so many layers. Presumably there are underlying issues that perhaps you have that your friends do not. Or perhaps you were vulnerable at that time in your life, triggered by stress or ... oh Talia, it could be a number of things.'

I hang my head, sit up, and look about the room.

'Is this difficult to talk about?' asks Grace.

'No,' I lie. What underlying issues?!

'What we do know is ... those that do develop eating disorders have some kind of body image disturbance,' says Grace.

'What?' I say. 'Like I see myself as fat.'

'Yeah,' says Grace, 'or perhaps you know you are slim but feel fat ... always feel fat. Never slim enough because inside there is a feeling of never being enough. Not good enough.'

I nod.

'Of course an eating disorder is also perpetuated by the culture we live in. Where being fat is detested and being thin is idealised. We are constantly bombarded with messages of perfection and, for most, impossible thinness.'

Again I nod.

'I never read women's magazines … full of diet tips and idealising thin women. And I refuse to watch anything on TV that features starving looking actresses. And Talia,' she smiles, 'that doesn't leave much.'

'I read something once,' I say, 'can't remember where … but it said in some countries … generally poorer places, being larger is desirable. Means you're wealthy.'

'That's right, Talia,' smiles Grace. 'It's the Western world that says thin is attractive. That being thin will solve all your problems. But you know what … it's just a body size. Not right or wrong … won't fix the hurt inside … yes being healthy is important but it doesn't make you better or less.'

And I look at her, sitting there with her skinny ankles protruding from her faded jeans.

What hurt inside, I want to scream!

March 30

I'm sitting at the kitchen table drawing with Sol; Mac was, but only lasted two minutes, had to get up and charge round like Buzz Lightyear. Mum comes in and says, 'You remember it's Lola's birthday this weekend, don't you? It would be nice if you could come.'

'Yeah …,' I say, 'I remembered.' Not! 'When was it?'

'Sunday, 10: 30 at Aunty Maxine's. Oh and,' she beams, 'guess what I got her?'

'What,' I say, 'Barbie.'

'A Snow White dress up, just like the one you had. And Aunty Maxine wanted to give her. She'll love it.'

'Who,' I say, frowning, 'Aunty Maxine or Lola?'

'Well both, you loved yours,' she says, 'Lola will be the same age as you when you got yours, four. I'll go get it.'

And before I could say, "don't bother", she was gone.

'Here it is,' says Mum, pulling it out of a white plastic bag. 'Exactly the same as yours.'

And there it is ... the precious dress up. Emerald blue with a big white color and yellow apron. Puffy sleeves.

'Can I wear it?' Sol grins.

'Don't be silly,' says Mum, 'you're a boy, boys don't wear dresses.'

'Why not?' asks Sol.

'Because they don't, anyway it's for Lola,' says Mum. 'Her present not yours. I'll put it away.' And off she trots like the wicked stepmother only she's not a stepmother just wicked. And if not wicked ... definitely vain.

Sol's like, 'Talia, will you get me a Snow White dress up for my birthday?'

I so wanted to say, "Of course, sweetie, of course, why not."

But I'm like, 'No.'

March 30

Do I really want to go to a four years old's party? No I do not. Why?

Who the fuck knows and who the fuck cares.

I just don't.

March 31

So I'm like, 'I have a headache.'

Mum's like, handing me two Panadols, 'I told you, these will sort it.'

'And lots of homework,' I say, rubbing my eyes.

'A break will do you good,' she says, 'come on, she's your niece.'

'Ok,' I sigh, swallowing both Panadol … what I really want to say was, 'get fucked.'

Aunty Maxine is her usual obnoxious self, dressed like a pink fairy, glittery pink wings and all. Reminded me of a flamingo … a fat one; "don't rest on one leg Aunty Maxine you'll tip the fuck over!"

Mums like, 'You never said dress-ups,' looking down at her blue floral dress.

'The invitation did say, fairy party,' says Aunty Maxine, with this … can't you read look.

'Oh well,' Mum half smiles, 'fairies are no good for the boys anyhow.'

'Elves,' said Aunty Maxine, touching her slicked down, glittery blond hair, 'they could've been elves.'

"Cut off her wings," I want to tell Mum, looking about at all the little fairies; fluttering their wings and waving their wands. Lola looks so cute ... freckles across her nose like fairy dust. Strawberry blond hair in French braids. A pretty lavender fairy dress with white sparkly wings. She even had pretty little ballet shoes, lavender too. 'Happy Birthday,' I say to her, wanting to grab her wand and spread fairy dust ... magic dust all about the garden. But I guess the fairies already have because the sun is shining. The sky is big and blue and clear.

There was a huge leafy green blow up castle ... of course with fairies on it. In retrospect it could have been Tinkerbell ... or not. I was so busy jumping about myself with all the fairies and Mac; Sol was sulking because he wanted sparkly wings too; that I didn't notice.

Apparently, Sol got to wear not just wings but a whole fairy outfit. Lavender with sparkly white wings. Even the lavender ballet shoes. Yep ... Lola's. I didn't get to see because I'd left by then.

All the food came out ... of course fairy bread ... and chocolate rice bubbles – my childhood favorite; chippies, sausage rolls, little homemade pizzas, lollies and oh just too much food. Aunty Maxine looks at me and smiles, 'Help yourself, Talia, plates are over there.' Paper plates with fairies on them. Cups too.

'I'm good,' I say.

'It's nearly lunchtime, you must be hungry,' she smiles. What is it with her?

Grant says, mouth full of sausage roll, 'She bought her own food … it's in Kim's bag.'

And I look at him and could … could something. He stepped in and yeah.

'I'll go get it,' says Grant, grabbing another sausage roll and returning with my lunch box, containing my sandwich and fruit.

'Thanks,' I smile, 'thanks Grant.'

He smiles back and yep, grabs another sausage roll. I look at Grant and for a fleeting moment wonder if my Dad eats sausage rolls.

If he eats at all.

Not long after Aunty Maxine brings out an enormous fairy cake. 'I didn't make it,' she smiles, 'had it made.'

We all sing happy birthday to a glowing Lola. She really did look sprinkled from head to toe in fairy dust.

'Cake everyone,' says Aunty Maxine, 'it's chocolate under all that lavender icing … looks delicious.' And she proceeds to hand out pieces.

Little Lola comes running in the room dressed in only her knickers; mauve with a little pink fairy, 'Look what I got Mum,' waving about the Snow White dress up.

'Oh Lola, you were supposed to wait to unwrap your presents,' says Aunty Maxine, 'did you help yourself?'

'Sol ... Sol give it to me,' she beams. 'Wanna put it on ... please.'

'Talia,' says Aunty Maxine, 'will you hand out the cake, I've only done the children.'

'Sure,' I smile.

'I'll help with the dress up,' Aunty Maxine says, grabbing the dress from Lola. 'Oh ... oh lovely, it's a Snow White dress. Kim, oh Kim where did you get it? I looked everywhere.'

Mum beams proudly, 'In that little boutique children's store that's just opened.'

'Oh ... thanks so much, Lola loves it,' says Aunty Maxine, putting the dress over Lola's head. 'Say thank you to Aunty Kim.'

'Thank you,' says Lola, 'do I look pretty?' Twirling about with her hands on her hips.

'Oh beautiful,' says Mum.

'Like a Snow White princess,' says Aunty Maxine's friend, Karen.

'The fairest in the land,' Aunty Maxine kisses Lola on the cheek. 'A photo Lola let Mummy take a photo.'

And Lola stands in her emerald blue dress with its big white collar, yellow apron. Puffy sleeves. And smiles cutely like the princess she thinks she is while Aunty Maxine clicks her camera over and over.

I look down at the chocolate cake slices with lavender icing I'm holding … fight the urge to lick it.

To eat it.

Grant grabs a piece from the plate, 'My second, delicious.'

I watch him take two bites before the cake disappears … he follows this up by licking his fingers. I look back to Lola and think, who ever saw a Snow White with strawberry blond hair. And freckles. Snow White had pure white skin. Give the kid some foundation, I'm sure Mum will have some in her bag.

The lavender icing keeps staring at me, urging me to dip in my finger and I don't know why but I just want to fall on the floor and weep.

Cry.

So next thing I know I'm out the door, a piece of cake in my hand.

I so wanted to eat it, just a taste … but I throw it on to a neighbour's yard, hoping a flock of birds will see it. Peck at it with their little sharp beaks and make it disappear.

I walk the two hours home feeling like I'm going fucken crazy which I still think I am.

April 1

Blah!

April 2

I never did eat lunch that day … or dinner. Refused to come out my room. No matter how much or long Mum stood outside it, crying like she'd lost her make-up purse.

'You embarrassed me,' she cries. 'How could you just walk out like that on your own cousin? On Aunty Maxine? On me?'

'As if they missed me,' I yell back.

'It was rude,' says Mum, blowing her nose and sniffing. 'How could you be so rude?'

'Go away,' I yell, 'just go away.'

'I won't go away,' she cries, 'not until you explain yourself.'

'I'm a rude thoughtless uncaring bitch,' I say.

'You said it,' agrees Mum. 'Especially the bitch.'

'You got your explanation, now piss off and leave me alone,' I say, throwing a book at the door.

I hear Grant, 'Kim, sweetheart … just give her some space.'

'Space,' says Mum, 'she owes us all an apology.'

'Maybe so, but you're not going to get it … not now anyhow,' says Grant. Wise fucken man!

'Come on … lets go, I made you a hot cup of tea.'

I hear them leave … Mum sobbing.

Sobbing like I am inside.

April 3

I admit missing two meals has reminded me how wonderful it is to feel empty inside. To hear my stomach rumble … to feel light. To feel like I'm in control of something that is so uncontrollable it terrifies the shit outta me.

But as much as I never want to eat again … I hear Julie's voice, 'Twenty percent become chronic, six percent die.'

Truth … sometimes I don't know why … I want to die. I want to dissolve into nothing and never return.

But I'm trying diary, I'm really and truly trying to unscrew my screwed up head.

April 4

Mum hasn't spoken to me since the other night … obviously still hasn't found her make-up purse.

Grant joins me at the basketball hoop, 'Can I play?' he says.

'Ok,' I say, chucking him the ball.

And that was it. I was so expecting a lecture but nothing. Just B ball … shooting hoops. I let him win.

April 5

I said to Grace, 'You're skinny ... how come, I mean do you diet? Never eaten breakfast in twenty years?'

Grace smiles, 'Oh gosh no, I have porridge dribbled in honey and cream, just about every morning.'

'Really,' I say, and bite my thumb, 'cream?

'Talia,' she smiles, 'I know I'm thin. When I was a child and adolescent, I was really thin. My mother used to feed me Complan, a high energy drink. As she said, "to put some fat on those bones." I ... when I became a therapist and was interested in food disorders I did consider the fact that I am naturally very thin. And never dieted. Not even once.'

I nod ... but can't help but frown. Another extraterrestrial?

'But Talia ...,' she smiles, 'then I considered the fact that I was thin ... a thin adolescent but felt ugly and not good enough ... because I was thin. Skinny. I was teased ... bullied. Emu. Ostrich legs. My nickname was Bones.'

'Oh,' leaning forward in my chair.

'As I evolved or grew up,' she says, 'I came to accept my thin body and understand that size or shape has little to do with our worth as human beings. That we are good enough ... just because, just because we're born ... and it has nothing, absolutely nothing to do with the size of our thighs or tummies.'

'I've never felt good enough,' I say.

'And that feeling probably runs deep ...,' she says, 'but ask yourself ... did you feel good enough when you were thin?' Oh fuck ... does that mean I'm not now?

'I felt ... I felt ... I don't know,' I say. Because I really don't.

'That's ok,' she says. 'As we talked about before ... society or culture says, you have to be thin, to be beautiful, to be liked, to be popular, to be accepted. But it's a lie. Being thin is a body size. Nothing more. Being slim ... well it's healthy, nothing more.'

'You think?' I say, confused.

'It does not determine your worth as a person who deserves love and care.'

'Maybe,' I say. 'Maybe.'

April 6

Then again maybe not.

I saw Hippo girl on the bus coming home from seeing Elli at the mall.

Fat fat hippo girl.

She clambers on the bus and sits herself down a few seats ahead; she takes up the whole seat. Really she could do with the walk!

An elderly lady, wrinkled like a dried up raisin boards the bus at the next stop. The bus is full and hippo girl stands up, smiles at the elderly woman and points to her seat. The elderly lady shuffles herself over to the very edge and says, 'Sit here.'

'I'm good,' says the hippo girl, hanging her head. She knows ... she cannot fit.

I want to throw a blanket over her so that nobody can see her enormous size. Wave a magic wand, "Abracadabra ... make hippo girl disappear."

The way she hangs her head and chews on her finger nails; still eating; I think she wishes she had a blanket or wand too. And yet there she is ... standing for a frail old lady with a wrinkled face, someone she's never met before. Baring the humiliation of stares.

I think ... dear dear diary, what a kind kind girl. I forget she's a hippo and want to crown her beauty queen.

April 7

I see Mum sitting there ... filing her nails, reading the latest woman's magazines and think of my newly crowned beauty queen. Mum looks at me, 'Talia, go do your hair ... you look like something the cat dragged in.'

And I know the truth.

If I came home one day, looking like the hippo girl, my mother would not only like me less than she already does now. She would despise me.

Not good enough.

You better believe it.

April 8

I introduced Elli to Chrissy and Stacey today. 'You're pretty,' says Chrissy, 'bet you had lots of boyfriends.'

'Not really,' blushes Elli. 'You're pretty too, lovely eyes, do you have a boyfriend?'

'No,' giggles Chrissy, 'but …'

'I do,' interrupts Stacey, 'Jona.'

'They have sex,' says Chrissy, wide-eyed. Not them too!

Elli looks at me and we smile, 'Oh, that's … um … nice … and you're protected.'

'I'm on the injection,' says Stacey, pointing to her bottom, 'it hurts.'

'That's great,' says Elli, 'but does he wear a condom?'

'No,' laughs Stacey, 'cause I get the injection.'

'That stops you getting pregnant … but a condom stops you getting diseases,' says Elli, looking at me for help.

'What diseases?' asks Chrissy, 'oh you mean like … like scorpions or something?'

'Scorpions,' cries Stacey.

'Crabs,' says Elli, 'I think you mean Crabs.'

'Oh,' says Chrissy and Stacey.

'Don't worry,' says Elli, 'forget what I said. As long as you're on the injection … that's great.'

'I'm on the injection too,' smiles Chrissy, 'my foster Mum said I don't get a period so I don't have to worry.'

'Good,' says Elli. 'That's great.'

When the girls go off arm in arm, in search of hotdogs, I say to Elli, 'Are you on the injection?'

'No,' smiles Elli, shaking her head.

'The pill?'

'No.'

'Minipill?'

'No …'

'Oh,' I sigh. So you're not having sex!

April 8

It's fortunate I have one kindred spirit that's not sex mad. Anna rings last night and is like, 'I've been seeing three guys.'

'Three,' I say, astounded, 'do they know?'

'Sure,' she says, 'I've told them I just want casual and that I want to see other people if I like.'

'But are you,' I say, 'are you … you know?'

'Shagging,' laughs Anna.

'Yeah,' I say. I'm not sure if I like university life.

'Maggie seems to be over Liam,' says Anna. 'Seeing some musician.'

'Oh that's great,' I say, 'I wondered if she was still seeing him, haven't heard from her in ages.'

'Too busy shagging,' laughs Anna. Yeah singing.

'I won't be up these holidays,' continues Anna, 'I have a job here but I'll come back next time ok.'

'Ok,' I say, 'ok.'

'You doing ok?' she says softly.

'Yeah, good, I got another A in English the other day.'

'That's great … maybe you should do journalism.'

'That's exactly what Mr Reiding said. He's like, "Talia, ever thought of doing journalism. You'd be very good."'

'And,' says Anna, 'have you?'

'Nah … I …nah,' I sigh, shaking my head, 'people have to read your work and I'm not that good.'

'Mr Reiding thinks you are,' says Anna. 'Does he still tug at that beard and always look like he needs a good sleep?'

'Yeah,' I laugh, 'he's a nice man.'

'Nice and tired,' laughs Anna. 'Maybe he needs a good shag, might lift those bags.'

'He's alright,' I say. 'He suits looking tired.'

'He is married aye,' says Anna, 'wears a ring from memory. Maybe his wife doesn't give him any.'

'Yeah, he's married,' I say, 'apparently a teacher too.'

I conclude three things when I hang up.

1 Mr Reiding is far from grumpy so must be getting it ... being that he's a man.

2 Condoms are of paramount importance at university.

3 My friends have become sluts.

April 10

So I'm in class ... English that is and I look across at Mr Reiding. He looks back at me, grins from ear to ear.

Ah ha ... my conclusions ... correct.

April 11

I was telling Elli about my friends ... how university had unleashed their slut side. I show her their photos on my phone. 'You must miss them,' she says, looking sad.

'I do,' I say, 'but it's good they are … you know studying and stuff.'

'True,' she nods, removing her glasses. I wish she wouldn't.

'This is my friend, Bella,' she says, handing me her phone. 'Isabella.'

'She's looks lovely,' I say, looking at a smiling pretty face. Dark hair pulled up in a pony. A silver nose ring.

'She is,' says Elli, 'miss her heaps.'

And paint my skin black because here comes Othello. Green eyed and nasty. 'Ah uh,' I say, 'do you think we should go to class now?'

'We used to hang out all the time, do everything together,' says Elli.

'I've gotta go toilet,' I say, 'better go.'

'Oh ok,' says Elli, 'sorry, I'll see you tomorrow.'

'Bye,' I say, 'yeah see you tomorrow.' But I'm not sure if I really want to.

I sit on the toilet, peeing until there's not a drop of liquid left in my bladder. How come I can have friends but she can't?

April 12

'Grace,' I say, 'if … say if … doesn't matter.'

'If what?' she asks, smiling and leaning her head to the side. 'If what Talia?'

'Are your daughters skinny … I mean slim, built like you?'
I ask.

'Actually … they are a healthy weight but more built like their father. They never got called, "Bones".'

'Well …' I say, squeezing the cushion on my lap, 'if one day one of them came home fat, really fat. Hippopotamus fat. Would you be grossed out?'

'Grossed out,' repeats Grace, looking sad. 'At my daughter … no.' And she says no with such a soft gentle tone I almost believed her.

'Really,' I say, 'no?'

'Talia,' she says, shaking her head, 'no. If my daughter came home one day looking like a hippopotamus I might be concerned for her health. I would be concerned about her health. But I think most of all I'd be concerned about what it was that was making her so unhappy or sad that she wanted to eat to absolute excess. What was it she was stuffing down and what was it she was hiding from.'

'I see,' I say.

'Talia,' Grace says, 'if you had a daughter that was the size of a hippopotamus how would you feel?'

'Well,' I say, 'um … I don't know, never had a daughter.'

'What if Sol or Mac became fat, really fat,' says Grace. 'How would you feel about that?'

'That's different,' I say, 'they're boys.'

'How is that different?' she asks.

'I don't know,' I frown, 'just seems it.'

'What makes it seem different?'

'It's just different that's all ... boys ... I don't know why.'

'Ok,' sighs Grace, 'all I can say is, if my daughter or son, if I had one, was very overweight it would concern me, sadden me, worry me somewhat but I would love my child all the same.'

'But wouldn't you look at her and feel disgusted,' I ask, 'even ashamed.'

'Talia, no,' she says gently.

And I look at her, her warm brown eyes and feel like I want to run.

'Does that make you sad?' she asks.

'No,' I say, standing up.

'You're crying,' she says.

'I'd like to go now,' I say, 'see you next week.'

'Talia, a wise woman once told me, "feelings pass, tears are not the enemy, just an expression of sadness..." And you know what ... have a good look at a Hippopotamus some time, they're actually very cute ... I think gorgeous.'

'Whatever,' I say, 'bye.'

Cute ... gorgeous, think I'll look for another counsellor.

April 13

I've decided to be a far more positive fucked up person than a wallowing negative bitch and furthermore, embrace the fact that I'm doing exceedingly well despite the wallowing bitch trying her best to drag me under. So well done me.

Congrats ... yay yay yay.

Ps ... and in keeping with that philosophy I'm considering a new counsellor that promotes positivity as opposed to tears.

April 14

Think you can and you can ... I'm sure I read that somewhere.

Behold I am therefore I am.

I am a fantastic person with ... ok that's pushing it.

April 15

I'm going to be more like Elli. Not as tall or not as blond ... actually not blond at all. In my own dark haired short legged way, more of a person that doesn't seem to give a shit. Not only does she eat Big Macs, chocolate thick shakes and cake, she seems oblivious to any guys that seem to stare. I see them ... their drooling tongues, like a working sheep dog. In fact, she says to this guy, Peter, whose tongue was like a waterfall, 'Will you move your ass, you're sitting in our seat.'

'Oh its ok, Elli,' I say, 'we can sit somewhere else.'

'We always sit there in the library ... oh come on then,' she says, turning her back oblivious to poor Peter's red face ... getting even redder as he checked out her moving ass.

Ps ... Found that quote

If you think you can do a thing or think you can't do a thing, you're right. HENRY FORD

April 16

Still I think she's hiding something ... there's this lost part to her. I mean she's as Alien as any Mars creature could be ... doesn't seem to care about stuff that I agonize over. But there's something she's hiding ... something that makes her feet unbalanced like they don't belong on the earth. I guess she'll tell me when she's ready or perhaps not ... I mean there's a lot I don't tell her.

A lot I don't tell myself.

April 17

I was thinking about Elli ... what was it that made earthquakes beneath her feet, when I get this call from Maggie. 'I had coffee with Liam,' she says.

'Coffee,' I say, 'how?'

'In a cup ... actually a glass at the uni cafeteria,' she laughs.

And I'm like, 'He's there … I didn't know you were at the same university. Is that why you didn't go to Teachers College?'

'Um … no … not really … I changed my mind that's all … didn't wanna be as busy as my Mum.'

'You didn't have to be a Principal.'

'I know … I just decided I wanted to do a Bachelor of Arts and I love it.'

'Oh,' I say, 'so how was coffee?'

'Oh Talia,' she says, sounding like Peter with the waterfall tongue, 'he was so gorgeous. Hahhhh…'

'And,' I say.

'And he was … oh … I could've fucked him there … on the table.'

'Oh …,' I say, having images of all the onlookers 'is he still with Macy?'

'No,' she sighs, 'a new girl … and guess what, she's like a size 16. All boob and ass and ass and boob.'

'Really,' I say, absolutely fascinated. 'A size 16.'

'Well, maybe a 14, but an ass like a giraffe. Though I bet not as firm.'

'Wow, gorgeous Liam likes big ass,' I hear myself saying; astounding myself.

'Sorry ... Talia,' says Maggie, 'I shouldn't be talking about body sizes, not to you.'

'Well,' I say, 'we always did ... didn't we.'

'True,' she says, 'but ... I'm sorry. I didn't think.'

'It's ok,' I say, 'I'm over it any way.'

'Over it, what anorexia?' she asks. 'I don't know if you can just be over it, Talia.'

'Sure I can,' I say.

'I hope so, but look at me ... am I over Liam ... no. Much as I try and anorexia ... fuck you were so sick.'

'And now I'm not,' I say.

Told you I was a new and improved positive me.

April 18

I so wanted to keep walking right past the entrance to Grace's building. Now that I think about it my feet wanna run every time I go there.

Sprint.

But did I?

No.

Do I?

No.

Why?

Good fucken question.

So anyhow I said to her, 'Who was that wise woman?'

'My grandma,' she says. 'She lived with us.'

'Oh,' I say.

'She was a beautiful kind woman,' Grace grins, 'taught me so much about life. She adored me.'

'Adored,' I say.

She nods and smiles.

'I've never met my grandma,' I say.

'And why is that Talia?' she asks.

'Mum says she's a 'bitter fat bitch' and that's about it. She could have died for all I know.'

'So they don't have any contact,' says Grace.

'Not as far as I know,' I say.

'And your Dad's parents?' says Grace.

'I used to see them sometimes, even after my father left. They were old and weird and stunk of cigarettes and I don't know … Granddad he freaked me out. And I stopped wanting to go and that was that, haven't seen them in years. But … they still send me a birthday card and money every year … and at Christmas. They must be old as now.'

'What was it about your granddad that freaked you out?' asked Grace.

'Umm … I … not sure,' I say.

Grace nods, 'So you can't remember or you're not sure what it was?'

'He … I … he was … Nana used to wait on him like a slave. Butter his bread, his toast and if it wasn't done as he liked it … he'd yell at her and she'd have to do it again.'

'Oh,' says Grace, 'a bully.'

'And,' I say, 'it was real weird because he couldn't drive the car or wouldn't … I'm not sure but the whole trip was spent with him criticising Nana's driving. He was always mean, calling her names.'

'What sort of names?' asked Grace.

'Like … lazy, wrinkly, useless … "You're bloody hopeless," he'd say. And I'd look at Nana … all kind of childlike even though she was old. And sometimes her eyes would be glazed with tears. And …' I say, wiping a tear.

'Just sit with the feeling, Talia,' says Grace. 'Just let it come.'

So diary … I absolutely try, even though it feels stupid and fucked up.

'I just felt sorry for her,' I say. 'I guess it's her that still sends me cards and little bit of money. Probably behind the asshole's back.'

'And Talia,' says Grace, 'how did he treat you ... did he bully you also?'

'No,' I say, shaking my head, 'he just kinda ignored me. I could've been a pot plant in the corner of the room. A cobweb on the ceiling ... if you know what I mean.'

'He sounds like a cruel man,' says Grace. 'And was your own father like that. Do you remember?'

'Nah,' I say, 'can't remember. I was about four when he left, so you know ... I was little.'

'And you haven't seen him since?' says Grace.

'Nah,' I say.

'And how does that make you feel?'

I shrug my shoulders.

'So you're not sure how that makes you feel ... your father leaving and then not making any contact with you again.'

'Glad,' I say, 'makes me feel glad.'

'And why is that, Talia ... why does that make you feel glad?'

'Because,' I say, 'what I do remember is arguing ... being woken up at night to Mum screaming and crying and one time I crept out of bed ... saw her throwing a plate at him. And a mug. Maybe that's why he left ... anyhow can't believe it's the end of term and its school holidays.'

Which is true because I can't.

April 20

Oh yay the house is full of easter eggs. If Grant eats any more I swear his skin will start changing color.

April 21

Grant's like, 'Oh for god's sake, Kim … just have a taste, a bite.'

'I don't eat chocolate,' says Mum.

'Seriously, Kim,' says Grant, 'you need to loosen up.'

'I loosen up when I want to,' says Mum, wrapping her arms around him and kissing him on the lips. Oh shit here she comes … queen of porn.

I'm gone.

Later 10pm …

Yep … I was spot on … can hear heaving and ahhing and dear diary I quote, 'Oh fuck me Grant. Fuck me.' We seriously need soundproof walls or a much larger house. Say a castle.

You'd think when a man got to nearly fifty he'd have hung up his construction hat … laid down that jackhammer.

Instead he's showing off how well hung he is … at his age, probably with the help of Viagra.

April 22

And there he is looking somewhat dazed from that overdose of Viagra. At least I guess he's tending to the kids … making toast and milky drinks.

Mother … in the bath no doubt soaking that vagina.

I said to Elli, 'Wanna help me take the boys to the zoo?' There are some animals I want to check out.

'Oh yeah,' she says, 'haven't been for … shit … a long time.'

'Cool,' I smile. Cool.

April 23

We had the best day at the zoo. Caught the bus and train and bus again which was fun for the boys in itself. Sol especially was wide eyed and said, 'I'm gonna be a train driver when I get big like Grant.'

'Great idea,' smiles Elli, looking even more Barbie like in that pink sweater and lip gloss.

'I'm gonna be Spiderman,' says Mac. He insisted on wearing his Spiderman suit and got so many stares you'd think he really was the real thing.

'Cool,' I say.

'What you gonna be?' asks Mac.

'Dunno,' I say.

'You could be a princess,' says Mac.

'I don't think so,' I say … trying not to frown. 'But Elli might want to be.'

'I'm gonna be a vet or dentist,' she says, 'well if I study hard enough.'

'I didn't know that,' I say.

'Yeah,' she says, 'I love animals … that's why I'm soo excited today,' squeezing my hand. 'What about you Talia, what you gonna do … was it a dietitian?'

'Yeah,' I say, 'think so.'

'That's why you're such a health freak aye,' she smiles. Has she not heard yet? I wanna ask but don't.

Anyhow the zoo was fantastic. So much better than I remember as a kid. Lush green vegetation and bush. And the animal enclosures were as natural as possible with streams and more bush and the elephant even had a waterfall. There was hardly a cage in sight. And I only felt a little sorry for the animals being locked up.

The boys were so excited but wanted to rush from one animal to the next. Elli and I could have spent much longer at each one.

I have to say … if Liam's new girlfriend has an ass the size of a giraffe … I'm impressed. They are enormous … but what amazing creatures and check out those eyes and eyelashes. 'They're bigger than Grant,' says Mac.

'That's so they can reach up high and eat leaves from the trees,' says Elli, lifting Mac up so he could see clearer.

'I like the zebra,' says Sol, running off to the next enclosure.

I run off after him and we stand gazing at the zebras, 'How'd they get their stripes,' asks Sol.

'I dunno,' I smile, 'it's like someone painted them isn't it.'

'Yeah, I think they painted a horse,' says Sol, again running off.

Funny enough the longest we stayed at any enclosure was the hippopotamus. The boys were fascinated, 'Look at his teeth,' cried Mac, pointing as the fat fat hippo opened its mouth almost one hundred & eighty degrees.

'The biggest yawn I've ever seen,' says Sol, wide eyed.

And it truly was ... I had no idea a hippo could open its mouth like that or that its teeth were so large. They were the length of Sol or Mac's arm. Enormous. All the better for eating with!

'I don't think he brushes,' laughs Elli.

'No,' I nod, 'dirty teeth, yuck.'

'Oh he's ... I think that's the male, he's beautiful,' sighs Elli, 'look at the size of that body compared to its legs.'

'You wonder how those tiny legs hold up that huge body,' I say.

'Yeah,' agrees Elli, 'I love him … amazing.' Elli loves the hippo.

'It says here,' I say, 'they can stay under water for up to half an hour.'

'Wow,' says Elli. 'Hear that boys, those hippos can stay under water a long, long time.'

'I can too,' says Sol. 'I make bubbles. Mac can't he won't put his head in.'

'I can too,' says Mac. 'Can.'

'No,' says Sol. 'I'm only a hippo hippot hipp ppot mus.'

I look down at Sol and Mac and smile, 'You can both be hippopotamuses if you want.'

'I can be one too,' says Elli, walking slowly and waddling. 'Lets go aye, I'm starved.'

So we do … we eat at the children's park. Elli orders hot chips with tomato sauce which she shares with the boys … she hands me the carton and says, 'Oh you don't eat chips do you?'

'I do,' I lied, 'but I'm good thanks … I have a sandwich.'

'So what was your favorite animal?' asks Elli.

'I like the tortoise,' says Mac.

'Really,' I say fascinated, 'why.'

'Cause he has a big shell on his back,' says Mac, licking his fingers. 'And he's looks old and beautiful.' Old and beautiful ... I ... almost cried.

'I like the hippot ...hippotmus,' says Sol, 'cause he's got big teeth.'

'Me too,' says Elli, 'the hippo was definitely my favourite. We should go back after lunch on the way back.'

'Yeah,' yells Sol.

'And one more look at the tortoise,' I say.

'Yay,' says Mac, waving his arms. 'I love the tortoise.'

'And what animal was your favourite, Talia,' asks Elli, 'what animal do you want to see again?'

'Arh ... umm,' I say, 'not sure ... probably the giraffe. I have a thing for big eyes and eyelashes. And long necks too.'

'Did you see the size of their bottoms?' says Elli.

'Yeah,' I laugh.

Gorgeous Liam likes big ass.

April 24

I was bathing the boys, Sol blowing bubbles and popping up every now and then just to say, 'I'm a hipotmus.'

Mac sitting upright looking at Sol like he really was from the zoo.

Anyhow, I hear Mum and Grant arguing in their bedroom. It kinda freaked me out so I stood outside the door to listen and Grant's like, 'You have to tell her.'

'No,' says Mum.

'Kim,' says Grant, 'she deserves to know.'

'No,' yells Mum, 'I said no.'

'Kim ... this is crap ... you're being selfish.'

'I'm not selfish,' yells Mum. 'He's the selfish fucken one and you can piss off and go fuck yourself.'

Oh dear ... that must be where I learnt the art of communication.

I was outta there and back with the oblivious boys. But diary ... who is she and what is it she deserves to know?

April 25

Grant is sucking it up but I know is still bothered by something. And with the way he looks across at me I can only conclude that she ... she is me.

April 26

What worries me a bit is Grant having finally worked out that he's hooked up with a yes ... a somewhat selfish bitch. Porn star she may be ... but perhaps he needs more after all, say maturity and kindness. And now what ... will he pack his bags and leave? Because ... well he might be a hairy man that tucks in his t-shirt into his trousers looking somewhat dorkish but he is the best stepfather the boys could possibly have. Better than their own flesh and blood who turns up or should I say doesn't turn up on occasion.

What the fuck is it with the modern day father?

Perhaps ... perhaps it's the selfish woman they breed with that they can't handle. Then again ... perhaps not.

Maybe when most men breed, wings replace their arms and they have to fly the fuck off for winter ... nearing summer they lose their senses and can't find their way back.

Fuck ... surely at nearly forty Mums too old to breed with Grant.

April 27

Caught up with Maggie today which was lovely lovely lovely. She's only back for a few days.

She has a stepfather too ... whom she says is a bastard, I guess more stereotypical like Cinderella or... or Snow the fuck White. And her Dad grew wings for the winter too and lost most his senses turning up only now and then. Still now and then is better than then and not. Perhaps anyway.

She says, 'I hate the fact I look just like him. Tall and muscular, dark hair with olive skin.'

'Weird,' I say, 'cause apparently I look like my father too. Actually it grosses me out.'

'Never mind,' says Maggie, putting her arm across my shoulder, 'we don't have to be like them.'

'Yeah,' I smile.

We sit just chilling in silence for a while until I say, 'So how's the musician … still making music?'

She laughs, 'Yeah … he's good and kind and funny and he's an expert downstairs which is fun.'

'But,' I say, 'I can hear a but.'

'Liam broke up with the giraffe … the girl with a big ass,' she says, hanging her head.

'And,' I say, trying to hide my disappointment.

'And,' she sighs, 'that means he's single.'

'You got it bad haven't you,' I say, not really sure how to help.

'I know,' she sighs, 'Anna says real grumpy like, "Wake up Maggie, he's not interested … might want to fuck you because guys are always up for any easy fuck but he's not into you." And then she's like, "You have a nice guy … move on … you're driving me fucken crazy with your pitiful face."'

'Oh,' I say, 'she's always pretty much straight to the point aye.'

'Sure is,' smiles Maggie, 'like an arrow … bulls-eye.'

'Maybe,' I say, 'we should book you in for a heart transplant.'

'Yeah,' smiles Maggie, 'that might fix it.'

April 28

Perhaps it is true ... issues of the heart can only be fixed with a transplant or lobotomy.

April 30

I took Elli to meet Maggie today and I noticed that Elli seemed a little nervous. We hung out at Maggie's place and Elli seemed more interested in playing with Maggie's cats than conversation.

I tried to include her and Maggie asked her lots of questions like, 'How long have you been living here?' and 'Why did you move?'

And Elli's like, 'Can't remember,' and 'Dad got transferred in his job.'

And ... just kinda awkward.

'She's really pretty,' whispers Maggie, when Elli went to use the toilet. 'Shy though.'

'Yeah,' I nod, 'she is but she's not normally shy.'

'Maybe she doesn't like sharing you.'

'Don't be silly,' I frown.

In reflection ... perhaps it's true.

May 1

Went to the movies last night with Maggie and stayed the night. Her stepdad is a bastard … speaks to her Mum like she's trash. You'd think a career woman like a Principal wouldn't put up with that crap. He's like, 'You put flour in the casserole … you know I don't like flour in a casserole … when do you ever think of me? Oh I'm only your husband, the last on your to do list. I'm not eating it … give it to your furry fucken mongrels.'

And he's up out of his chair; disappears into the lounge to watch the news. Wanker!

I look across at Maggie's Mum, Dawn, pushing her food about on her plate … and no she doesn't have an eating disorder … I don't think. She looks like a worn out teacher like they do, like Mr Reiding. I bet she hopes dawn doesn't arise tomorrow morning so she can just sleep and sleep … not wake up next to that prickly faced prick.

Flour? … what about venom … I'll spit some out on his plate.

Had to say my farewells to Maggie in the morning. She was heading off to stay with her grandparents for a few days before returning to University.

'They're getting old,' she's says, 'don't know how much longer they'll be around.'

'How old?' I ask.

'Well in their eighties,' she says, kissing me on the cheek.

I miss her already.

May 2

Oh fuck, Mum and Grant are arguing again.

'You need to tell her,' says Grant.

'No,' says Mum.

'She should know,' says Grant, in a sad kinda tone.

'No,' says Mum. 'No.'

'I don't understand,' says Grant. 'Why?'

'Why?' says Mum, 'Fucken why. Because he doesn't deserve her to know. That's why. Now just drop it. Just leave it alone.'

'I think,' says Grant, 'you're being bitter and mean and I don't like it and right now I don't like you.'

Oh shit what did I tell you ... If she doesn't get a personality transplant or perhaps a heart one like Maggie ... he's gonna fuck off and then the boys will be left with a Cinderella or Snow fucken White step-parent.

May 3

Oh shit shit shit. And fuck.

The atmosphere is very icy and I need to wear twice the amount of clothes just to keep warm.

May 4

I never thought I'd say this but oh joy … Grant had his construction hat back on last night. I thought their headboard might make a hole in the wall.

May 5

Grant still looks at me with these sad kinda eyes and it's freakin me out. I wish the sun would shine and he'd put on shades. The darker the better.

I wanna say, "What?"

But I don't … cause I'm with Mum on this one … I get some vibe that I don't need to know.

May 6

I'll be glad when school starts back. The boys are driving me batty. Elli is away somewhere with her parents and I miss her.

I don't miss Grace though … it's fantastic she's away. In fact not having to sit in that chair with two cushions on my lap is what can I say … blissful.

May 7

I get a call from Anna, she's like, 'Sorry I didn't get up to see you, just had this work opportunity.'

'It's ok,' I say.

'Did you catch up with Maggie?'

'Yeah, it was lovely,' I say.

'To be honest,' she says, 'she's driving me fucken mad.'

'Oh,' I say, a little freaked.

'Over Liam ... she needs her head read. I should book her in to see a fucken psychiatrist.'

'Oh,' I laugh, 'like me.'

'Oh sorry ... I didn't mean you ... but you know what ... if you had got help earlier you might not have ended up in hospital ... we all could see something was up.'

'But I would've refused,' I said, 'anyhow. I was too sick. And remember ... you did keep telling me I was too thin and you were worried and I just drifted away into my own skinny fucked up world.'

'Yeah ... you did,' said Anna, 'I felt like we let ... like I ... it was my idea to go on that stupid diet.'

'And it was my idea to not come off it.'

'Talia,' she sniffs, like she's holding back tears, 'I always felt bad like it was my fault and I'm so so sorry.' Then oh fuck ... she is crying and I want to pass tissues to her down the phone.

'Anna,' I say, 'it's not your fault. It's nobody's. People just get sick sometimes.'

'But,' she weeps, 'if we hadn't started that diet ... you would've been alright. And at university ... instead ... instead you're repeating your year.'

'Anna,' I say, 'I didn't know you felt so bad. Please don't ... it makes me feel bad ...' Beginning to sniff myself.

'I felt so awful, I'd go home from the hospital after seeing you and just cry.'

'I'm sorry,' I softly weep. 'I'm sorry.' Where the fuck is Grace when I need her ... "tears are not the enemy," her Grandma said or someone like that.

'I'm so so sorry Talia ... in fact Maggie had to drag me to the hospital ... I didn't even want to come. Not because I didn't care but because I did. Because seeing you there locked up and so thin and sick ... it just did my head in.'

'It's not ... it wasn't your fault,' I sigh, closing my eyes ... shutting off the light to those tears. Things can't grow without light ... right?

'I just ...' says Anna.

'No,' shaking my head, 'just no.'

No.

May 7

I wish Anna hadn't told me she felt so bad because now I can't shake off this bad feeling myself.

And ... I don't want to eat lunch.

Or dinner.

May 8

Oh yay! School today.

May 9

So it was soo good to see Elli, good to be around someone that doesn't feel bad because I was sick. She smiles when she sees me, teeth showing, eyes beaming. I almost felt shy, but happy happy happy.

After she tells me about her holiday and how her parents drove her crazy she's like, 'Talia … wanna come to mine after school sometime this week?'

'Oh cool,' I say.

'I know I haven't asked you before,' she says, 'and I've been to yours heaps and that's kinda rude but … I didn't want you to meet my parents.'

'Oh,' I frown.

'Not because of you,' she says, putting her hand on my back, 'because of them.'

'Oh,' I say. Is this what she was hiding? Perhaps she really is extraterrestrial and she somehow came out human looking. Ok now I'm being fucken extraterrestrial myself.

'And,' she says, lowering her head, 'there's something I want to tell you.' Ah uh!

'Ok,' I say. 'I have to watch the boys tomorrow and the next day ... Mum's somewhere ... some appointment or something ... probably beautician having her nails done.'

'I noticed she had well-groomed nails,' says Elli.

'She's got well-groomed everything,' I say, 'like something outta a TV soap.'

'Yeah ... she's very attractive,' says Elli.

'If you like fancy wallpaper I guess. You should see her in the mornings ... no makeup ... without her hair puffed up.'

'You don't like her much,' says Elli, 'do you?'

'Oh,' I say, feeling bad. 'She's just annoying. Aren't most parents?'

'I guess,' sighs Elli, looking sad. 'Mine sure annoy me. Can't wait until I can go to university.'

'Me too,' I nod.

Me too.

May 10

It's possible I have a crush on Mr Reiding. He smiles at me from across the room looking somewhat refreshed and again I think ... oh you beautiful man. Maybe I have a thing for men or boys that smile. Well smile at me.

Hey boys, all you need to do is smile and she's all yours!

Pretty much.

That's all Jason had to do ... smile ... make me laugh and next thing I'm having fantasies of ... well just fantasies anyhow.

And Mr Reiding ... I guess the fantasies are different. I imagine sitting at the dining room table discussing books and him telling me how brilliant I am. Tugging at his beard and smiling. And I'd be like, "Can I get you anything Dad ... another glass of water?"

Oh my God ... did you just see what I just called him ... Dad.

Well at least I know I'm not after a married man.

Just a taken Dad.

May 11

Diary ... went to Ellie's. Her parents aren't aliens and she doesn't live in a spacecraft.

But ... is she more alien now? ... hope not.

Her home is pretty flash ... expensive looking furniture, big leather couches and lots of big ornamental pieces; vases with tall flowers and flaxy looking sticks. And this extremely expensive looking collection of tiny crystal or glass ornaments ... little swans and little people and little pieces of furniture. I was scared to pass it in case I knocked it. Broke a tiny swan or head of a tiny person ... or like Goldilocks visiting and broke a leg of a chair. Only a tiny little glass or perhaps crystal chair.

'Something to eat?' she says.

I almost said, "Porridge … the smallest bowl thanks."

'Oh … umm … oh …do you have any fruit?' I say, 'an apple and a glass of water would be great.'

'Umm,' she says, 'sure … we do,' rummaging about in the huge metallic fridge. 'Granny smith ok?'

'Please,' I say.

She shows me about while we munch on our apples.

'Big place,' I say. 'Especially for just the three of you.'

'Yeah,' she says, 'it's a rental.'

'Uh ha,' I nod. 'Not gonna buy.'

'No,' she says, putting her core in the bin, 'Dad will probably get transferred back at the end of the year.'

'Oh,' I say, 'do they want to … don't they like it here?'

She gives me this look like she's gonna tell me something … something important, 'Don't know.'

'Oh,' I nod.

'Talia …' she says.

'Yeah,' I say.

'Nothing,' she says, 'doesn't matter.'

'Show me your room,' I say.

She's got that hesitant look again but says, 'Ok … ok.'

So I enter and her room is messy; stuff …clothes, papers and books everywhere. Even a damp purple towel on her unmade bed. 'Oh sorry,' she says, when I lift it up to sit down. 'Mum says I'm a lazy slob … I know your room is immaculate. Mum would love you as a daughter.'

I smile but somehow doubt exchanging her Barbie doll beauty for a dark haired fucked up version of a daughter would go down well. Even if I was extremely tidy. Probably part of my disorder!

'Oh I love Adam Lambert,' I say, looking at a large poster of him, on the wall above her dresser.

'Yeah,' she smiles coyly, 'he's cool.'

'And gorgeous,' I say, 'even Mum fancies him … and what she's like twice his age. I heard on the radio not long ago he got voted the sexiest popstar in America.'

'Really,' she says, looking up at him too. 'I didn't know that.'

'Yeah,' I say, 'they were interviewing him about the release of his new album. Congratulating him because it went straight to number one in America.'

'Yeah I knew that,' Elli says, 'the first out of the closet gay man to do so.'

'Yeah that's right,' I say, 'he's so gay and sooo gorgeous.'

'Talia,' says Elli, looking down, 'that's why I have his poster.'

'Sorry,' I say, 'because he's gorgeous.'

'No,' she says, shaking her head.

'You love his music,' I say, 'his voice.'

'Well yeah,' she smiles, 'but no ... because he's a role model.'

'A role model,' I say, 'for what?'

'For being out of the closest,' she says, biting her thumb.

'Yeah,' I smile 'he is that.'

'He's not only out,' she says, 'he's proud ... and he follows his dreams ... and he believes in himself and his music.'

'He does sound like a really nice guy,' I say. 'Really positive and kind on the radio.'

'Talia,' Elli sighs, 'I used to have a poster of Ellen DeGeneres.'

'Oh yeah,' I laugh, 'she's so funny. Grant loves watching her show ... and he's like a real man's man.'

'Mum,' Elli says softly, 'she tore the poster down. Ripped it up into tiny shreds ... came home and there it was all over the floor.'

'Oh,' I say, 'why ... I mean Ellen ... what did she ever do wrong ... she's funny?'

'She's gay,' says Elli, 'lesbian.'

'Oh,' I say, 'but ... so your Mum has a thing for lesbians.'

'She has a thing,' sighs Elli, her eyes beginning to water, 'for her daughter being a lesbian.'

I look at her ... beautiful Barbie ... long blond hair, legs up to her neck, big blue eyes, pink sweater ... so pretty ... I know it sounds pathetic but I said, 'But you're so pretty.'

And she looks at me with tears now falling and says, 'That's just what my Dad said. "But you're beautiful. Beautiful." Fuck Talia ... what the fuck has how you look got to do with being gay? You just said Adam Lambert was gorgeous.'

'Oh,' I say, 'I don't know ... it's just all the boys like you.'

'And,' she says, standing up, 'what has that got to do with being gay? You and every other female fancy Adam. And anyhow isn't Ellen gorgeous?'

'Well yeah,' I say, 'but she ... you know wears trousers has short hair.'

'Talia, get on the fucken internet and check out Ellen's wife,' says Elli, 'long blond hair, wears dresses. Guess what? ... lesbian.'

'I'm sorry,' I say.

'I think you better go,' she says, wiping her eyes.

'I'm sorry,' I say again ... because I truly am.

'Talia,' she says, 'I think you're pretty fucked up sometimes. You seem to think everything is about how someone looks. You think because I look a certain way ... I'm a certain person ... that I have it easy ... you are fucked up ... I might be gay with parents that loathe me for being so but you ... you're shallow.'

Oh so she finally got me figured out.

'Shallow,' she continues. 'Just like my parents. Mum walked in on me kissing Bella ... yeah that's right she's my girlfriend and I miss her. Next thing I know Dad's being transferred ... as if moving towns can change who I am.

'Who I love.

'Well I'll be with her soon ... we're going to try and get into the same University next year. So there ... now you know and now I'd like you to leave.'

'Elli,' I say, 'I was ...'

'Just go,' she says, 'I'll stay here with Adam Lambert ... because ... because he gets it. He knows what it's like. He's my friend.'

I slowly walk towards the door ... turn round to see her crying into a pillow and instead of going back and putting my arm across her shoulder like a good friend would, I keep walking. Close the door as I leave.

I never have been too good with tears.

May 12

I know I have a lot of negative traits ... a lot ... but I had never really considered shallow as being one of them. Bitch ... granted ... fucked up ... definitely ... selfish ... oh yes ... but shallow.

Dictionary definition ... shallow ...1 having a short distance between the top and the bottom

2 not thinking or thought out seriously.

Conclusion.

An absolute accurate description. 1 I do have a short distance from the top of my head to my feet. And … 2 I … I didn't think. Well actually I did think … it just wasn't thought out seriously.

May 13

'Grace,' I say, 'my friend Elli isn't talking to me.'

'Why is that Talia?' she says.

'Because … because,' I say, 'I was shocked she was gay. And to be honest I still can't get my head round it.'

She nods and says, 'What was it that shocked you and why can't you get your head around it?'

'She's like really beautiful,' I say. 'All the boys stare when she's around.'

'And beautiful looking people can't be gay?' she asks.

'I know,' I say, 'that's shallow. It's just … I'd look at her like she had it all … and now.'

'She can still have it all,' says Grace. 'She's just gay with it.'

'She says I'm shallow.'

'I don't think you're shallow Talia … just pretty confused. Just mixed up. You place so much emphasis on a person's appearance … as if that determines who they are. How does that sound to you?'

'Shallow,' I say.

'What does being beautiful mean to you?'

'Means,' I say, 'being slim. Pretty I guess.'

'And what does being slim mean?'

'Being liked I guess ... being accepted,' wanting to stand up and run out the room.

'So being fat,' says Grace, 'what does that mean to you?'

'Being ugly,' I say, scratching my head, 'ugly and fat.'

'And ugly and fat means?'

'Ugly and fat means ... ugly ... yuck ... like I'm not good enough and ... and just like this feeling of being small even though I'm fat.'

'You look sad,' says Grace. 'What's making you sad about this conversation?'

'I just don't want to be fat,' I say, beginning to cry.

'Why?' she asks, leaning forward.

And diary I look at her and have this image of grabbing her throat and squeezing it. Told you I was like Othello.

'Why Talia,' she asks again. 'Why don't you want to be fat?'

'Because,' I say, 'I don't want to be ugly ... yuck ... I ... it scares me ... something scares me inside.'

Grace passes me some tissues and says, 'Talia ... you're safe.'

And I look at her, her kind lined face, her white dreadlocks pulled up in a thick multi-coloured band, like a rainbow in a white sky ... and I ... I'm terrified.

May 14

Of course now that Elli's not talking to me ... it truly is silent at the library ... haven't even seen Chrissy and Stacey. And now that it's the weekend ...dah! ... what the fuck to do!

Found myself with my nose in one of Mum's magazine and woe and behold there was a picture of Ellen and her wife, Portia. And shit diary ... she's a looka like Elli. Not that Ellen's not pretty ... she's ... well Portia has long blond hair and wears this glamorous turquoise gown while Ellen's in a tux. A white tux.

And oh shit ... dig a hole for me and bury me in it. Make sure it's wide enough because although I'm shallow ... I feel fat.

May 15

So I rang Elli's house to apologise again. And her mum burst into tears. She's like, 'We don't know where she is, she's taken off.'

'Oh,' I say.

'You don't know anything do you,' weeps her Mum, 'where she would go ... or if ...?'

'We had a disagreement,' I say, feeling like someone should put handcuffs on my wrists.

'So did we …' says her Mum, 'her father he … he …'

'He what?' I say, hoping it was worse than what I did.

'He told her to get out,' sniffs her Mum.

'To get out,' I say, wanting to use those handcuffs on her father now.

'He lost his temper,' she weeps, 'he … he didn't mean it.'

'Oh,' I say, 'how long has she been gone?'

'Just a night.'

'Have you tried … have you tried Isabella's number … maybe she caught a plane somehow there?'

'Isabella,' she sniffs, 'you know then.'

'That she's a lesbian,' I say, 'Mrs Gibb… it doesn't make her bad or any different … she's still the same Elli … just … just gay.'

'I know,' she says, 'her father … he … he …'

'Yeah,' I say.

'He …,' she says, 'he just doesn't want her to be.'

'But she is,' I say, 'she is.'

May 16

I'm soo worried about Elli. I'm sure she's gone to Bella's. But what if ... what if her parents are fucked up over the whole gay thing too. I think she mentioned that Bella had a solo Mum ... so at least having one parent to deal with gives better odds.

May 17

If I had've been more supportive and didn't have such a short fucken distance between the top and the bottom ... she ... might've come to me. And I could've said, "Don't worry, most parents are fucked up and assholes anyhow."

And she would've cried in a heap at the end of my bed and I would've placed a soft warm blanket over her. And she would've looked at me with those sad blue eyes, mascara running down her face and whispered, "Thanks."

May 18

Yeah Talia ... thanks a fucken lot you shallow bitch.

May 19

I rang Elli's mum and oh yay, she's like, 'She was at Isabella's ... her mother contacted us last night. She hitchhiked can you believe?'

'Oh god,' I say, 'really, how dangerous.'

'I know,' she sighs, 'thank god she's alright.'

'Is she coming home?' I ask ... hopeful ... the library is so quiet.

'No,' she says, 'Isabella's mum said she can stay for a while. I'm going to fly down in a few days, maybe a week.'

'What about school?' I ask. 'If she misses too much ... she wants to be a vet or a dentist.'

'Does she?' says Elli's mum. 'Oh that's lovely ... she always did love animals, always wanted a dog, her father doesn't like mess. And,' she laughs, 'she has great teeth.'

'She does,' I say.

'Cost a lot of money those teeth ... thousands worth of straightening.'

'She had braces?' I ask.

'Sure did, she used to have buck teeth.'

'Really,' I say, trying to imagine Elli with buck teeth. Did give her an average alien look especially if I added twenty to thirty pounds.

'Talia,' she says, 'it is Talia isn't it?'

'Yes,' I say.

'Are you ... are you gay too?'

'No,' I say, 'I'm not.'

'How do you think she knows she is?'

'I don't know,' I say, 'you should ask her sometime … but I think … well from what I understand if you're gay … you just kinda know you are. Like you know what your favorite colour is or food.'

'You don't think she'll grow out of it?'

'She's gay Mrs Gibb,' I say, 'it's not a shoe size.'

'Ok,' she says, 'thanks Talia … you're a good friend.'

I wish I was.

May 19

I'm so glad she's safe. I think I'll give her some time and then make some contact with her. Say sorry and stuff.

Tell her I've grown a few inches and I'm not so shallow anymore.

May 20

I so didn't want to go to see Grace today but … I did. I told her I didn't want to talk because I just didn't.

And she said, 'I like the way you asked for what you needed … some days we just aren't in the right space to talk … as long as that's not always.'

'Thanks,' I say, 'it's just … remember my friend that I told you about? She took off and I just feel like it's my fault.'

'How,' she asks, 'how is it your fault?'

'Because the way I reacted to her being gay ... because I'm a bitch.'

'Talia ... you're very hard on yourself,' she smiles. 'It just wasn't what you were expecting and you apologised ... you did what a good friend does. I don't think you're a bitch at all ... I think you're actually very kind.'

'Kind,' I frown, 'I don't think you know me.'

'Well from what I do know,' she says, leaning forward, 'you seem like a very kind and gentle young woman.'

And that proved it ... she obviously can't have passed her counselling exams and was acting under someone else's name.

With legs like hers I bet her real name is ... dipstick.

May 21

As if my life could get any worse Mum has invited Aunty Maxine and clan to dinner. Oh yay ... oh fucken yay.

May 22

So Aunty Maxine's like, 'Your hair looks nice now that it's grown.'

I rub my nose.

'Talia,' she says, 'your hair looks nice.'

'Does it,' I say.

'Well, I think so,' she smiles, 'sets off those pretty brown eyes. Gosh doesn't she look like her father. Kim ... doesn't Talia look more and more like her father.'

Mum looks at me ... from head to toe and toe to head and I swear if I had a shotgun I'd shoot them both. See ... Grace is so a fraud!

'Well,' says Mum, 'she certainly doesn't look like me.'

'Or me,' laughs Grant ... but I know ... I feel that icy draught and ... he looks sad and why the fuck why?

'Or me,' laughs Aunty Maxine, 'way too thin.'

'I'm going outside,' I say.

'In the dark,' says Grant.

'Gonna shoot some hoops.'

'I'll come too,' says Grant, 'could do with some air.'

Mum ... she gave him this glare ... the kind that used to tear at my heart when I was kid. Yeah ... I used to have a heart way back then.

Put it like this, he may as well leave that construction hat at work because he won't be using that jackhammer for some time.

'I don't want to play with you,' I say, in a tone unfortunately just like my mother's glare.

He looks dejected and I feel real mean ... but ... and then Mum's like, 'I'm just gonna make tea ... you'd love a cuppa wouldn't you Grant.'

I shoot hoops the best I can; considering there's only a slither of moon in the sky. I wish there were more stars ... but they seem scarce too. I was just remembering being on a school camp once out in the country. The stars were amazing ... they seemed to light up the entire sky. It was a warm summer evening and this boy, Steven and I lay under the stars. Just looking, saying nothing. I'd had a crush on him for about a year. He had auburn frizzy hair, freckles and I thought he was just gorgeous. 'Talia,' he said softly, 'can I kiss you.'

You would have thought he'd asked for a blowjob because I stood up and said, 'Go fuck yourself.' Just like that. God knows what he thought ... I was thunder and he was like a bolt of lightning ... outta there.

I had a lucky escape really because not long later he hooked up with this girl Emily. And nine months later they had a baby girl.

Anyhow ... I was thinking about that story; the stars, Steven, red frizzy hair which apparently the baby ended up with, when Grant says, 'Wanna play?'

'It's too dark,' I say, 'no moon.'

'Oh yeah,' he says, looking up at the sky, 'just a slither.'

'And I'm getting cold,' walking towards the door.

'Talia,' he says, 'before you go in ... can I ask you something?'

'No,' I say.

'Talia, please,' he says, 'it's important.'

'Mum looked mad at you,' I say.

'Don't worry about your mother … I'll deal with her,' he says. 'Talia … do you think about your father?'

'What's to think about?' I say.

'Would you want to see him if he wanted to see you?' he asks.

'Why would I want to see him?' I say. 'Not even a birthday card in fourteen years he can go drop dead for all I care.' And diary I feel this … this … like if a shotgun was handy and he, as in my father, walked up the drive right then and there I could blow his fucken brains to bits.

And Grace says I'm a gentle and kind young woman … I so need a new counsellor … one that works with psychopaths.

'Talia,' says Grant. I almost forgot he was there. 'It's him that has missed out … missed out on being your Dad.'

'Yeah right,' I say.

'Yeah I am right,' he says, 'you're a good kid.'

You heard him … good fucken kid.

I bet if the moon was full and he had brighter light he would've said, "I know why your father stayed away … he didn't wanna see his own reflection."

And I would've said, "Yeah ... I'm just like him ... fucked and fucken awful."

May 23

So I'm walking around school today ... just can't seem to bear the library and I don't know why but that shotgun feeling won't go away. It's like I have fire inside. I was half expecting someone to say, "Talia, what's that coming out your ears ... and nose?"

"Oh ... it's smoke," I'd smile. "So fuck the hell off before I fucken burn you."

And the next thing you'd know sirens would be wailing and some firemen would blast me with an enormous hose. And because one hose couldn't put out the fire they'd have to call for backup and evacuate the entire school.

May 26

I haven't been writing because I thought by doing so the flames might burn themselves out. I'm a grouchy bitch ... even intolerant of Sol and Mac. Found myself after school today in a book shop in the health section looking at diet books.

This plump middle-aged woman looks me up and down and says, 'Surely that's not for you?'

'No,' I say. But you could certainly do with it!

May 27

'You seem very agitated,' says Grace.

'Nah,' I say, 'I'm all good.'

'Your foot, it keeps going up and down, tapping the floor, what is it trying to say.'

I look down at my tapping foot and try to make it stop but the wires aren't connected and it keeps bouncing about like a baby on someone's knee.

'A foot says something,' I laugh.

'Yeah,' she says softly. 'Like perhaps it says … I want to stand up or I want to kick or I want to dance … perhaps. So if your foot could talk what would it say?'

'That I … I … it wants to kick,' I say.

'Who?' Who would it like to kick?'

'I don't know … anyone … everyone.'

'So it's angry?'

'Yeah I guess.'

'If anger was a colour what colour would it be?'

'I don't know … like fire I guess … red and orange and black smoke.'

'I have some paper and crayons … what say you draw your anger.'

So I sit on the floor like I'm five years old and feel even younger and draw this anger that is apparently in my foot. Except it feels like it's in my feet and hands and legs and wrists and shoulders and ... and ... in my gut.

'I've had enough,' I say ... looking at my picture of scribbled red and orange and black fire. I scribbled sooo hard I put holes in the paper.

'Have some water, says Grace. 'You've worked hard.'

And now ... I'm sitting here in my room, on my bed, phone in my hand, seriously considering calling the fire brigade myself.

May 28

I keep thinking if I just lose a little weight ... a couple of pounds, everything will be alright. I'm sure somehow ... someway it will help.

Grace says, 'Feelings pass Talia, if you just sit with it or express what you feel even a little of it ... it will pass.'

But I feel like I'm waiting for a bus to arrive ... everyone else waiting boards their home ... but the one with my address just won't arrive.

Perhaps ... I know diary ... six percent die. Twenty percent chronic.

I'm chronic with a fire burning my insides and I don't understand why.

I wish Elli was here … I wish I wasn't so shallow … maybe I could inject myself with lesbian hormones and turn up at Isabella's and say, "Can we be a threesome?"

Or better still I could find out where Jason lives … Jay from the Bay and say, "Can you kiss me and fill me with your laughter and fun?"

And I'd melt in his gorgeous arms and he'd kiss me, gentle and passionate all at once. And when he released me I'd be full to overflowing with his high. And we'd laugh together forever … anytime I felt bad I'd just say, "Kiss me."

May 29

'Kiss me Jason, kiss me.'

May 30

I'm sitting in English gazing about the room … looking at the grey clouds out the window … wishing it would piss down so I could stand under the rain. Stand and let the drops seep through my body … cold and wet.

Wet.

Mr Reiding is absent … the lesson is not the same without him. I don't even know what it's about. I miss his beautiful tired face and most of all I miss his, 'Well done, Talia … excellent work.'

And for a fleeting moment I think I might miss my father … and then … not.

No I do not.

May 31

I know the ice in this house and the lack of construction work is some disagreement over him. My father.

Perhaps he has made contact after all these years and perhaps … just perhaps he wants to see me. And Mum, she doesn't want to tell me and Grant, he thinks she should.

And me, what do I think? Good question.

Library Definition …

1 Father … male parent … an important figure in the early history of something … priest … the father God.

2 Dad … father

3 Daddy … father; oldest or most important person or thing.

Interesting. I therefore conclude Clay asshole fuckwit McKenna is no more my father than Father fucken Christmas. The only thing he qualifies in is being male. An important person in my early history … whatever. Definitely no priest … though I understand they too like their alcohol. And he sure ain't no God.

Unless God is a scary drunk.

I soo hope that's not true … I'm hoping for … well someone more like Father Christmas. Kind and happy and gives out lots of gifts.

So ... back to the question what do I think? I'm with Mum on this one ... rare but true. And ... I'm going to investigate how I can change my last name.

June 1

Thank God for exams ... gives me something to do.

June 2

Just got off the phone to Maggie. She's like, 'Oh Talia ... I slept with him.'

'Who?' I ask.

'Liam ... I slept with Liam.'

'Oh,' I say, 'so you broke up with the musician?'

'Arh ... no,' she says softly, as if the musician was in the room.

'Oh,' I say, 'how did that happen then?'

'Scott ... oh Talia I feel sooo bad ... he was out at some gig. I was supposed to go too but then some of the girls from my hostel asked me out for a night on the town. So I thought why not ... be fun. And it was ... we were dancing up a storm ... having a great time. And then there he was ... Liam. I thought my chest was gonna explode. He comes on over and he's like, "Good to see you Maggie ... looking hot." He was drunk.'

'Were you?' I ask.

'Hardly ... only had a little to drink ... too busy dancing.'

'So what happened then?' I ask.

'He was all over me ... hands and kissing my neck. And I know ... oh fuck what have I done ... Scott will be soo hurt.'

'You gonna tell him?' I say.

'I don't know. I'm confused, in the morning Liam was awkward and like giving me negative vibes. I guess Anna was right ... he just wanted sex ... and I was there.'

'Oh Maggie,' I say, 'I'm sorry.'

'It's me that's sorry ... I was dumb ... maybe I just wanted him because I couldn't have him. He's still gorgeous but so is Scott.'

'So what now?'

'I don't know Talia, I don't know. I've never been good at lying ... and someone might tell Scott they saw us kissing at the club.'

'Yeah,' I say, 'but kissing isn't sex.'

'No,' she begins to cry, 'but we did ... we did have sex. I didn't even make him use a condom.'

'Oh,' I say.

'Don't worry, I'm on the pill ... but you know ... Liam's had a few.'

'I'm sure you'll be fine,' I say.

'Yeah,' she says, sniffing.

'What about you, Talia ... how you going?'

'Ok,' I say. 'But ... but I have wanted to ask you something.'

'Go for it,' she sniffs.

'If your Dad turned up and wanted to see you what would you do?'

'Well,' she says, 'it's kinda different for me Talia ... because he has and does turn up now and then. Less of the now ... not much of the then either really. But I've always seen him ... take what I can get I guess.'

'Don't you hate him?' I ask.

'No,' she says, 'don't think so anyhow.'

'Do you hate your father?'

'Don't know either,' I say, because I don't. 'I think he wants to make contact.'

'Oh,' she says. 'Be good to see what he looks like.'

'Maybe,' I say, beginning to sweat ... smoking ears.

'All I know is,' says Maggie, 'whatever he is ... useless or not ... he's my father. And I might not even like him ... I'm not sure I do ... but I'm not sure I don't either. So in a way ... seeing him, helps me to work that out. Helps me to decide whether I want him in my life or if I don't.'

'True,' I say.

'But saying that sounds kinda weird kinda stupid.'

'Why?' I ask.

'Well,' she laughs, 'it's not like I have a choice really. He turns up ... he disappears been like that for ... shit how many years.'

'But even so ... you still want to see him?'

'I guess,' she sighs, 'how else can I work it out. Know if I actually want to unless I'm given the option. So what about you ... what you gonna do?'

'Nothing,' I say. 'Nothing.'

I don't think diary that I want to work it out.

I'll just stick with the not.

June 4

The boys and I had a lovely time at the park ... I think I enjoyed the swings more than them. I swung as high as my legs would take me ... my feet almost touching the sky. It reminded me of being a little girl and my Dad taking me to the park. The same park. Sitting on his knee while he swung us both. I was too scared to sit by myself. I remember him going down the slide with me too. He'd hold me close and we'd slide down ... him saying, 'Weeeee!' I loved the slide back then ... I loved being held by my Dad.

But do I want to see him ... No. No. No.

Diary ... but ... I really and truly could kill him. Or at least I could kill someone. I could smoother him with my hands. Am ashamed to say but I could stab him a hundred times with a knife.

What the fuck is wrong with me? ... I think I was far saner when I was on a diet. Far saner when I was locked up in a mental asylum.

June 5

The boys were at Aunty Maxine's ... Grant had just got back from dropping them off. I hear Mum's thumping voice, 'Well, you tell her then, and you live with the repercussions. I'm going out.'

'Kim, please,' says Grant, 'she's your daughter ... you should be doing this. You should be the one to tell her.'

'I don't think she should know,' she yells, 'I've told you that.'

And diary ... I didn't know if I should hide in the wardrobe and pretend I couldn't hear or storm out like a soldier and demand to know what it was I should and shouldn't know.

I'm frozen like a fat snowman in the entrance of the hall ... I hear a car roar off and then Grant ... he's standing in front of me with tears in his eyes. I've never seen such a big man-bear with tears in his eyes and I want to say, "Don't you realise it's winter ... fuck off!"

He looks at me, half smiles and says, 'I need to talk to you ... come and sit down.'

I drag myself to the lounge and sit in an armchair; hold a cushion tight. He sits on the couch.

'I don't want to see him,' I say.

'Who?' he asks.

'My father, I don't want to see him. I know that's what you've been arguing about.'

'Talia ... I understand you don't want to see him.'

'Yeah well, thanks,' I say, standing up.

'Talia,' says Grant softly ... gently, 'he's dying.'

'What?'

'He has a brain tumor ... he's in a hospice ... I'm sorry,' he says, wiping tears.

'Dying,' I say.

'Yeah ... your nana contacted us some months ago. She thought you should say good bye.' Goodbye ... I never said hello.

'Did he,' I ask, swallowing the melting ice in my throat, 'did he want to see me?'

'I really don't know, Talia' says Grant, leaning forward in his chair.

'Oh,' I say, 'so it's Nana's idea.'

'Talia ... he's dying. Nana says any day now. I'm not even sure he's conscious. Do you want to see him? I will take you.'

And diary ... I don't know why but I burst into tears ... but at the same time, smoke is blowing and steaming and puffing out my ears. Out my nose.

I shiver and rub my sweaty palms, 'Can I think about it?'

'Sure,' says Grant, 'sure. But remember ... he could die any time.' And I hear this voice ... this little voice that says, 'Good.'

Good.

June 7

So the following morning, after being told the terminal news, Grant and I set out for a four hour drive. We got up at six am and left after breakfast. Mum, she got up too ... she made Grant bacon and eggs and coffee and sat looking at him like he was some kinda superhero. She never looked at me though, not even once. She kissed him on the top of his head and then on his left cheek. She did though make me my food for the day. She put it in Sol's lunch box; red with Spiderman on it. I couldn't help thinking she'd rather have given it to Grant. But he got his own lunch box; plain blue. My lunch box was broken so I got Spiderman. All day I worried that Sol would find out his lunchbox was missing ... and be sad. And mad ... mad at me.

The trip seemed to take forever, we listened over and over to the same CD; it was the only one in Grant's car. A collaboration of recent number ones. Fortunately for me it wasn't Grant's usual eighties sounds … he loves eighties music. Duran Duran and is it Boy George or George Boy. And then of course …Kiss and George Thoro-someone and all this loud stuff. Mum had cleaned the car the other day … she likes up-to-date music.

Surprise surprise another minor detail we have in common.

The sky was big and bright and clear; like the sun was smiling, sending rays of warmth and happiness all over the hospice grounds and building. And that seemed weird to me. Why wasn't it grey and cloudy and sad … like it had been for most of the trip?

We got out of the car and the first thing I saw was a gaunt looking elderly man being pushed in a wheelchair. He had a crochet blanket on his lap … pink and white and blue and yellow and orange and red and purple and … it looked so pretty and he looked so thin and so tired. And yet when I looked at him, which I had tried not to, he smiled. 'Beautiful day,' he said.

The man pushing the wheelchair … old as well, thin on top, lined and sad looking, put his hand on his shoulder and said, 'Sure is Dad.'

Dad.

And Grant he smiled when I couldn't and said, 'It was cloudy all the way here … beautiful gardens.'

The old man pushing the wheelchair said, 'Dad loves gardening ... don't you Dad?'

And the elderly man ... he beamed with this look of contentment, 'I grew the best roses didn't I son.'

'You sure did,' said his son, 'you sure did.'

And then they both smiled at us as if to say, "Goodbye ... have a nice stay."

Before I entered the door which Grant was holding open for me, I turned to see the elderly man and his old man son looking at a winter rose bush. It was red.

A deep, deep red.

Nana greeted us ... she looked like she was a patient not a Mum. She smiled but there were tears falling down her face. She wrapped her arms around me. She was thin. I could feel the bones in her back. Even through a hand knitted white jersey, cable knit, I think it's called. She used to post me cable knit jerseys just like that ... I refused to wear them, said, 'They make me itchy.'

She let go and lowered her head. 'You're too late,' she said, 'he passed ... about an hour ago.'

And Grant he looked at me and I looked at him and then everywhere else. At the cream walls. The painting of butterflies to my left. A vase of white flowers to my right. A woman walking past. Middle aged, three quarter sky-blue pants, making her chunky legs look even chunkier... name badge, Silvia ... who the fuck would work here?

The carpet was beige and … had had too many feet trample on it … it could do with a good lay down. Which has to say something … considering it already was.

'Let's get out of the hall,' sniffs Nana, wiping her eyes. 'Do you want to see him? He looks peaceful.'

'That would be good,' said Grant, looking at me.

I don't know why he thinks seeing my dead asshole father would be good … he ushers me into the room behind Nana. The name of the room is called Rose and I think how rude … how fucken rude that the elderly man in the garden who loved roses didn't have this room.

I expected to see a skinny gaunt looking man … but he was puffy and full. Apparently brain tumors can be different from other cancers where your body disintegrates.

Disappears.

No … he was larger than life … and dead.

In fact, that's why he died here … Nana and Granddad couldn't manage him at home. No there was no new wife or half brothers and sisters to meet. Just Clay fucken McKenna.

Fat.

And dead.

Granddad stands up and shakes Grant's hand, 'Sorry for your loss,' says Grant. And I look at Grant … big fucken man bear, "Stop fucken crying." I want to say, "he was an asshole anyway."

'He was our only son,' says Granddad, swallowing and twisting his neck. He so needs to pull down his grey slacks; they're sticking up his ass. Cable knit jersey too. Dark Blue.

'I know,' says Grant, 'Kim told me. She sends her condolences … she's looking after the twins.'

'Would you like me to make some tea?' says Nana, 'there's a family kitchen where we can make whatever we like.'

'I'll help,' I say.

She nods.

So we make tea in a silver pot and bring it back on a floral tray. With biscuits … Superwine and Mellowpuffs. And we sit in the room called Rose and sip hot and then later, cold tea. Grant eats at least half a dozen biscuits. And I sit looking at the Mellowpuffs … the chocolate, trying to recall the last time I had eaten one.

I can't.

June 9

Nana wanted us to stay the night but I … I was so glad when Grant said we couldn't. All the way home I kept thinking of Sol's Spiderman lunchbox and hoping like crazy that we got back before he realised it was gone. We didn't play the only CD we had … we sat in silence. Just the hum of the car … the car humming.

As we walked up the drive Grant put his hand on my shoulder and said, 'Talia … you've said nothing … not a word … are you ok?'

'It's not like I knew him,' I said. Because it was true. I didn't.

And now diary … I'm up again at six am … about to go on that four hour drive … to a funeral for a fat dead man. Dark hair with flecks of grey. What color were his eyes? … I couldn't see they were shut.

June 10

Funerals are weird things … Dictionary Definition: Ceremony in which a dead person is buried or cremated.

Buried or cremated. I would've liked Clay to have been cremated then buried. Unfortunately Nana and Granddad decided only on burial. And why they chose the most expensive coffin I will never know. Beautiful white wood with gold handles and white silk … pure white silk for his fat dead body to lie on. And diary … there were baskets of single red roses. Deep, deep red just like the elderly man was admiring. The elderly man that should've had the room named after a rose.

What did he have instead? … Lily or Magnolia or perhaps Sunflower. I hope Sunflower … big and bright and shining like the sun that day I met him. I hope he grew sunflowers too.

Anyhow … everyone was supposed to take a single red rose from those baskets, those woven wicker baskets and place it in Clay's open coffin. People lined up, red rose in their hand

and said their goodbyes … many crying. Grant turned to me and said, 'You going up?'

I looked at him, scratched my head and said, 'No.'

'Talia,' he said, looking confused, 'this is your chance to say goodbye.'

'I said no,' looking straight ahead.

'Talia,' he whispered, 'I know he wasn't there for you but he's your father.'

'I said no.'

So silly fucken Grant is up out of his chair, taking a single red rose from the basket.

Deep, deep red.

And he walks up the front of the church and places the rose gently on the fat dead body of my father. And the whole time smoke's rising from my nostrils and ears.

He walks back. He has tears. Tears in his eyes. He sits down next to me. I glare, 'You better not have said goodbye on my behalf.'

And he looks back, sighs and says, 'Oh Talia.'

I stand up; climb over Grant and storm out of that horrible old church to the sound of Amazing Grace. How amazing is Grace … not even fucken here when I need something or someone to be on my side. I'm soo mad at Grant … so mad.

So mad.

I still am.

I never saw the rest of the funeral … the lowering of the coffin into the ground. It's a shame about that part. I would've enjoyed that.

I walked and walked and walked some more. Enjoyed the feeling of my pounding heart … my heaving chest. I smiled … knowing Clay's heart had stopped.

When I had walked enough, I waited back at the car. Grant arrived not long later … 'Where have you been?' he said.

'Nowhere.'

'It was rude,' he said.

'I don't care,' I said. Because I don't.

I don't fucken care.

He lowers his head, 'I'm trying to understand … why you're so angry … why … why you don't cry, he's your father.'

'I didn't know him,' I said.

'My Mum died when I was three years old,' he said. 'I didn't know her but I … I'll always love her. Always.'

I nod. Look at the ground. My black heels on the road.

'I still miss her.'

I look up at Grant … big man bear, tears falling from his big man bear eyes and I want to say sorry. I want to say, "Sorry Grant."

But I keep seeing him walking up the aisle, single red rose in his hand, deep, deep red ... him placing it gently on my fat, dead father and I could scream.

So I don't say sorry ... I mutter, 'Well ... I don't miss him.'

And he hangs his head like I've broken his heart ... and I ... I just don't care.

We never went to the afternoon tea put on by Nana and Granddad ... of course Grant had to say our apologies.

Our goodbyes.

I waited in the car ... listening to Adam Lambert. Made me feel like Elli was with me.

He looked sad the entire trip back. The entire four fucken hours. And I don't think it was Adam Lambert singing over and over and over again that made his face hang. It was probably the embarrassment of having to say to my elderly grandparents who had just buried their son, "Talia, your only grandchild is such a bitch she refuses to come."

June 11

Sol never missed his Spiderman lunchbox which was such a relief.

June 12

I wonder why birds sing and tweet and hum so early in the morning. What are they saying to one another? Is it the young ones saying, "Mum I'm cold ... fluff up your feathers and wrap me up." Or perhaps, "Mum ... I'm hungry ... I'm starving, please get me some food." Or are they just singing for the joy of life. Perhaps the lady bird wakes up and sees her lover bird and she tweets her love. In love.

Either way I think it's strange ... what are they singing about at four thirty am? And why the silence by five?

June 13

I'm listening to the birds again and I've decided it's the babies ... the baby birds tweeting to their Mums. 'Fluff up your feathers Mummy,' they tweet, 'I'm cold. Wrap me up.'

And so the Mummy bird she puffs up her feathers and breathes out her chest and wraps her wings around her little cold birds.

June 14

I hope there is such a thing as reincarnation. And ... I ... I can come back as a baby bird.

June 15

'I'm going to school today,' I said to Grant.

'Are you sure?' he said. 'Are you sure you're ready?'

I nod.

'Talia …' he said. 'I'm sorry.'

And I look at him … a spoonful of cereal in his hand. And I still feel this … I still feel … smoke is still puffing out of my ears. 'Doesn't matter,' I say.

Mum enters the room … all glammed up. 'Good to see you in your uniform, Talia. School is exactly what you need.'

'You look lovely,' smiles Grant, looking her up and down.

Personally I think that skirt is way too short. Thank god she's wearing stockings. I guess being a man he's thinking … can't wait until I can get my head up that skirt. It's hardly surprising I feel so nauseous.

June 16

Mr Reiding calls me back after the class. He's like, 'Take a seat Talia.'

I sit down.

'So,' he smiles, 'I have your exam results … excellent marks … top of the class … 88%'

I nod.

'I wanted to personally congratulate you,' he beams. You'd have thought I'd won gold at the Olympics.

I look out the window … a puffy, white cloud that looks like a bird. A baby bird. 'Thanks,' I say.

'And,' he says, scratching his ear, pulling at the lobe, 'I wanted to say ... I heard about your father and I'm so sorry for your loss.'

'I didn't know him,' I said.

This time, he nods.

So we sit like that ... me looking out the window at the puffy, white cloud that looks like a baby bird and him nodding.

'Well thanks for that,' I finally say, standing up.

'Talia,' he says, tugging now at his beard, 'you're doing really well.'

'Am I?' I say.

Am I?

June 17

I passed all my exams. But ... I'm not sure I want to go to university anymore. Not sure I want to be a dietitian.

Not sure.

June 18

I didn't turn up for my appointment with Grace yesterday. I know that's rude and I ... I guess I am. Rude.

She rang this morning, I was still in bed. She's like, 'Talia ... you don't have to do this alone.'

'I just forgot,' I said

'Ok,' she said. 'Let's make an appointment for next Friday then … ok. Four o'clock after school as usual. How does that sound?'

'Ok,' I lie. Ok.

June 19

Maggie's like, 'Oh Talia … Mum only just told me … about your Dad.'

'Oh,' I say.

'Oh Talia … I'm so sorry … why didn't you ring me … text me … let me or Anna know?'

'Don't know,' I said.

'Do you want to talk about it?' she asks.

'Not really … no,' I say. Because I don't.

'Ok,' she says, 'but if you ever do … I'm here ok.'

'Ok,' I say. 'So what happened … with Scott … with Liam?'

'You sure you want to talk about my shit?' she asks.

'Maggie … just be normal with me, please.'

'Ok.'

'So what happened?'

'I never told Scott … which I know is bad … and I feel terrible. And Liam nothing … seen him a couple of times around campus. Could hardly look his way. And he … he seemed oblivious.'

'Really,' I said, 'oblivious.'

'Yeah really. I was such an idiot.'

'He sounds like such a wanker,' I said.

'Nah,' she says, 'I'm such a stupid bitch.'

'No you're not,' I said.

'Yeah I am.'

'Nah,' I say.

'I am Talia. I'm a stupid bitch because I still want him. Even now. I think … I think I just want him to want me … like I want him. But he doesn't which makes me pretty screwed up.'

'Oh Maggie,' I say. 'What you gonna do?'

'I think about breaking up with Scott because it's so unfair. What do you think?'

'Shit … I don't know … I don't know anything about love.'

'But … it's not … well poor Scott.'

'Maggie … maybe just think about it for longer. I know it hurts but Liam … he well … I guess he doesn't feel the same.'

'I know,' she says, 'I know. I get that.'

So we talk a bit longer but don't really come to any conclusion as to whether she should break up with Scott or not. And then she's like, 'So Talia … how's it all going food-wise. You doing ok?'

'Yeah ok,' I lie.

June 22

It's not that I want to diet or necessarily lose weight … it's just … just that I feel kinda sick inside. Nauseous.

Like food just turns my stomach and then and now, oh joy oh delight, I can feel the weight disappearing from my body. And I like that. I like that diary. I like the feeling that I'm thin and light and disappearing where no one can find me not even myself.

It's not that I think I'm fat … sure I feel fat …well sometimes. It's like this panic … this feeling that I'm ugly and disgusting and yuck and like it's all over me and I can't get it off. That's being fat.

Fat.

But … rationally I realise I am slim … smaller than most. But diary … I'm whispering as I write … I don't want to eat. I want to relish in the feeling of being lighter than light.

It's like that mother bird wrapping its wings around her young. I am her young and losing weight … not eating is her wings.

June 24

Grace is like, 'Talia, I'm so sorry to hear about your father … how have you been … what's been going on for you?'

I shake my head and say, 'Not much.'

'Do you want to talk about it or would you rather talk about something else?'

'Well,' I frown, 'there's really not much to say … except he was fat … puffed up.'

'He was fat,' she repeats.

'Apparently the steroids he was on … they can … I expected him to be thin and frail … like a cancer patient.'

'And how did that make you feel … seeing him fat?' asks Grace.

'I don't think I felt anything,' I say, 'I just was surprised.'

'So seeing him fat shocked you,' says Grace.

'And,' I say, 'I just thought he's kinda gross … kinda ugly … which I know is mean because he's dead … he died before Grant and I got there. Did you know that?'

'Oh,' she says, 'so you never got to say goodbye … not while he was alive anyway.'

'Well,' I say, 'he was unconscious … had been for a few days … so that's almost dead anyway … isn't it.'

'They do say many unconscious people have some awareness of those around ... but I can see how for you he may have appeared almost dead.'

'Grace ...' I say, 'at the hospice ... each room was named after a flower.'

'Oh that's lovely ... what a lovely idea,' smiles Grace, 'and what was your father's room.'

I lower my head, 'Rose.'

'Rose ... such an amazing flower. Do you like roses, Talia?'

'I think all flowers are amazing ... they are don't you think?'

'I do,' smiles Grace, 'all flowers have some beauty ... some gift ... a gift from nature ... I think my favourite flower is the sunflower.'

'Really,' I say, 'mine too. Why do you like it?'

'I love the color ... I wear a lot of yellow, you may have noticed. But what I love the most is the way it stands upright on one thick stem and seems to reach out ... reach out to the sun. I love the sun,' she glows, 'the petals seem to love the sun too. They open themselves wide ... wide like arms embracing ... embracing arms ... I just find the sunflower fascinating. And you?'

'Oh,' I say, trying to absorb all she said and hoping the elderly man did get the Sunflower room, 'I guess ... they ... look alive. Big and bright and hopeful.'

'Yeah,' beams Grace, 'they do look hopeful ... they do ... maybe this summer you could plant some with Sol and Mac and watch them grow.'

'Oh yeah,' I smile, 'they would love that. I remember when I was about six we grew some at school. They were soo big and soo bright and the only thing ... I was sad when they died.'

'But,' smiles Grace, 'they leave behind seeds. Sunflower seeds ... and from that a new flower will grow.'

'But only if you plant it.'

'Yes,' she smiles, 'only if you plant it. Feed it ... water it ... and of course place it in the sun,'

'The sun,' I say.

'Talia ... when you think about it, the sunflower symbolises so much doesn't it.'

'Does it?' I say, frowning.

'Yeah ... I think so,' she says.

'What?'

'For me,' she says, 'the seed is the spirit of someone that passes ... dies. The flower and stem like the body ... dies. But the seeds, the seeds live on. And from that seed an all embracing sunflower can appear.'

'Oh,' I say, 'so you mean ... the seed is the spirit of someone that has died.'

'Yeah,' she says, 'least that's how I see it … and from that seed … that spirit … the deceased lives on. It's only the physical body that dies. Just like the sunflower … that eventually goes brown and wilts and dies. But the seed … it's still there … alive.'

'Oh,' I say, starting to feel that bloody smoke begin to rise, 'I hadn't really thought about that.'

But what I really wanted to say is … "So it's only my Dad's fat body that died … and there's some seed, some fucken spirit that didn't."

Well I'm glad for Gloria … who really might be singing Hallelujah with some angels in heaven and glad for the elderly man that loved roses and should have rightfully had my father's room. But … the thought that my father's spirit is still alive is enough to turn my stomach.

Another reason to avoid dinner tonight.

June 25

No doubt as you can appreciate … Sol and Mac won't be growing sunflowers this summer and I'm hoping that the elderly man got to be in a room say, Magnolia or Lily.

June 26

I've just realised that's why the hospice must name each room after a flower. Because it's not just the sunflower that leaves behind a seed … a spirit. They all do.

All flowers.

I guess all plants in fact.

So when the body … the sick and tired body can no longer breathe in that room … just like the flower the room is named after … a seed remains and lives.

June 27

I've been walking endlessly … looking at gardens. Flowers. And I get this bitch feeling like I want to trample over the flowers that gardeners have carefully and lovingly grown. It seems that flowers are everywhere … despite the fact it's winter. I'm not looking forward to spring.

June 29

What can I tell you … its 4:30 am … the birds are chirping. I'm cold too and need wings.

June 30

Oh fuck me … have Grace tomorrow and I sooo don't want to go.

July 1

I was fifteen minutes late … lied, 'Missed my bus.'

'Never mind,' she said, 'you're here now. Take a seat ... would you like me to take your jacket ... it's warm ... the heater's on.'

'No,' I say, 'I'm good.'

'So what's been happening, Talia?'

'Same old,' I say, 'school. Homework. School. Assignments.'

'And you're doing ok ... did you ever contact your friend Elli?'

'No,' I say, 'she's living at her girlfriend's house with their family ... going to school there now.'

'You must miss her,' she says.

'I guess,' I nod.

'Have you made any other friends?'

'I have lots of people I say hi to and have short conversations with ... but nah not really ... can't really be bothered ... just want to finish school and get on with university or something. Try and get into the same university as my friend Maggie ... I'll try where my other friend Anna is too.'

'And do you still want to be a dietitian?'

'I'm not sure ... maybe I'll just ... don't know.'

'And what is it that has made you change your mind ... about becoming a dietitian?'

'I ... I don't know ... I pass biology and chemistry and that but it's kinda boring and sometimes I think ... well studying food and health and stuff … maybe that's not such a good idea.'

'Perhaps,' smiles Grace, 'whatever you learn is never wasted, that's what I always told my girls.'

'You think,' I say, hopeful.

'Everything you learn whether it is through study or just life, life experience, it all becomes part of who you are. And you become wiser and often kinder for it.'

'I hope so,' I say. 'I hope one day I'm wise … and kind.'

'Are you not kind now?' she asks, leaning forward, placing her long fingers on her thorn cotton trousers.

'I like your earrings,' I say, 'hoops.'

'Thank you,' she smiles, touching one. 'So, Talia, are you not kind now?'

'I'm definitely not wise … that's for sure … thick at times, where did you buy your headband?'

'This one,' she says, touching the thick woven band around her head, 'my daughter bought it for me once … years ago … for a birthday I think. Do you like it?'

'You suit it … with your dreadlocks … it looks great on you … I've never worn headbands,' I say, rubbing my hand over my head.

'And why is that?'

236 | NATASHA JENNINGS

'I think … well I tried my friend's on once, Anna's, and I just felt like I stood out too much and I didn't like that.'

'So you don't like to feel like you stand out too much?'

'I guess.'

'How does it make you feel? Standing out?' she smiles.

'Like … it freaks me out … feels like everyone's looking at me … makes me … I get this feeling like I want to disappear.' And yuck.

'Disappear … Talia, I want to read something I read just the other day,' and she reaches over and picks up a book from the floor to her left, 'ah … here it is, "*With Anorexia there is a denying of yourself and an unconscious longing to disappear, as if by becoming small your needs and presence also diminish, especially your need to be loved.*"

'Nah,' I laugh, 'I just want to be thin … I'm vain.'

'It also says,' she says gently, '"*Anorexia Nervosa is intimately bound up with the complexities of receiving nourishment and love. With longing to be nurtured and loved, we reduce our presence so as to reduce our need for that love.*"'

And I look at the thin bitch of a counsellor … thin … and consider the fact that she must feel deeply unloved. And lonely too. I stand up, 'I know we have ten minutes to go but I'd like to finish now.'

She smiles and gently says, 'Talia … just sit down, have your glass of water … feel your feet connected to the ground and then leave.'

'Ok,' I say but really I want to smash that thin bitch in the teeth.

Kind? … fucken unkind me.

July 2

Dictionary definition: Anorexia Nervosa … lack of appetite for food … as in chronic illness.

Second dictionary, just to make sure.

Dictionary definition: Anorexia Nervosa … a disorder in which a person refuses to eat because they are afraid of becoming fat.

As I said … 'I just want to be thin … because I'm vain.' A vain unkind bitch.

Therefore I conclude once again … Grace is obviously a fraud. And, I so need a new therapist.

I think I'd like a fat one … a big roly poly obese one that wears nothing but elastic slacks and big tank dresses and whose ankles are like trunks not stems from a sunflower.

July 3

Happy birthday Grant.

I didn't buy him anything because I still find it hard to look at the bastard after taking that single red rose and placing it on my fat dead father.

But then I felt guilty so me and the boys made him three big cards one from each of us. Sol drew some kind of robot or transformer or something like that, I didn't like to ask because I so often get it wrong and he gets all indignant and upset. And Mac ... his was definitely just some kind of scribble but I'm sure there's something in there that has meaning ... at least to him. Perhaps it's a bomb.

Gone off.

And me ... I just wrote in block letters ... Happy Birthday.

I took the boys hand in hand and we strolled to the dairy. Bought a box of chocolates. Roses. Because that's all they fucken had.

I made the boys give the cards and fucken Roses to him. He hugged each of them, like they had just given him gold. I gave him a ... don't even think about it look ... and fortunately he didn't wrap his bear arms around me.

Mum was all over him giving him about ten different gifts. Books, socks, a shirt ... blue demin, aftershave, a red bucket full of everything you need to clean your car and a couple of CD's. And then she whisper's, 'I'll give you the main present tonight!' And of course he gets that ridiculous smile. What's she got him ... a new construction hat?

I just wish they'd move sites.

Happy Birthday Grant ... hope you choke on a Rose.

July 4

I forgot to mention Grant was forty-eight which I guess makes him officially old. The boys and I made him a chocolate cake. We put forty-one candles on it ... that's all we had. I was tempted to poke out my tongue and squirt out a drop or two of venom into the cake mixture but then I realised Sol and Mac eat cake too.

So I didn't.

July 5

I know I am fast becoming one of those 20%. Chronic.

But ... I can't ... my collar bone aches ... I can feel fat dissolving ... leaving my body. And I like it. I like it a lot.

And I cannot ... I can't stop.

July 6

I don't know if Grant or Mum notices that my breakfast now consists of a quarter piece of toast. No butter just a slither of Vegemite. Vegemite has lots of vitamin B's ... and when I was sick last time, I remember overhearing I was low on those.

Those 4:30am chirpy birds must be getting well fluffed up ... which is lovely ... their babies will be soo wrapped up. I hope they like Vegemite ... perhaps I should put butter on their three quarters ... just for the extra fluff up.

I heard them this morning as usual ... tweet tweet and chirp chirp ... I started feeling anxious ... "Come on Mum ... listen to your babies ... they're cold ... wrap them up."

The relief that came over me when those babies stopped chirping was like warm water on a minus four degree day. Hooray.

I do have a black tea as well. Apparently tea, even gumboot has antioxidants. Perhaps I should get some green tea ... super full of antioxidants.

Grant is usually so busy scoffing his own face, running late for work and Mum ... dragging herself out of bed to reach for her second black coffee. Grant always brings her first. And Sol and Mac ... running about, or watching TV or jumping off the couch.

They both have two pieces of toast every morning. Sol Vegemite. Mac peanut butter or jam. Has to be plum jam. If I don't cut off the crusts ... I get this, 'Tala,' yelling from the lounge. 'No crusts.'

It used to annoy me, having to cut off the crusts. Meant changing knifes to get a better cut ... I guess that sounds lazy ... perhaps I am. These days I never forget and don't mind ... happy to think those mother birds are getting extra fluff.

July 8

So on the way to see Grace: oh joy! ... I see hippo girl. It was raining and she wasn't wearing a coat ... probably couldn't get one to fit her. Her hair was even more curly ... more bedraggled ... more mousy brown. I could see her in the distance on the other side of the road; I crossed over.

For some weird reason ... I just wanted to see her. Look her in the eyes. See what color they were. The tremours in the pavement got closer and closer until there she was ... hippo girl. 'Hi,' I said, smiling.

She lifted her head, half smiled. Her eyes were charcoal ... deep ... dark ... almost black. Lovely eyelashes that curled around them. And, believe it or not, she had a beauty spot on her left inner cheek. A pretty mole signifying beauty. The way her head drooped after that half smile ... she must hate it, that mole.

Or perhaps ... she hates herself.

I really wanted to say, "would you like to have coffee ... or hot chocolate full cream if that suits? Extra marshmallows."

But I didn't. I just stood watching her behind waddle along the pavement ... bedraggled, fat and wet.

I was half an hour late for Grace.

'Sorry,' I said. I really was ... and felt really bad and rude and unkind and fat.

She gave me this ... "what's going on Talia?" look and I just started talking about the rain and the cold air and the rain again and how I had noticed lots of people don't wear coats and how cold they must get.

'Unless you're really fat, perhaps,' I hear myself say.

'I'm sure fat people feel cold and wet too,' she says, looking me up and down.

And diary ... I don't like that, hippo girl cold and wet.

'What are you feeling Talia ... why are there tears in your eyes?'

'I just ... I don't like ... I don't know ... 'I say, wiping my eyes.

She passes me the tissues. 'You look really sad, can you tell me about it ... what's that sadness about?'

'I ... I ... don't like ... there's this girl ... she's fat ... really fat and she looks so sad and lonely and she's wet.'

'And what's her name?'

'I don't know ... I just see her sometimes ... I saw her today.'

'So something about her makes you feel really sad ... perhaps it triggers some of your own sadness. What is it about her that makes you feel so sad?'

'I just feel sorry for her,' blowing my nose.

'Some people are probably ok with being overweight, Talia. She could be perhaps ... what do you think?'

'She's not happy,' I say, 'she's sad ... she's got dark eyes ... deep eyes ... sad.'

Grace smiles warmly, 'And Talia, you know how that feels don't you ... to feel deep sadness. To feel alone. To feel fat.'

I hang my head.

We sit like that for several minutes … me hanging my head … Grace probably watching me like I watched hippo girl waddle away.

'Grace,' I say, 'that book … what does it say about overeating? Can you read it to me, please?'

'Sure,' she smiles, reaching into a pale yellow crochet bag with black beads and pulling out a book.

'Ok … here we are … Obesity … *obesity seems to have happened in tandem with social pressure to be model-thin; two extremes of the same problem. Eating has a wonderfully soporific effect. It numbs your feelings, leaving you emotionally satiated. The more you eat, the less you feel, as if the food becomes ballast against the tides of emotion washing your insides. Eating beyond your needs occurs at times of emotional stress, grief, loss, depression, fear, guilt or shame. Remember, most of these feelings are unconscious.*'

I nod and half smile at Grace … sip from my glass of water.

'Want to hear more?' she smiles.

'Ok,' I say, leaning forward.

'*Excessive eating then leads to excessive weight gain, constructing a wall that serves to ward off potential causes of hurt, or rejection, but also blocking out your own feelings. The wall may be a layer of protection but inside is someone longing to love and be loved.*

Many women put on excess weight following sexual assault. By covering up … feelings are shut away beneath layers of fear and mistrust.'

I nod … and begin to cry like I haven't for years. If ever.

'I'd like to go now,' I say, standing up.

'Talia ...' Grace says, like a puffed up mother bird. 'Sit down ... and just be with those tears for a minute or two.'

I sit back down. Breathe heavily. Suck it up.

'I'm ok,' I say, blowing my nose. 'I just feel sorry for that fat girl.'

'Yeah,' smiles Grace, 'me too.'

Yeah ... me too.

July 10

I'm so over counselling ... waste of fucken time.

July 11

Gonna start wearing earmuffs to bed. Chirp fucken chirp.

July 13

Anna rang, 'did you get my card ... sorry about your Dad?'

'Yeah,' I say, 'thanks.'

'I ... I should've called ... I didn't know what to say ... I'm not a very good friend.'

'Sure you are,' I say, 'I'm glad you didn't ring because I don't want to talk about him or him dying anyway.'

'Really?' she says, so soft … like velvet.

'Really,' I say, 'really really … tell me about life … about what you been doing and stuff.'

She laughs, 'I'm in love.'

'Oh wow,' I say, 'and is he in love too?'

'I hope so,' she says, so coy like, sweet … where has Anna gone?

'So what's his name; how'd you meet and stuff?'

'Blair … his name is Blair; he's not my usual type.'

'I didn't know you had a type,' I interrupt. All blokes were in the radar!

'I suppose,' she laughs, 'he's just really sweet and kind and buys me flowers and we go on real dates to the movies and dinner and walks through the botanical gardens. He loves playing on the swings and we have competitions to see who can swing the highest.'

'Cool,' I say, 'I love swings too.'

'Yeah, I know you do,' she says, 'we've had lots of competitions … and you usually win.'

'And did you meet at university?'

'I did, he's a second year law student … twenty and just between you and me,' and she starts to whisper, 'he's a virgin.'

'A virgin,' I repeat, not sure what to say next. Is that a good thing?

'So of course we haven't done it,' she says. 'I think Talia, I'm gonna get tested.'

'For what?'

'You know … tested for Aids and any other sexually transmitted diseases … I have been a bit loose.' Only a bit!

'Oh,' I say, 'yeah … got you … be a bit embarrassing though won't it?'

'No,' she says, 'I'm not embarrassed … just want to make sure I'm all good to go … for when Blair wants to do it.'

'So he hasn't tried?'

'No,' she says, 'he's sweet and romantic … fuck knows what he sees in a tart like me.' She said it! Not me.

'Maybe he wants a tart like you,' I laugh.

'I hope so,' she giggles, 'because I'm in love.'

July 14

I guess I'm a tart too … because I'm really starting to think I'm in love with Mr Reiding. And he's a married man. Has a silver wedding band which I'd very much like to remove.

He must be the kindest teacher that ever existed … kindness seems to be a recurring feature because that's what Anna said about Blair, 'He's sweet and kind …' she said. And she's in love too.

So perhaps it's not muscles or good looks that really take hold of a girl's heart … its kindness.

Mr Reiding certainly doesn't work out in a gym … he's slim but not muscular. Lines form around his eyes and mouth where I know he has done a lot of smiling … a lot of laughing. And his hands look soft … but I bet they have done a lot of dishes and cleaning. I'm sure he would help his wife even though he'd rather have his nose in a book.

I wish he could put me in his tweed jacket pocket and take me home. He could put me on the mantelpiece … like an ornament … and I'd just stay right there. Close to him.

In his home.

I guess he'd make love to his wife at night … but that would be ok … she could have that part of him.

I'd be like a special ornament dear to his heart and in that way … in his heart.

July 15

I tried really hard not to be late today … made my feet walk one foot in front of the other … even though they soo wanted to run.

In the other direction.

I was distracted by these workers; yellow construction hats! … digging up the pavement, apparently laying new cables for the internet. No doubt trying to lay their own cables tonight. And then there was this jewelry shop I'd always wanted to look in … even though I don't wear jewelry. Just earrings. And then I bumped into Chrissy with her foster Mum. She's like, 'Oh Talia,' so excited, 'this is my friend Talia, Mum.'

'Hello dear,' says a frumpy grey haired woman, wearing pink lipstick, 'lovely to meet you.'

'Talia's our friend,' repeats Chrissy. 'We visit her in the library. She's real brainy … always working hard in the library, aye Talia.'

'I don't know about the brainy bit,' I smile, 'but I do work hard.'

'You are brainy,' laughs Chrissy, 'sometimes she helps us with our homework.'

'That's lovely dear,' smiles foster Mum. She has crooked front teeth. Blue eyes. Some kind of blue uniform. Worn flat black shoes. Thick legs. She turns towards me, 'Talia, I'm Francis and I just want to say thank you.'

'For what?'

'For looking out for my beautiful girl,' she smiles, putting her arm across Chrissy's shoulder and pulling her close.

Chrissy beamed and I half smiled. 'Oh I … I like Chrissy and Stacey popping in to see me. They … make me smile.'

'Lovely,' she says, 'they make me smile too.'

'Well, I better move,' I say, 'I'm late for an appointment.' Because now I really am.

And they walk off … hand in hand, 'She's very thin,' I hear Francis say. 'Very thin.'

So when I finally arrive at Grace's little counselling room I'm forty minutes late.

I sit down … she's drinking tea or perhaps whiskey to calm her nerves. Her frustration.

'I'm sorry,' I say. My feet are tapping but I am.

'Talia,' she says, 'coming here is very difficult for you isn't it?'

'No, I just … get busy and bump into people and forget the time and stuff.'

'Talia,' she smiles, 'have you heard the saying, the only way out is through.'

'Yes,' I nod.

'Well,' she says, 'it's true … the only way out is through … by facing up to whatever it is that terrifies you so much.'

I nod.

'By discovering what it is that hurts so much that you don't know how to deal with it other than by not eating. By getting thin. And I can see … each week you come … you are thinner. And I'm concerned … I'm worried.'

'Don't be,' I say, feeling guilty and pissed off and afraid ...
terrified all at once.

'Talia ... it is a choice ... healing ... getting well ... it is a
choice. You have to decide ... ask yourself, do I want to get
well ... more than well ... do I want to heal?'

'I see,' I say, wanting to stand up and kick her skinny shins
... then run out the room, screeching, "bitch what do
you know? You're a fraud ... got your qualifications in a
rubbish bin."

'Talia,' she smiles ... gently ... kindly ... and you know I
have a weakness for all things kind, 'I know it's hard ... I
know you are terrified and I know part of you wants to run
out of this room screaming ... but Talia, the only way out
is through.'

'I'll try harder,' I say. But the truth is ... I'm not sure I can.

July 17

Dictionary Definition: heal ... become sound or healthy
again, cause to do this; put right, alleviate sorrow; archaic
cure. Old English ... whole.

Whole. To become whole. True ... I am perhaps a third of
a third ... on a good day. But then who is whole ... Grace?

Alleviate sorrow. Am I sad?

Just between you and me ... please don't tell anyone else ...
I think I am.

July 19

Grant's been looking at me ... I know he is. I don't fucken care if he thinks I'm too thin or skinny ... I'm nowhere near what I was when I had to be admitted. We don't have scales in the house any more ... which must annoy the shit out of my mother.

He followed me outside this morning and said, 'What are you chucking?'

'The crusts from the boy's toast ... the birds eat it,' I say, putting my three quarters up my sleeve. Getting vegemite all over my wrists.

Fortunately he's been working a lot of overtime ... not usually home till well after dinner. Eats his reheated in the microwave, on the couch. Feet up, watching the news. I eat with the boys ... I've gone vegetarian ... apparently it's much better for you. And that's true ... fact ... not just because I'm ... I'm a relapsing fucked up anorexic. But I'm sure this time I will ... I won't get too thin ... just ... I don't know.

Hope he stops staring ... gives me the creeps.

Jerk.

July 21

Guess what? Elli rang. 'I'm sorry,' she said, 'really sorry.'

'No I'm sorry,' I say, 'you're right I was shallow.'

'I guess you were just surprised,' she says, 'most people are.'

'I was,' I say, 'but I really don't care you know ... I love lesbians ... if you know what I mean?'

She laughs, 'I know what you mean.'

'So you still with Isabella? Living at her place?'

'Yeah,' she says. And I could hear this contentment ... is it love? ... in her voice.

'You sound happy,' I say.

'I am, Talia, I really am.'

'Bella's Mum is soo cool and funny and kind and doesn't care that her daughter is gay ... not at all. She just loves her, no matter what. And she has made me welcome like ... well just like I'm welcome.'

'Oh that's great,' I say, 'really great. She sounds lovely ... what's her name?'

'Hilary,' she says. 'And Bella's Dad, he's cool too, they're divorced ... but they get on really well which is soo cool. It was Bella's birthday last night ... eighteen and we all went for dinner. Her Dad and his partner included. She's nice too.'

'Oh that's cool,' I say, 'Cool that they all get on and cool that everyone is ... that they don't care you guys are lesbians.'

'I know,' she says, 'we are so lucky.'

'And your parents,' I ask, 'how are they?'

'Dad, he's still not talking to me. Mum rings me every second day ... we Skype on occasion too. We should Skype.'

'Oh … we don't have the connection,' I lie.

'Oh never mind,' she says. 'It's good talking to you. I've missed you. You were a good friend.'

'I miss you too,' I say. Man I really do.

'Maybe you could come down in the school holidays … Bella would love to meet you … I'm sure her Mum would be cool.'

'That would be nice,' I say.

'I better go, have loads of homework to do.'

'Still want to be a vet?'

'Absolutely,' she laughs, 'Bella's Mum has two cats, Indy and Rat. I love them so much. Rat sleeps on my bed. He's a big black ball of fluff. Indy … she's more of a bitch; I've got scratches all up my arms. She's ginger.'

'Rat,' I laugh, 'who named a cat Rat?'

'Bella's brother, Lloyd, it was his cat but he moved out … actually he's overseas … London. Doing the big O.E.'

'Does Bella have any more siblings?'

'Her Dad and his partner they have a three year old. Cute as. Reminded me of your brothers. Are they well?'

'Yeah,' I sigh, 'they are good … going to kindergarten and driving my Mum bananas jumping all over the furniture … being superheroes and stuff.'

'And your Mum … and Grant … they ok?'

'Ok,' I lie. Fucken marvelous.

'And you, Talia ... you doing ok?'

'I'm good,' I say, 'got another A in English and I'm ... you know, just plodding on.'

'Call me sometime,' she says, 'I'd love to hear from you.'

'I will,' I say. But will I? I don't honestly know. Not because she's lesbian ... who cares about that ... just because ... just ... I ... don't know.

July 22

I was right on time. Four o'clock on the dot ... sitting in my chair, cushion on my lap. 'Hi,' I say.

'Hi,' smiles Grace. And then she looks at me ... looks with intent and then ... then the bitch frowns.

Can you believe ... I'm sitting there, on time, and she's frowning? What the fuck!

'Talia,' she says, 'are you going to remove your coat?'

'No,' I say. Because I'm not. And why the fuck should I. Its twelve degrees outside.

'It's warm in here,' she says. 'The heater has been on all day. Look I'm in bare feet.'

Skinny fucken feet too. Her toes are long ... the second one longer than the big toe.

'Talia,' she says, 'how much are you eating?'

'I'm eating,' I say.

'What did you have for lunch?'

'An apple,' I say, 'and a sandwich,' I lie.

'Talia, please be honest,' she says, 'let's be honest. Be honest with me.'

'I know I've lost weight,' I say, 'after my Dad died I felt nauseous and just couldn't eat much … I wanted to. I just felt sick … all the time.'

'That's normal,' she smiles, 'grief and sadness can bring about changes in appetite.'

'I'm not sad,' I say. 'In fact … I couldn't care less.'

'So you don't care that your father died … you don't feel sad at all?'

'No,' I say, 'I don't.'

'So how do you feel?'

'Nothing,' I say. 'I feel nothing.'

'So what is the feeling nauseous related to? What is it that is making you feel sick?'

'Maybe it was a bug,' I say, folding my arms. 'And I got it the same time as his funeral.' It's possible!

'Perhaps,' she says. 'But what I'm seeing is … you losing weight which began about the time your father died. And … that is somewhat normal with grief Talia. Makes it very hard for someone that has anorexia.'

'I'm not fucken grieving,' I say.

'You're not fucken grieving,' she repeats.

'I'm not fucken grieving,' I laugh. And diary … weird as she may have found it … I laugh and I laugh and I laugh.

'Something's going on Talia,' she says gently, 'something you find very hard to talk about. Isn't that true?'

And I laugh again. Like I'm in some live comedy show.

Grace sits looking at me thinking fuck knows what, until she finally says, 'The way I see it … you keep losing … you're heading back into hospital.'

'I won't lose any more,' I say. 'I'll eat, I promise.'

'I'm not sure you can make that promise … not sure how much the anorexia has taken you over.'

'Nah,' I say, 'I'm alright.'

'Perhaps,' she sighs, 'what about going to hospital voluntarily. Getting back on your meal plan. Getting help, Talia … you could still do your school work from hospital. Perhaps even attend school.'

'I … I … I'll think about it,' I say. And I'm not lying … I really will.

July 24

I am thinking. I am. It's two am and I'm lying here with the light on. Thinking and thinking and thinking.

Diary … I haven't told you but I've been sleeping with the light on most nights. Sleeping with the light on because I'm scared my Dad's seed or spirit is gonna float in and pay me a visit.

And I really don't want that. I truly wish he was cremated and buried and cremated again … just to be sure and just to … well perhaps a seed couldn't survive all that. Especially a faulty seed like my father must have.

Probably why I'm faulty … his fucken seed.

Yuck that grosses me fucken out.

Help.

July 26

So I put the boys to bed … read them a story … A Hungry Caterpillar.

Hungry. Interesting that the caterpillar eats everything in sight, gets fat … turns into a beautiful butterfly. Whatever!

Return to the lounge to collect Sol's blankey and Sharkey Pillow Pet and find Mum and Grant deep in discussion. Whispering. He's holding her hand.

Once the boys are asleep … I go to my room and try real hard to complete my biology assignment which is already overdue. And who barges in but mother.

She stands in the doorway, floral dressing gown, fluffy mauve slippers, hands on her hips. 'Stand up,' she says.

I look at her… say nothing. Keep rereading my essay.

'You skinny stupid bitch,' she says. 'How could you do this to me?'

'Do what?' shuffling my papers.

'You're sick again,' she screeches. 'Sick … how could you be so selfish?'

And diary … I look across at her … look down at my papers and feel like I'm lost somewhere. Somewhere I neither belong nor understand.

'Talia,' she cries, tears falling, fists clenched, 'I knew I couldn't trust you … knew you'd let me down. So what now?'

I bite my finger.

'What now?' she yells. 'I said what now?'

I bite harder.

She stands there … yelling … I don't really hear the rest but I do hear Mac crying. I hear his little sad voice, 'Stop it,' it says.

I walk past my hysterical mother, scoop him up in my arms and take him back to his bedroom. Past Grant … the tearful man bear. Lay with little Mac, until he goes back to sleep. 'It's ok,' I whisper, 'everything's ok.'

Everything's ok.

Ok.

July 27

Four-thirty am ... I wish I was a baby bird, tucked up in a nest. Chirp chirp tweet tweet and Mummy bird puffs up and fluffs up and wraps her warm wings around me.

And I am warm. Safe.

Later ... My mother looks more like a scarecrow ... I'm the crow. She, according to Grant is, 'extremely worried, hardly slept ... Talia she cried nearly all night.'

And there she is ... standing in the doorway of the kitchen, tissues in her hand ... mascara like smeared mud ... 'We need to talk ...'

'I'm eating my breakfast,' I say, sipping my hot black tea.

'Don't lie to me,' she crows. Got that wrong she's both the scare fucken crow and the 'arh arh' crow.

'I'm off to school,' I say, standing up and walking past her like I'm not afraid.

'Talia,' she says, bursting into tears.

I grab my coat, my bag ... kiss the boys on the cheek and leave.

Goodbye.

July 29

Mr Reiding asks me to stay behind after class. Because I'm in love with him, beard 'n all ... I do.

'Sit down, Talia,' he says. Gentle. Kind.

So I do.

'Talia,' he smiles, leans his head to the side, 'I have your assignment here ... the one on film. I've given you a C. And quite honestly I'm not sure ... it's even that good. I've reread it and reread it and it's ... just not you.'

'Umm,' I say, 'I've had a bug.'

'The staff and I,' he sighs, 'can see you are looking very thin.'

'I've felt nauseous,' I say, wanting to cry in his lap, 'some kind of virus, I think.'

'Talia,' he says, 'we are worried about you. I'm worried. You are such a bright kid ... have so much potential. Looks to me like anorexia is winning ... it will rob you of that potential Talia. It is robbing you.'

'I ... I'

He smiles. Gentle. Kind.

Tears begin to fall.

He hands me some tissues from his desk.

'Is ... are you getting help?' he asks.

'I … I … I have a counsellor. And a caseworker … she left or something to go overseas and I haven't seen my new one. Yet.'

'I see,' he says. 'Talia … I don't understand anorexia … but I know it must be very hard, especially after the loss of your father. But Talia … don't let it win. You deserve to be well.'

I sit at his desk in that chair sobbing like a little girl who had lost her favorite doll. Mr Reiding he doesn't say anything. Just sits opposite me.

Quiet.

Listening.

Nodding.

'I'm sorry,' I finally sniff.

He gently smiles.

'I … I'm really sorry,' I say again, wiping my eyes, breathing heavily.

'Don't be,' he says, 'just get well, Talia. Get well.'

A few minutes later he walks me to the door. Smiles, 'See you later.'

I nod … so wishing I was small enough to fit in his pocket. His tweed jacket pocket.

I just couldn't make it to Grace's later that day. Couldn't do any more tears. I texted her. Told her I was unwell. Which is true. I'm feeling more nauseous than ever.

I walked and walked ... went to the mall. One shop to the next. When it closed I walked some more. It got dark and I kept walking. It got cold and I kept walking.

I didn't know where to go or what to do. Perhaps I should've seen Grace after all. Because diary ... I really am not feeling that great.

Lost.

Alone.

Afraid.

The light is on ... my stomach ... it's sick and rumbling all at once. It's Mum's birthday on Sunday and I guess I ruined it for her. What does she get? ... a fucked up daughter that's forgotten how to eat.

July 30

Grant knocks on the door. Enters. 'Talia,' he says, 'here's a hundred dollars ... I'll take you and the boys to the mall. Get something for your Mum. She's ... she's stressed.'

'I'm sorry,' I say. I am... I think.

'Is half an hour ok?'

'Yeah,' I say. 'I'll just have a quick shower.'

And I do. I have a quick shower … have a long look in the bathroom mirror. I am thin. But not nearly as thin as when I was admitted to hospital. Surely they can all see that. I guess the problem is … I can't eat. I'm trying … that piece of toast has been staring at me for over an hour and a half. I've had one bite. But I did eat a whole teaspoon of Vegemite … just for the vitamin B's. That's trying … right?

So we go to the mall. I wander around first with the boys. But all they want to do is look at the toys. 'Mum will like this,' says Mac, picking up a Woody. From the movie, Toy Story. 'Look it talks.'

Well being a porn star … I'm sure she does love a woody but not that sort.

And Sol, he's like, 'What about this,' picking up a skipping rope with glittery ends. Now that we could both use … unfortunately it's probably too short for Mum's long legs.

Grant finds us in the toy department, about half a dozen bags in his hands and says, 'I'll stay here with them … you go find something and we'll meet in the food court in say half an hour.'

So I wander off and roam from store to store. What do you get a mother that hates you? Don't think a hundred bucks would cover it.

Eventually I decide on a voucher at a beautician. She could have a deluxe facial with a neck and shoulder massage for that. I think … she'll like it.

I find Grant and the boys eating McDonald's. The boys waving some little plastic toy about. 'We got a happy meal,' they both say at once.

I smile.

Grant hands me ten dollars. 'Get some lunch, Talia. Something.'

So I buy two pieces of avocado sushi and a diet coke. I can only eat one. But one is better than none. Grant looks at the sushi left on my plate, 'You not gonna eat it?'

'No,' I say.

He gives me this, what the fuck am I suppose to do? look, picks up the remaining sushi and two bites later … gone.

'What did you get your Mum?' he asks later, on the drive home.

'A voucher for a facial … a deluxe one with a shoulder and neck massage.'

He nods. 'She'll like that.'

July 31

And she does … like that. I wrap it up in paper the boys have drawn on. And we make a card. Cut out pictures from her old magazines and stick it on the front. Sol picks a cat … white with a cute pink collar. Mac, he picks a truck. Funny enough, a big Mack. Orange and blazing. I cut out a dog … which I think is real cute, even though she doesn't like dogs. And a waterfall scene … don't know why, just do. I know what she'd really like ... pictures of skinny bitch models but I resist the urge.

The card and voucher is from us all so I get Sol and Mac to give it to her together. I stand and watch. She kisses them both on the cheek. Mac climbs on her lap, Sol runs off. She looks across at me, mutters, 'Thanks.'

She's definitely like some royal porn queen sitting on the couch surrounded by her servants opening parcel after parcel of lingerie. No wonder I feel so fucken sick.

He gives her a huge bunch of flowers too. Huge. And perfume. And make-up. And a sloppy fucken kiss that just about made me vomit. Oh great ... I'm not only anorexic but bulimic too.

Did the boys and I make her a cake? No. What's the point? ... she doesn't eat it.

But lucky us ... her lovely sister arrived mid afternoon with an enormous cake. Apparently banana ... chocolate icing with two candles. Where's the other thirty-seven?

I heard Aunty Maxine whisper to Grant, 'Talia's looking thin ... what's going on?'

Grant shrugs.

'How's Kim coping? Poor Kim,' she sighs.

'Not so good,' he sighs.

Not so good.

Good enough to open her royal legs and let Grant's jackhammer pound the fuck out of her, no doubt.

August 1

I felt so embarrassed to go to English today … considered wagging. I didn't … I went and sat, head down … afraid to look anywhere other than my books. I caught him glancing at me … I half smiled … put my head back down. So glad when the bell rang.

And so glad to see Chrissy and Stacey smiling at me, handing me a bag of lollies.

'No thanks,' I say.

'Mum says you're too skinny,' says Chrissy.

I smile and sigh, touch the cracks on my lips.

'Gee Talia, what a big pimple,' says Stacey. 'Can I squeeze it?'

'No,' I laugh, 'it's one of those ones that don't have a head, not yet anyhow.'

'Lollies give you pimples,' says Chrissy, putting one in her mouth. 'That's what Jona says aye Stacey.'

'Yeah,' she says, 'he doesn't eat them, cause he gets heaps of pimples.'

'You still go out?' I ask.

'We're in love,' smiles Stacey. 'He says he loves me all the time.'

'That's nice,' I smile.

'We gonna get married one day.'

'Cool,' I say. 'Can I come to your wedding?'

'Yeah,' laughs Stacey.

'I'm gonna be bridesmaid aye, Stacey,' beams Chrissy. 'What colour's gonna be my dress?'

'I don't know … lavender or purple or maybe pink … bright pink or maybe … maybe … like umm … what do you think Talia?'

'Has to be,' I smile, 'what you like. What colour you like.'

'She can't wear white though, aye Stacey,' says Chrissy, chewing on another lolly.

'Yes I can,' says Stacey, pouting her lips.

'She's having sex,' says Chrissy, 'so she can't.'

'Can too,' says Stacey, hands on her hips.

'I think a bride can wear any colour she likes,' I say. 'White is nice.'

'But she's sexing,' smiles Chrissy.

'Doesn't matter,' I say. 'Least she knows what she's in for.'

'Jona loves me,' says Stacey. 'So we have sex … cause he loves me and I love him.'

'Yeah,' I say, 'that's nice,' placing my hand on Stacey's. I mean … perhaps it is.

'Your Mum, your foster Mum,' I say, 'she's nice, Chrissy.'

'Oh yeah,' Chrissy beams, 'she's real nice … better than my own Mum.'

I nod. 'What does she do?'

'Looks after me and my foster Dad and my foster sister and foster brother and she works at an old people's home because she says, "I love oldies."'

'She must be very busy,' I say.

'She is,' smiles Chrissy, 'but never too busy for me.'

Any chance she wants another foster kid?

August 2

Mum and Grant are like a couple of detectives trying to investigate what I am and what I'm not eating … and I just don't think I can take much more. Suddenly Mum wants to sit down all together at dinner … 'like a real family'.

'I have so much homework,' I say. It's true … I do. Struggling to keep up.

'Talia,' she bursts into tears, 'I'm trying.'

Grant puts his hand on her shoulder, kisses her on the back of the head, 'Talia, please.'

Wanker.

So I sit at the table … like a real person in a real family feeling unreal.

Lost.

I eat half a plate of broccoli and that's like full of thousands of important minerals and vitamins, right. I drink a few sips of pineapple juice because Grant poured it into my glass. Then I get up and tip it down the sink, 'I really prefer water,' I said.

Grant looks up at me, mouth full of food and there it is, "the what the fuck do I do?" look.

Mum she's like … giving me the scarecrow look … manages to keep the crow under wraps.

Sol and Mac … I help them eat. They're slower than me.

August 3

Mum arrives back from Zumba, 'We had a new instructor,' she tells someone, perhaps Aunty Maxine or Chris her friend, over the phone.

'You didn't miss much,' she says.

'Well actually,' she says, 'the music and dancing was great, she was pretty funky.'

'Yeah but,' she says, 'the instructor she was like … she had fat hips and tummy … I mean Zumba's supposed to tone all that. I just didn't think she was a very good representative.

'Yeah … yeah.

'Exactly,' she says, 'I mean what kind of advertisement is that?

'Ar ha … yep … I know!

'And,' she says, 'she so needed her roots done.

'Yeah … shocking aye, you could see her dark grey hair down her middle part. It was actually pretty gross.

'Ah ha … yep … exactly … I just think Zumba instructors should be well … slimmer for a start … and roots done … a bonus.'

That was all I heard … I grabbed my ball and shot some hoops with Jason. Didn't last long … felt a bit dizzy.

August 4

Grant's like, 'Talia … I've found a copy of your meal plan … it says two pieces of toast. Glass of juice or milk.'

I look at him … look down at my one piece, pull at my ear. 'Yeah … well I'm not hungry.'

He shakes his head, bites his lip. Sighs.

I take a bite, chew. Chew again. Swallow.

'Talia …' he says. 'Doesn't matter.' Stands up, walks towards the door. Turns round, 'I'm worried … I'm worried about your mother.'

I nod. Want to say, "Go fuck yourself!" but I don't … I just nod.

August 5

I arrive at Grace's … two minutes late which is really not late at all. She smiles. I smile back.

'Talia,' she says, 'Carly Piro … your case manager … she's arriving in ten minutes. I did text you … not sure if you got the message.'

'Why?' I say.

'I think you know why,' she smiles.

'No,' I say.

'You can't keep losing weight,' she says, 'let's review what's going on … find out how thin you are.'

I nod.

'I didn't want … I … I talked with Carly and she thought perhaps it was best she came here … I wasn't sure if that was best … I'm just aware … you're getting thinner … I'm trying to … I think you need help that I can't give you.'

I nod.

There's a knock at the door.

Carly enters … she's pretty, long brown hair, green or perhaps blue eyes. Slim. Not skinny.

'Hi,' she smiles.

'Hi,' I say.

And then it's blah blah blah … trying to review my mental state … risk of suicide even … for fucks sake … how much I'm eating and everything else.

'What we are hoping,' says Carly, 'is that you'll come to hospital as a voluntary patient … get you back to a healthy weight … and … before you are at real risk.'

'Can I think about it?' I ask. 'I promise I will.'

Grace smiles.

Carly sighs. 'I'll talk to Doctor Adelaide … she really would like to see you. See what she thinks … I have discussed your case with her this morning … she's concerned … we all are.'

I nod. I don't know what else to do or say.

'I'm going to talk to your Mum, Kim this evening,' she continues. Oh fucken great!

I frown … look down at the floor. Carly's wearing black pulps, I like them. Not sure I like her … pretty bitch.

'I understand that's difficult for you to hear,' she continues. Does she? 'So … I'm thinking … let's make an appointment for Monday. You know where the community mental health team is … say four pm. How does that sound Talia?'

'Whatever,' I mutter. Wonder where she got those shoes?

'So four pm it is,' smiles Carly, marking the time in a big black diary. Handing me a card with the appointment time.

'Thanks,' I say. Fucken marvelous.

August 6

Do I want to go hospital? No I do not. And … yet … I do. I know I am falling. Like a brown leaf from a tree … I am falling … drifting … lost. And if I land … among the thousands of brown leaves on the damp ground … I don't know if I can or could be found.

Eventually I would break down … dissolve into the earth. I want that … but I don't.

I guess I've really fucked up … and yet diary I still don't want or can't or … I can't eat.

I can't.

And I'm scared.

And afraid.

Nana called this evening; she wanted to speak to me. I told Grant no.

So he lied … said I'd ring back later. That I was busy.

Then he enters my room. I'm lying on my bed. He sits down on the floor.

His eyes are full of tears, 'Talia, help me understand.'

'What?' I say, 'understand what?'

'Why you won't eat,' wiping his eyes, 'why you refuse to talk to an old lady … an old lady that says that you're her only link to her son.'

I look at him, shake my head, sigh heavily, 'I'm just not a very nice person.'

'You can be,' he says, 'you can be a really lovely ... you're so loving with your brothers.'

I don't know what to say ... so I say nothing.

'Are you going to go voluntarily, Talia ... back to hospital?'

'Probably,' I say.

'I'll take you on Monday,' he says, 'pick you up from school.'

'But you'll be working,' I say, rubbing my shaking hands.

'Talia ... I'll take time off ... no problem ... your Mum ... she's ... she's ... she won't be able to attend.'

'I can catch a bus,' I say.

'I will take you,' he says. 'I'll be there at the school gates ... if we've got time we could have a coffee first. And,' he laughs, 'I could have cake.'

'I'll watch,' I say and smile.

August 7

Sneezed last night; woke up with a cold this morning. Drank a tall glass of freshly squeezed orange juice for breakfast. A short glass for lunch. Dinner ... perhaps broccoli, half a plate. Aren't they full of vitamin C too? Hope so.

Feel like snotty shit.

August 8

Another tall glass of freshly squeezed orange juice ... who said I was anorexic? ... two Panadols and I'm off to school. I'm so behind ... just need to go ... I'm hoping like crazy that at my consultation today, they will decide to work with me while I'm still at home. I don't want to miss school. I know I need a little help ... get back on track and stuff ... but perhaps hospital isn't the answer. And I'm sooo sure I'm only about ... say forty-two kilos; almost fat, well almost within the healthy range.

I'm going to try real hard to be assertive and tell Carly and Doctor Adelaide, if she's there, what I think is best for me. And surely they can see ... I'm not nearly as thin as last time.

Diary ... say a little prayer to umm ... God ... Mother Mary ... Muhammad ... anyone that could possibly help.

August 12

Well I don't know if you prayed but a fat... excuse the pun! ... actually don't excuse it... lot of use God, Mother Mary or Muhammad were.

I'm in hospital. Not the mental asylum full of fucked up mentals ... talking to themselves or staring into space, or hanging from the ceiling ... no ... the general hospital. The general hospital for nice normal sane sick people.

Why am I here? Now there's a story.

So ... I go to school ... class, one after the next, eat an orange for lunch; vitamin C ... taking good care of myself!

… go to English … love Mr Reiding as per usual, bastard … and on my way to my next class, I fall down the stairs. Land flat on my face. I have two black eyes, a broken nose, cuts on the inside of my lips, bruising and a huge lump on my forehead. I look so good!

Could've been worse … as everyone keeps saying. 'Least you didn't knock out or chip any teeth.'

What happened after the fall … I really don't know. I woke up in an ambulance … this totally bald officer looking down at me. 'You've had a fall,' he said. 'I'm Grant.' That sounds familiar … where have I heard that name before?

So here I am … and here I've been for the past few days. I only just realised I had you … you were in my school bag.

Not much eating going on … how the fuck can I with cuts in my mouth. There was some talk of tubing me. But now … the general hospital is handing the black eyed broken nosed anorexic problem over to the mental asylum. I'm being transferred later today.

My nurse … she's … I actually really like her. Eva. She's black … big assed, white teeth and Jewish.

I said to her once, 'What's it like to be black … a black woman in a pretty much white country?'

I don't think I've ever seen a black … real black model; coloured perhaps, on TV or in magazines.

She laughed, writing down my recordings; pulse and blood pressure on to a chart, 'Not only am I a black woman, I'm Jewish too.'

'Wow,' I say, 'that must be … wow.'

She laughed again, flashing those white teeth.

'I used to straighten my hair,' she smiled, touching her short frizzy hair, 'it was the one thing I could do to make myself more white … I got over that.'

And I looked at her … perhaps it was because I had a gollywog as a child; short black frizzy hair, gold hooped earrings, wide smile, purple polka dot dress … she was beautiful, I loved her … I really liked Eva too. She was funny and kind and black. She knew what it was like to feel like you don't belong, you don't fit in … yet she did. She had this … who gives a fuck attitude! … I missed her when the nurses changed shifts.

And today, this morning … she sat on the edge of my bed … put her hand, her so black hand on my knee and smiled, 'You sure is skinny.'

'I'm thirty-eight kilos,' I said.

'I know,' she laughs, 'I'm more than twice that … inherited my Ma's big bust and butt.'

'I was about thirty kilos or just under … last time I was sick.'

'Ooh girl,' shaking her head, 'you lucky you didn't snap.'

I smile.

'I've come in to say my goodbyes,' she says, ''case I miss you later … I gotta take a patient for a scan 'bout the time you leave.'

'Oh,' I say ... am I small enough to fit in her uniform pocket?

'Gonna miss you girl,' she says, squeezing my knee, 'hope you ... learn how to eat.' She laughs, 'I could teach you a thing or two 'bout that.'

I laugh too. 'Thanks Eva ... you been great.' Put a purple polka dot dress on you, gold hooped earrings and I'd squeeze you tight. Rest my bruised face in your big busted chest.

August 13

Grant wheeled me into the psych unit, even though I insisted on walking. Had my review ... with Doctor Adelaide, Carly and some new nurse ... Erin. 'You got new glasses,' I say to Doctor Adelaide, 'blue.'

'I have,' she smiles, touching the frame.

'And ... your hair,' I say, 'it's different.'

'It's longer,' she says, 'decided to grow it.'

'Looks nice,' I say. It does.

And they say ... not much changes. But then it was the same old ... trying to get into my head and work out why I have relapsed and where to go from here. Apparently I'm at risk of something called, Refeeding Syndrome. My phosphorus and potassium levels are low. This means food has to be reintroduced slowly. 'I think,' says Doctor Adelaide, 'that tubing until your mouth is completely healed is the best option ... how do you feel about that Talia?'

'I don't care,' I shrug. It's weird … I honestly don't.

'Ok,' she smiles, 'a nurse will insert it when we've finished here.'

'Whatever.'

'You'll need your bloods taken again,' she says. 'Bed rest … temperature, pulse and blood pressure taken twice daily.'

'What can this Refeeding Syndrome do?' I ask.

"It's rare,' says Doctor Adelaide, 'but … the shifting of electrolytes and fluid increases cardiac workload and heart rate. Can lead to heart failure … most commonly caused by cardiac arrhythmias.'

'Ah … I see,' I say.

'It can also cause confusion, convulsions and coma … but,' she continues, smiling, 'I'm sure you'll be fine … we'll monitor you closely.'

Right then … bed rest … blood tests it is.

August 13

You will never believe what I'm about to tell you … Jason, 'yo … Jay from the Bay,' is here.

Though there was no, "yo yo's," going on. Just, 'Talia … what happened?'

'I fell down some stairs at school,' I say, barely able to look at him. Definitely at risk of heart failure.

'And …' he says, 'the skinny?'

'Oh,' I say, 'yeah … sorry.'

'Don't be sorry,' he says, sitting down on the couch next to me. Me … battered face … skinny, in a wheelchair, waiting in the corridor for my room to be made up by Erin.

'I … you look well,' I say. 'You're different.'

'Yeah,' he grins, 'this is the … the not manic me … the calmed down, slowed down version.'

And he sure was … like he had grown up … or something.

I nod and try to smile.

'Looks like we won't be shooting any hoops,' he says.

'No,' I sigh, placing my hand on my chest. My heart … in need of support right now.

'I'm getting discharged in the morning,' he says.

'Have you been here all those months?' I ask.

'Nah …' shakes his head, 'I went home a few weeks after you.'

'Yeah … so what happened?'

'Pot … cannabis is what happened,' he says, 'me and my bro's … it's something we've always done … for too long. Anyhow I was told, "Bipolar and cannabis don't mix," … didn't listen. Tried to … sort of … this time I will. I've got a building apprenticeship … with my Uncle. Start next week. I'm totally buzzed out.'

'That's awesome,' I smile.

'Any pot smoking,' he says, 'and I'm out. Plus I'll probably end up back here.'

It was about then, Erin came out my room, smiled and said, 'All ready … bed made … ready to go.'

'Oh,' I say, not wanting to leave … hoping that the first thing Jason did when he got home was smoke a joint the size of a cigar. Two.

He put his beautiful hand … long fingers, on my shoulder, 'I'll pop in before I go tomorrow,' turning to Erin, 'is that ok?'

'Sure,' she smiles, 'that's fine … you two meet another time?'

'Yeah,' he smiles, 'Talia's my basketball bro. She's mean.'

I blush … though not sure about the bro part. And mean?

August 14

Jason just left. Feel like crying. Miss him already. He looked so cute wearing this grey beanie and grey cardigan … though I did miss seeing those lovely tattooed arms.

I'm like, touching my tube, 'I can't eat … I would, just want to get well, get back to school … my mouth is cut to pieces inside.'

'Oh shit,' he says, pulling up his chair, closer to my bed. 'You did a good job falling down the stairs. Did you actually faint or something?'

'Yeah ... probably I guess,' I nod, 'well least that's what they think.'

'You're lucky you didn't break something, especially with those skinny legs,' squeezing my foot with that gorgeous hand.

'Yeah,' I blush, 'I was.'

'Was there something that happened to ... that ... like started you back not eating?'

'My father ... he died,' I say, looking down.

'Oh,' he nods. 'Must've been hard,'

'Well,' I say, 'not like ... I didn't know him ... he left when I was little, four or something.'

'And now you never will ... that sucks.'

'Well ... I don't know,' I say, 'just want to get well ... I'm not nearly as thin as last time I came in.'

'Really,' he says.

'I was at least six or seven kilos lighter,' I say.

'Fuck,' he said, 'you must have looked hideous.'

'I guess,' I nod.

'Did you think you were still fat?'

'I ... sometimes,' I say. 'Sometimes I felt thin and old ... bones ... but inside still fat. Still yuck.'

'And now?' he asks.

'I'm saner,' I say, 'I think when you get really thin ... you kinda lose your mind ... sort've almost mad, like psychotic I guess.'

'Like me ... feeling high,' he laughs.

'Yeah,' I smile.

'I gotta go,' he says, 'my Uncle ... he's probably already here.'

'Ok,' I say.

'Get well Talia,' he smiles. 'Get well ... you look heaps better with some meat on your bones.'

'I will.'

I will.

And just when I think he's gone forever ... he's standing at my bedside. 'I gotta run, Uncle's waiting and Mum ... I just thought ... here's my number,' handing me a piece of yellow paper, 'when you get well ... get outta here ... we ... if you wanna catch up sometime, that'll be cool.'

'Ok,' I smile, hand on my heart again.

'Next time,' he waves.

Next time ... you never know.

August 15

Julie is my nurse today ... back from her two days off. She sat down on my bed and wrapped her arms around me... only she could hardly fit because of a big belly.

'You're pregnant,' I say.

'I am,' she laughs, patting her tummy.

'I'm six months,' she laughs, 'yeap big for six months I know ... no I'm not having twins.'

'You look beautiful,' I say. She does. Full and overflowing with boobs and tummy, glowing skin ... little tired around the eyes, but beautiful.

'Thanks,' she says, 'I'm excited,' resting her hands on her belly.

'Do you know what you're having?'

'A baby,' she laughs. 'I've always liked surprises.'

'Is it a surprise to see me?'

'Well ... we always hope, our patients don't come back ... hope when you leave, you stay well. But it can be a revolving door, sometimes.'

I nod.

'Sometimes it takes a couple of times to get it right, so this time aye Talia. This time.'

'Grant is bringing me in work to do from my teachers,' I say, 'give me something to do ... and so I don't fall so far behind.'

'Great,' she smiles, 'that's great.'

'Hopefully, I'll be able to concentrate.'

'Well ... you're not nearly as thin as last time ... so that will help.'

'Yeah,' I say. 'I'm glad I didn't get that thin.' Because diary ... I really am.

I actually really am.

August 16

I am glad I'm here. Somewhat embarrassed ... a little ashamed, perhaps a lot ... but I want to be well. I want to be healthy. Whole.

August 17

'I'm thinking that in the next day or two,' says Doctor Adelaide, nodding her head, 'the tube could come out, and we introduce you back to food ... slowly of course.'

'So does slowly,' I say, 'mean small amounts?'

'Yes,' replies Doctor Adelaide, looking down at what I presume is my file, 'because you had barely been eating for weeks ... let's see a quarter piece of toast, an apple and broccoli for dinner.'

'Something like that,' I say. A teaspoon of Vegemite too, and actually, half an apple.

'Ok,' says Doctor Adelaide, 'great ... the house surgeon said the inside of your mouth is looking good.'

'Arh ha,' I nod.

'I'll speak with India and she'll put together a meal plan.'

'Ok,' I say.

'Do you want to be part of that process,' Doctor Adelaide asks, 'work with her to come up with a plan?'

'Nah,' I sigh, 'I just want to get well ... don't want to argue ... not anymore.'

Doctor Adelaide smiles and nods her head.

August 18

India looks as super slim and super fit as ever. She pulls up a chair and smiles, 'Hi Talia.'

'I like your floral skirt,' I say.

'Thanks,' she smiles, 'just bought it. I'm not usually a floral girl or a navy blue ... but it works doesn't it, the navy blue with the floral design.'

'It's lovely,' I say, 'pencil skirts are in.'

'Yeah,' touching the skirt, 'but because it's polyester or something ... it looks tight but moves with you.'

'You always look nice,' I say. She does.

'And what about you,' she says, 'look at your bruised face … falling down stairs.'

'I look better than I did,' touching my face.

'I bet,' she laughs.

I laugh too.

'So,' she says, 'I have devised a meal plan … introducing back food … starting with about 40% of what should be your normal daily intake … build up gradually to 70% over the next week. Would you like to read it?'

'Nah,' shaking my head, 'you probably remember my likes and dislikes … and I just gotta eat.'

She nods and smiles. Lovely teeth.

August 19

So I'm eating and chewing and swallowing my food. Feel a little nauseated … but I'm doing it anyway. Yay! for me.

August 20

Eat.

August 21

Chew.

August 22

Swallow.

August 23

Swallow.

August 24

Chew.

August 25

Eat.

August 26

No cardiac arrest or convulsions ... perhaps a little comatose at times ... back on a full meal plan. Full cream milk and endless amounts of food. I'm now reintroduced to that cow in me ... that cow who chews and chews and chews again, swallows ... occasionally regurgitates and swallows again. And with the size of my growing stomach ... there's definitely more than one in there.

But ... and it's a big but ... I'm soo trying not to think about big stomachs, except for Julie's and she looks beautiful.

August 27

Quick phone call from Maggie … she's going to be up in a week. Yay! Feel kinda embarrassed that I'm here again … but she didn't seem to care. I kept saying, 'I'm not as thin as last time.'

And she's like, 'doesn't matter how thin you are or aren't … just get well babe, just get well.'

'I am …' I say, 'I will.'

'Good,' she says, 'you'll be in trouble with me if you don't,'

'What about you, what's happening, who's happening?'

'I have to run,' she says, 'I'll tell you later … when I see you.'

'Ok,' I say, 'ok.'

August 31

I …

It was Sunday.

Mum, who has hardly shown her made up face since I fell down the stairs, visited. She bought the boys and little Lola. Aunty Maxine has the flu or cold or something. Grant; he was called in to work.

Sol was wearing a Spiderman costume, all red and blue. Mac was wearing Batman, black with little pointed ears. Little Lola, she was wearing emerald blue. A big white collar and yellow apron. Puffy sleeves.

'Snow White,' I said, 'Snow White.'

Little Lola twirled around and curtsied like a little Princess. The boys charged about.

Her strawberry blond hair was long ... all the way down her back. Freckles across her little nose. Little wee hands. Tiny feet in tiny cream ballet shoes.

'I have a crown,' says little Lola, pulling out a little plastic tiara from Mum's navy blue handbag. 'It's got jewels.'

I smile, looking at the tiara ... silver with 'diamonds'. Diamonds are a girl's best friend.

'You can wear it,' says Lola, climbing up on my bed and placing it on my head. 'Now you're a princess too.'

I smile ... little Lola smiles ... Mum even smiles. The boys charge about.

Lola snuggles up against me ... the emerald blue touching my hand. It's cold ... silky. She wraps her little arms around my neck, presses her little lips against my cheek. 'There,' Lola says, 'all better.'

She climbs down. Sits down on the floor. Starts to roll about with the boys. Her emerald blue dress gets caught ... lifts up. She has little knees. Little legs coming out of tiny red undies. Deep, deep red.

I begin to cry.

Shake my head.

Wipe my eyes.

Forget to breathe.

'I'm tired,' I say, 'Mum … I'm really tired.'

'Oh,' she says, shaking her head, 'we haven't been here very long.'

'I'm sorry,' I say, 'I just … not feeling so good. Need to sleep.'

'Right then,' she says, nose in the air like Snow White's step-mum. 'Let's go kids … Talia's tired. Say goodbye.'

'Bye,' say all three kids.

'I'm sorry,' I whisper, as they leave.

Little Lola, skips back into my room. Emerald blue, white collar … yellow apron. Puffy sleeves. Hair all the way down her back. 'My crown,' she says, wide-eyed.

'Oh,' I say, removing the tiara from the top of my head.

Her little hand reaches up and takes the tiara. She places it on her little head. 'Now I look pretty,' she says, throwing her head back like a woman advertising shampoo. Like alien Barbie, Elli, used to do.

'You do,' I nod. 'You do.'

'Lola,' Mum calls out.

And she skips out of my room. Little Snow White wearing a plastic tiara. Diamonds are a girl's best friend.

September 2

'I found this ... a photo of you,' says Julie, sitting in a chair by my bed. She really did look beautiful ... green maternity dress setting off her eyes. Like cat's eyes. 'It's a photo taken when you were admitted last time ... dated October.'

'Can I see it?'

'Sure,' she says, handing me the photo.

'Oh ... fuck,' I frown. Jason was right; I did look hideous. Like something out of a concentration camp ... placed in a shallow grave. Only I was the Nazi ... the one that withheld the food ... and turned on the gas.

'So you were 30. 1 kilos,' smiles Julie, 'I think it says on the back.'

'Ar ha,' I say, turning the photo over, 'Julie ... I didn't look so good ... did I.'

'No you did not,' laughs Julie, resting her hands on her big green belly. 'A skeleton in a yellow singlet.'

'Can I keep it,' I ask, 'just for a while.'

'Sure,' she says. 'You're doing really well Talia. You're very quiet ... different than last admission ... you ok?'

'Sure,' I nod. 'Just want to get well ... trying to keep up with my school work ... I have exams in ... shit ... beginning of November.'

'Well,' she smiles, 'hopefully you can attend school in say a couple ... maybe three weeks.'

'So even if I'm here?'

'As long as you gain a couple more kilos and are committed to sticking to your meal plan.'

'I am.' I nod.

I am.

September 3

Anna and Maggie visited today. I actually ventured out my room and met them in the family room. I showed them the photo.

'Oh god,' says Anna.

'Oh Talia … fuck you were like a skeleton,' gasps Maggie 'look at those chest bones and your arms … no muscle … no fat.'

'And your face,' says Anna, 'chiseled cheekbones.'

'Yeah,' I say, 'my nurse Julie gave it to me … I'm keeping it by my bedside to remind me.'

They both nod.

'We bought nail polish in,' says Maggie, 'pink,' pulling a pink bottle out of her jeans pocket.

'Come on,' says Anna, 'put your feet up.'

So I do … take off my black socks and rest my feet on Anna's lap.

'Relax your legs,' says Anna. 'They're stiff ... like legs of metal.'

'Ok,' I say. And I try.

'Relax,' says Anna again, 'enjoy.'

And again ... I try.

'So Maggie ... still with the musician?' I ask, trying to divert attention from my stiff legs.

'Umm ...,' Maggie replies, biting her lip, 'I broke up with him. He was lovely ... really nice ... but I just felt so guilty ... you know after what happened with Liam.'

'Did you tell him?' I ask.

'Nah,' she sighs, 'should've ... wanted to ... freaked out.'

I nod. 'And Liam ... has he ever said anything?'

I hear Anna sigh heavily.

'Umm,' says Maggie, 'I'm seeing him ... kind of.'

'What's kind of?' I ask.

'She's fucking him,' says Anna. 'Letting him use her for sex.'

'Am not,' says Maggie, 'its mutual.'

'But Maggie,' I say, 'don't you want more ... you love him?'

Maggie sighs, looks down, 'I take what I can get I guess.'

And I remember those words, 'I take what I can get.' I want to say, "that's what you said about seeing your father," but I don't. I say, 'Maggie ... are you sure that's ok?'

'He does like me,' Maggie says.

'He likes his penis,' says Anna, beginning another coat on my nails.

'He ... he's just not ready to commit,' says Maggie, blushing.

'Yeah,' says Anna, 'so he can fuck you and other girls ... having fun.'

Maggie looks down ... she looks sad and lost. 'You'll work it out,' I say, nodding.

She looks at me ... half smiles, 'yeah ... hope so. Anna's in love.'

'I am,' beams Anna, looking up from my feet. 'And we haven't even fucked yet.'

'Still,' I say, 'that's nice.' I think.

'I got the all clear,' Anna smiles, putting the brush back in the bottle. 'No HIV or any other nasties. You wanna get tested Maggie ... fuck knows what you might catch from Liam.'

'Oh,' I say, 'my toes look good.'

They both smile. 'They do.'

'Pink,' I say, 'I like it. Can I paint either of yours?'

'Ok,' says Maggie.

So I do ... I paint Maggie's toes pink and Maggie paints Anna's toes pink.

'Gorgeous,' Anna says, 'when I get back to uni ... I'm gonna say to Blair, wanna suck my pink toes?'

We all laugh.

September 5

Four am ... not feeling so good. Had this yuck dream ... it's the second time.

I'm a skeleton ... wearing emerald blue. Big white collar and yellow apron. Little skeletal feet.

I'm in a coffin. It's white. Emerald blue, big white collar ... yellow apron; lying on the silky white.

It's cold. I'm hot. Sweating and shivering all at once.

I'm a skeleton in a Snow White dress up.

I want to disappear.

September 6

Help me diary ... I don't feel so good.

September 7

Where are you Jason? Here smoke this cigar. Shoot hoops with me ... make me laugh.

September 8

Mr Reiding, put me in your pocket. The pocket of your tweed jacket. I promise you won't even know I'm there.

Please.

September 9

The girls came in this morning … said their goodbyes. Both giving me a kiss on the cheek. I'm relieved really. Don't feel much like conversation. Just want to study. Put my face in my books.

Diary … I … I … I'm still a cow. Chewing and eating … swallowing and stuff. But I have this feeling inside like I just want to float away. Disappear.

Gone.

September 10

Grant and Mum came in this evening … sounds mean but I was glad they didn't bring the boys.

Grant's like, 'You're looking so much better, Talia. Face healed … just a little bruising now.'

I nod.

'You're very quiet,' he says, 'you ok?'

'Just tired,' I say.

'She's always tired these days,' says Mum.

I look about the visitor's room; listen to the howling wind, watch the trees outside the window sway, lean over.

'It's windy,' I say.

'It's so windy,' says Grant, 'Nearly blew me sidewards today … I was in town waiting to cross the road and a huge gust blew and I had to hold on to a lamp post.'

'Did not,' laughed Mum.

'Did,' said Grant.

Mum shakes her head. 'A gust of wind couldn't blow a man built like you over.' See man bear.

'Well it did,' he says, looking down at his body, rubbing his hefty thighs. 'It was bloody windy in town.'

And I watch the wind blow through the trees … listen to it howl. See a clear plastic bag fly through the air … wishing I was light enough, thin enough … to be lifted through the air.

Fly away.

September 12

I really have nothing to say to you or to anyone … other than hello and nod my head. I am well prepared for my up and coming exams.

September 13

Shanti's like, 'The wind has stopped blowing ... it's beautiful out ... want to eat lunch outside with me?'

I look outside my bedroom window ... blue sky. An enormous blue sky. I look at Shanti ... still soo beautiful, wearing a traditional Indian long top, baby pink over white trousers. I nod.

We prepare lunch together ... I exchange my normal sandwich for a cheese toastie. She has cheese and onion.

We sit in the sun and eat. I soak up Vitamin D. Apparently since I have lighter skin; I soak up more than Shanti ... least that's what she said.

I drink my full cream milk ... perhaps from one of my very own cow relatives. And what with all the cheese and milk and Vitamin D ... my bones are doing somersaults.

'You're doing so well,' says Shanti.

I nod.

'I'm tired,' I say, wiping my milky mouth.

'You look a bit tired,' she says, leaning her head to the side.

I nod.

'Back to your room?' she asks.

'Yes,' I nod.

'Perhaps have a little sleep.'

'Nah ... I want to finish a chemistry assignment ... all these calculations.'

'Oh,' she smiles, 'I remember those ... hated them ... but if you need any help ... I'm not that long out of school, plus we did some as part of our nursing degree. Or did we? ... actually I can't remember. We did do some chemistry.'

'Thank you,' I say, standing up, looking about when I hear a bird sing. A baby bird singing for its mother's wings?

'You look sad,' says Shanti.

'Nah,' I smile, 'see you later,' walking away with my plate and glass.

I have this fleeting ... psychopathic thought ... of chucking my glass and plate at that baby bird. Stop the chirp.

September 15

'Look Talia,' says Doctor Adelaide, 'you have been doing really well ... eating, gaining weight. And I'm aware you need to return to school ... we all want you to pass your exams. It's so important ... so important for your future.'

I nod.

'The nursing team and I have met this morning,' she sighs, 'we all want you to return to school. But there are some concerns.'

I nod.

'The nursing staff,' she half smiles, 'say that you are extremely quiet. Interact very little with them or other patients.'

'I just want to do my school work,' I say, breathing heavily.

'The night staff,' she says, straightening her white collar, 'they say you are often awake at night. You scream out on occasion. You sleep with the light on.'

I nod.

'I haven't as yet prescribed an antidepressant,' she says, looking at my file, 'I'm ... thinking perhaps it would help.'

'I'm not depressed,' I say.

'Your father recently passed,' she says.

'Yeah,' I frown, 'I hardly knew him ... I didn't know him.'

'That can be a huge loss,' she says, leaning forward in her chair.

'Why?' shaking my head.

'You'll never have the opportunity to get to know him.'

'Yeah well ... that suits me. I don't need an antidepressant,' I say, standing up, 'and I'll make more effort to converse, come out my room.'

Now she nods.

'I need to go to school, please.'

She nods again. 'I'm a little concerned but ... Monday ... all going well ... Monday.'

September 16

Two thirty am … I'm a skeleton in a coffin, emerald blue, a big white collar, yellow apron, skeletal little feet … lying on silky white. It's cold. I'm hot and sweaty.

The coffin is being lowered into the ground … down … down.

Down.

I smell beer.

September 17

I've been out of my room, attended the morning meeting. Ate breakfast with some girl … Sarah. Black, black hair, plump, pretty face. She showed me all these cuts up her wrists … like railway tracks. The inside of her ankles too. To tell you the truth I thought they looked disgusting. I said, 'Why do you do it?'

She's like, 'Why don't you eat?'

I shrug.

'Release,' she says, rubbing the scars on her left wrist.

I nod.

'And you … why don't you eat?' she asks, sipping her coffee.

'I am,' I say, biting my toast.

'But you didn't,' she says. And I'm not sure I like Sarah … railway tracks up her arms … up the inside of her legs. I even

heard that some girls like her put blades in their vaginas …
I mean … no wonder I want to stay in my room.

'Don't know,' I say.

'Just don't want to be fat?' she says, twirling a strand of her
black hair.

'I guess,' I say.

'What was your name?' she says, standing up with her plate
and cup.

'Talia.'

She nods. Walks away … towards the kitchen. I wonder
what it's like to walk with a blade between your legs.

Fuck!

September 18

So what if I'm in hospital … a mental one … I can still go
to school right. No doubt every fucka's gonna be looking at
me … there's Talia … she's mental. But there's always the
library. My friend.

And I'm sure Mr beautiful Reiding will be pleased to see
me.

A nurse will drop me off in the morning. Grant is going to
pick me up and then go back to work. I've been thinking
Mum is very lucky to have him. He is a kind man bear.

Doctor Adelaide thinks it's just too early for me to be discharged. That I need support to get back to a healthier weight. She's probably right.

September 20

So I was stared at ... muttered about. But I was right, Mr beautiful Reiding, he smiled. Praised my recent assignment. 'Excellent,' he said.

He put his hand on my shoulder, looked down at me, smiled, 'I'm glad you're back. Glad you get to finish school.'

I nod.

Chrissy and Stacey made a visit to the library. 'We was worried about you,' says Chrissy, wrapping her arms around me, 'Mum was right, you were too skinny.'

I nod.

'Have a lolly,' says Stacey, 'milk-bottles.'

I remember eating one of those once.

A long time ago.

I look in the white paper bag and take one.

I put it my mouth. Chew. Breathe. Chew. Swallow.

Diary ... it was yum.

September 21

I don't care who's staring at me or talking about me ... I'm gonna pass my exams. Leave school. Move on with my life. This time I'm gonna stay well.

Eat.

September 23

I've just come from seeing Doctor Adelaide. 'We've been talking and we think it might be best that Grace, your therapist sees you. It's not usual policy ... for psychotherapy while on the ward. But ... there's some concern about your sleep and quiet behavior.'

Still? Fuck's sake I've been trying to interact more. Concluding that Sarah is a complete and utter nutcase ... she has cuts even on her upper arms. When she's at home she uses clips or Steri Strips to pull the cuts back together. I mean slice and cut your own flesh then put it back together again. What the fuck!?

This is who they want me to interact with.

'So,' says Doctor Adelaide, 'I've spoken to Grace and she can come in tomorrow ... she'll be here at four pm ... just time enough for you to have afternoon tea after school.'

I nod. Oh gee thanks ... fucken marvellous!

September 24

I almost asked Julie if I could see Doctor Adelaide this morning ... wanted to discuss the issue of Grace's qualifications as a Psychotherapist. I mean to say ... she's extremely thin, has dreadlocks, does she smoke pot? ... and well ... just not sure she knows what she's on about.

But I didn't, now it's too late ... Julie is about to drive me to school. My uniform is getting so tight ... but that's good ... actually great ... least that's what I keep telling myself. Yay! ... I'm getting fat.

Till then ... or whenever ... hope Grace's car breaks down.

September 26

Three thirty am ... the Asian crocodile nurse ... and she does have big teeth ... and red lipstick. You'd think she wouldn't bother with lipstick on nightshift. Perhaps she fancies the other nurse on duty. Or the on call psychiatrist. Anyhow ... actually it's funny she was wearing green. Bottle green. Not exactly crocodile but close. Near enough.

So ... the Asian crocodile nurse ... she just gave me some hot milk and a hot water bottle. Not because I'm cold ... because I'm chilled, freezing. If I don't get some sleep soon ... I'll never be allowed to attend school.

So perhaps ... I'll just pull the covers over my head and pretend ... snore when the crocodile enters my room. Sounds like a good plan.

September 27

Two thirty am ... there's another nurse on duty. She's grumpy ... so like a crocodile ... and she's not even Asian. Blond ... blue eyed. Red lipstick ... I think she fancies herself! No hot milk or hot water bottles from her ... just this glare and a, 'Do you want a sleeping tablet? I'll page the on–call.'

September 28

One fifteen am ... diary do you think if I closed my eyes tight enough ... I'd disappear. Float away ... perhaps to heaven. Somewhere.

Only ... what if he's there ... his sunflower seed floating around ... smelling of beer.

September 29

Mum visited after school today, Grant and the boys too.

'You're looking good,' she said.

I almost choked.

'You are,' said Grant, 'really good and healthy.'

I nod, 'thanks.'

'Couple more kilos and you can come home,' smiles Mum. 'We'd like that wouldn't we boys.'

Sol and Mac push their trains about the floor.

I … I look at Mum and wonder where she's gone.

Grant puts his arm across her shoulder, kisses her on the side of her head. Is he proud … proud that she did know how to be kind after all?

'Hopefully,' she smiles, looking at Grant then back towards me, 'you'll be home for the boy's birthday.'

Oh my god … I'd forgotten about that. October thirtieth … I missed it last year … I was so sick.

'You gonna be four soon,' I say, 'wow what big boys.'

Sol looks up, 'Yeah,' he beams. 'We gonna be four.'

'And me too,' says Mac, standing up. 'See how big I am. I'm gonna be five.'

'You are,' I say, 'getting so big.'

'And me,' says Sol. 'I'm bigger too.'

'You're both getting such big boys,' I smile, 'big beautiful boys.'

'We gonna have a party,' beams Mac.

'Yeah,' I say, 'what sort of cake do you want?'

'A five,' says Mac, ''cause I'm five.'

'Four,' says Mum, 'you're gonna be four.'

'Five,' insists Mac.

'Whatever,' mutters Mum.

'I want,' says Sol, 'a train cake.'

'Yesterday it was Batman,' laughs Mum, putting her hand on Grant's knee. Is she on Prozac?

'Wow,' I say, 'how exciting … two birthday boys. And what present do you want?'

'Scooters,' they both say at once, 'and some more trains,' says Sol, holding up his train.

'And,' says Mac, 'you to come home,' climbing on my knee.

I look at him … his little face with big blue eyes … and get tears in mine.

September 30

Since I can't sleep … I've decided to study, which seems perfectly reasonable to me. Not like I'm doing a hundred sit ups or fifty press-ups. But not reasonable to Doctor Adelaide whose like, 'I'd like to prescribe an antidepressant.'

'Nah,' I say, 'I'm not depressed.' Least I don't think so. Give the pills to Sarah … now there's a problem … or two. Actually about one hundred all over her body.

She sighs, 'I understand your resistance … but … Talia it's just a support like a crutch with a broken leg.'

'I'm not broken,' I … I lie.

She sighs again … 'I'm thinking perhaps half a sleeping tablet … Imovane.'

I shake my head, 'Whatever.'

What Doctor Areleen Adelaide doesn't get ... is that I don't want to sleep. So Imovane ... how helpful is that?

October 1

Half a tablet later and I feel like groggy crap. Have this disgusting taste in my mouth. Yuck.

How I'm going to get through school today ... I do not know. Then fuck ... I have delightful Grace. I better get moving ... haven't even had breakfast and you know that takes time ... so much fucken food to consume.

An extra strong coffee ... about to be drunk.

October 2

It's Saturday morning ... being hassled by Kendall to get out of bed and ... I'm late for breakfast. It's actually time for morning tea. Time for a glass of full fat milk, a muesli bar and a piece of fruit. Am I hungry? ... not.

Last night I pretended to swallow my half a tablet. Wish I had.

Wish I had slept through the entire night.

I was a skeleton wearing emerald blue. Big white collar and yellow apron. Little skeletal feet. Lying in a coffin. Emerald blue against silky white. It was cold. I felt hot.

Red roses, deep, deep red ... were falling down on me. Like big drops of blood.

I smell beer.

October 4

I swallowed the entire tablet. Engulfed it like water in a desert.

But I still dreamed.

Diary ... please take me away ... somewhere ... anywhere.

Why aren't the birds singing ... chirping to their Mums? Perhaps they have died in the cold.

October 5

All I can do is work hard ... pass my exams. Isn't that true? Just work. Just study.

Just forget.

October 6

'Would you like weekend leave?' asks Doctor Adelaide.

I shake my head.

'Is that a no?'

I nod.

'I thought you'd want to ... no?'

'No,' I say, 'next weekend, perhaps.'

'Ok,' she nods, biting her thumb and studying me. Least that's how it felt.

'Is that all?' I ask.

She nods. 'You're doing very well, Talia ... I'm ... I'm pleased.'

'Thanks,' I say, scratching my head. I wonder if I could fit in her black suit jacket and if she has a mantelpiece.

October 7

I cannot believe I have exams in a few weeks. I am so glad I wasn't entirely eaten up by anorexia. Perhaps falling down the stairs was a good thing after all ... was God listening? Or Muhammad ... Mother Mary perhaps.

I saw Amanda this morning ... she was sitting with another patient at breakfast. A boy with a twitch in his left shoulder and big wide nervous eyes. Brown. He was wearing a jean jacket that looked like it hadn't been washed in years. I sat down next to Amanda. She nodded and half smiled. 'Hi,' I said.

'Hi, Talia,' said Amanda. 'This is Gordon.'

'Hi,' I said, nodding at Gordon.

The twitch in his shoulder got faster ... he nodded, looked about the room, over his shoulder, down at the floor.

Mumbled something ... looked at his cereal, picked up the spoon. Put it back down again.

'Eat it,' said Amanda, 'it's safe ... I promise.'

His shoulder twitching even faster ... faster still. 'It's poison.'

'No,' smiled Amanda, 'not poison ... not poison,' shaking her head.

'The CIA is trying to kill me,' said Gordon, looking over his shoulder again.

'The CIA isn't here Gordon,' said Amanda, 'eat your breakfast you must be hungry. You haven't eaten since you were admitted yesterday afternoon.'

'Who's the girl?' he said, pointing at me.

'This is Talia,' said Amanda, 'she's a patient here. And look she's eating her breakfast.' Me ... an example ... wow, I am doing well!

'It's all good,' I said, sipping my coffee.

Gordon stands up, spreads his arms like wings and spins around and around. Like a lopsided twitchy spinning top. 'You're all imposters,' he calls out. 'I cast you underground.'

With Gordon the lopsided spinning top still spinning about I turn to Amanda and say, 'I wanted to apologise.'

'For what?' asks Amanda.

'For hitting you with my bag ... last time I was in ... I made your nose bleed,' I said.

'You weren't well,' she smiled.

'Yeah ...' I nod, 'but I was pretty angry too.'

'And you were angry because you felt threatened ... scared ... that's the cause of a lot of anger ... especially in here.' And she smiled with forgiveness ... so kind.

I nodded. Thanks.

We both looked up at Gordon ... still spinning. Amanda stood up. 'Gordon,' she gently said, 'Gordon it's Amanda ... sit back down now.'

And he did. Just like that ... the lopsided spinning top came to a halt and he sat down. Breathless but looking somewhat relieved.

'I've been informed,' said Gordon, 'it's safe to eat toast and the coffee's fine. Has to have three sugars though.'

I laughed to myself ... three sugars aye ... so he's not anorexic after all.

October 8

'So,' says Grace, 'have you been having any more of those dreams.'

I nod.

'Do want to tell me about it ... has anything changed?' she says, leaning forward.

'Umm ... is that a new top?' I ask, 'it's a pretty blue.'

She nods. 'Yes it is ... I love it, it's lovely to wear.'

'Oh and it has tiny little flowers. Pretty. You always look nice,' I say, 'you have lovely loose ... kinda flowing clothes.'

She nods. 'Thank you. Talia ... so how's school going ... you managing to keep up?'

'I am,' I nod. 'Doctor Adelaide said I could have weekend leave but I said no.'

'Why's that?'

'I ... just feel ... like I'm more in control here. I don't want to slip back this time.'

She nods and rubs her chin with her hand, slowly ... back and forth.

'Talia ... remember the only way out is through ... if you really want to stay well ... heal, you need to go through ... but you don't have to do it alone ... we'll do it together. I'm here ... I support you.'

I look about the little room ... wishing it was more like Grace's with crystals and books and plants to look at. It's bare. Two chairs, a side table that Grace puts my glass of water on and that's pretty much it. She brings in a cushion for me to hold; it has a big beautiful yellow and orange butterfly. It's the one I always pick to hold in her room. She brings it in an enormous woven beach bag.

'I don't want to push you, Talia ... tell me if I am ... but see if you can tell me a little more about that dream.'

I sigh. 'The coffin is like the one my father lay in.'

'What colour?' she asks.

'It's white … I'm lying on the white,' I say, placing my hands in prayer position at my lips. 'Silky white.'

'And you're still wearing a Snow White dress?' she asks.

I nod.

'Tell me about it again … what colour was it?'

'Blue,' I sigh, nodding, 'emerald blue. It has a big white collar and yellow apron. Puffy sleeves.'

'And do you like it … the Snow White dress?'

'No,' I say, shaking my head, 'I hate it.'

'You hate the Snow White dress … what is it, that you hate about it?'

'I just have this feeling … this desperate need to disappear out of it. It's ripped. Torn.'

'So you don't like that it's ripped or torn?'

I shake my head; breathe heavily, 'I just hate it.'

'Can you remember if you ever liked it?'

'I … I think so. Hard to remember but I think so.'

She softly smiles, 'So … in the dream you're a skeleton, wearing a Snow White dress that you hate and want to disappear out of. What else is happening, Talia?'

'Roses,' I mutter, 'red, deep, deep red … they're falling down on me and as they fall they change into blood. And it's … the white … I'm lying in blood.'

Grace nods and says, 'You look really sad, Talia … what's happening for you.'

'I don't know … I don't feel so good.'

'Have some water, Talia … feel your feet on the ground.'

I sip from my glass … look up and say, 'He raped me. I was wearing my Snow White dress.'

Emerald blue, big white collar, yellow apron … against the brown of the living room couch. Tiny little feet.

October 10

Tiny little feet.

Not skeletal. Just tiny.

Just small.

Grace said she has to inform my psychiatrist … but everyone will respect that I don't want or need to discuss anything with anyone.

'And Mum, she doesn't have to know?'

'No,' she says. 'You're eighteen … nearly nineteen, she doesn't need to know.'

I nod, wipe my eyes. Try to remember to breathe.

'Talia, I'll come back on Tuesday, earlier … I think you might need some support.'

I nod.

I weep.

I nod.

October 11

So it turns out I wasn't raped on the living room couch at all … my Snow White dress torn apart like the inside of my tiny vagina. The blood … the deep, deep red … must have been tomato sauce between my legs. Staining the brown living room couch.

Dictionary Definition … rape … 1 forcible sexual intercourse with woman without her freely given consent: violent assault or interference.

2 commit rape on person (woman).

I've searched the dictionary from front to back and back to front for a word that describes forcible intercourse with a child.

Couldn't find one.

I'm relieved … so glad it wasn't rape after all.

October 12

I know Grace said something about feelings pass … but if I felt any more pain … I honestly think I'd rip apart like my little vagina. I'd break up … and I don't think all the king's horses and all the king's men could put me back together again.

October 13

I cried on the floor of my bedroom today while Grace sat opposite me not saying a word. "Please put me back together again," I wanted to say. But I didn't know how to talk.

"Please fix my vagina … it's bleeding … I don't feel so good."

October 14

'Can I have the whole tablet,' I say, 'please? I need to sleep.'

And Jenny the Asian night nurse looks at me with kind slitty brown eyes and I begin to weep.

'I'm tired,' I cry, rubbing my nose, 'please.'

'You're only charted half sweetie,' she says.

'Half's not enough,' I say. 'I just want … please.'

She nods and holds my shaking hand. 'I'll sit by you,' she says. 'I stay until you fall asleep.'

'Ok,' I nod, climbing back into bed ... burying my head under the covers.

'I'm scared,' I mutter.

'I know,' she says. 'I know.'

October 15

Julie sat in my room today and ate lunch with me ... I am eating diary ... I am.

She said, 'Are you feeling a little better now Doctor Adelaide has increased your Lorazepam?'

I nod.

'Just ... I know you didn't want to take it,' she says, leaning her head to one side, 'but it's just for a little while ... take the edge off all those hard feelings you're going through.'

I nod. Chew. Swallow my food.

'It's a beautiful day out,' she says, rubbing her big belly.

I pull back the blind and look outside at the blue sky. Sun shining. I nod.

'Maybe you'd like to go for a little walk in the sun later?' she asks. 'I could waddle alongside.'

And the word waddle ... it reminds me of hippo girl and I burst into tears.

'Sorry,' I murmur, 'sorry.'

I hang my head like the hippo girl and cry.

October 16

Last night I dreamed I was the hippo girl, bedraggled and wet. Wearing emerald blue. Big white collar. Yellow apron. Puffy sleeves. Enormous fat feet. Lying in the coffin of my dead father.

Only I lay on top.

Smothering him.

October 17

Mum and Grant brought the boys in to see me … I didn't want to see them. Not Mum, not Grant, not Sol or Mac. But I made myself venture out … Grant … he wrestled with the boys on the floor, play-fighting like cubs. Bear cubs.

Mum … she sat opposite me smiling at the boys … the bear cubs. And her man bear.

I tried my best to relax … kept having images of throwing myself out the window. Unfortunately we are only one story high.

I wonder … did she know? How did my father explain the blood on the couch?

I hear a bird sing … chirp and I feel so lost and alone … I say, 'Excuse me … I need to go to the toilet.'

So I sit on the toilet ... pee and pee ... wish I had drank so much more.

When I go back to the visitor's lounge, Mac is sitting on Mum's knee listening to a story. Sol and Grant ... still wrestling on the floor.

I look at the window ... hear the birds sing ... chirp chirp tweet tweet ... why doesn't my mother love me?

Where are her wings?

October 19

Dearest Diary ... thank you for loving me ... for accepting me with all my nasty flaws. You have never cared whether I am fat or slim or ... have short hair or long. You know that at times I have psychopathic tendencies ... am cruel and unkind. And you accept me ... you listen and don't judge. You are the very best of friend.

I love you.

Thanks.

October 20

I really and truly thought I could end my life. Join Gloria ... singing with the angels. But I ... I ... just can't.

I feel so lost and I don't know how to find my way out. But Grace keeps saying, 'The only way out is through.' She promises me, things will get better. So ... I'm holding on ... holding on to hope ... hoping that it will meet me more than halfway. I remember Julie saying, 'Hold on to hope and it will hold on to you.'

So I'm holding diary ... please help me ... don't let my hands slip.

October 21

So I went to school today. We only have a few more days left ... then it's study leave. Exams in twelve days. How I'm going to get through, I do not know. But I will try. I will.

Doctor Adelaide said I can get compensation because I'm unwell. But I'm not sick ... and I'm 46.9 kilos ... hardly anorexic thin.

Mr lovely Reiding put his hand on my shoulder. I looked at his hand, his wedding band ... up at him. He smiled. I nodded ... smiled back. 'You'll do well,' he said, touching his beard, 'I know you will.'

'Thanks,' I nod.

'Any more thoughts on university ... journalism perhaps?'

'I've put my applications in ... see what happens.'

He nods. 'You will do well,' he says again.

I nod, say nothing ... wish I could give him a hug.

Chrissy and Stacey sat with me on the grass outside the cafeteria. I'm so tired of hiding.

They as usual made me laugh … Stacey saying, 'Jona asked me to marry him. Down on one knee.'

'For real,' I laugh.

'Yeah,' she grins, 'not making it up.'

'But one day aye,' I say, ''cause you're what sixteen?'

Stacey nods. 'Jona's seventeen.'

'You gonna marry one day?' says Chrissy.

'Who knows … but I'm not really sure I believe in marriage.'

'Oh why?' gasps Chrissy.

I shrug. 'I think … maybe I believe in love … but … why do you have to marry someone?' Sign away your name.

'You get to wear a big dress,' says Chrissy, 'and look like a princess.'

I laugh.

Maybe that's it … I don't want to look like a princess … Snow White.

October 22

Four am … I smell beer.

October 23

Julie drove me to school today. 'You know it's my last day ... don't you?' she said.

I nod, looking at her enormous belly. Big breasts.

'So I might not be here when you get back from school.'

I nod.

'How you doing Talia?'

'Actually ... good ... kind of ... I've enjoyed going to school ... getting out my room.'

'That's great,' she nods, pulling into the entrance of the school. 'Oh look at those blossoms ... how lovely ... I love blossoms don't you?'

I nod, gazing at the row of blossom trees by the school gates. 'Yeah ... pretty pink.'

'Oh they are beautiful,' smiles Julie, 'and just think Talia ... not long ago those trees were brown and sparse.'

I nod, pulling out a card from my bag. Put the white envelope on Julie's lap. Open the car door.

'I'll see you,' I say.

She smiles. Nods. Picks up the white envelope.

'Open it later,' I say, climbing out the door. 'Thanks ... I'll ... thanks.' I'll miss you.

I walk away … turn back to see her waving … was it just me … or did she look sad?

I did.

October 24

Doctor Adelaide had asked me if I had wanted overnight leave. I was like, 'Not really … I'll just hang here if that's ok.'

She nods. 'I'm going to look at reducing your Lorazepam. How do you feel about that?'

'Good,' I say. I think.

She nods. Writes something down. 'It's probably good then that you're here. See how you manage on less medication.'

I nod. Aware that the ward is full … lots of sick adolescents. Sarah's been discharged … long gone and I must be the heaviest anorexic to still in hospital. 'Maybe … I … you could look at discharge … this coming week.'

She smiles, bites her thumb. 'That's why I was suggesting overnight leave. I'm aware you are still often awake at night … still bad dreams?'

I nod. 'Sometimes.'

'It will get better,' nods Doctor Adelaide. So she's a doctor … a psychiatrist … so she should know. I hope.

I hope.

October 25

Last night I dreamed I was the elderly man being pushed in a wheelchair looking at the hospice gardens. Pretty pink blossoms were everywhere. So pretty. So pink. Those branches were brown and sparse once.

My body was tired … dying but I smelt and saw and heard and felt in my heart the beauty of the cherry blossoms. I was an elderly man … dying … weeping with joy.

What was truly beautiful … even more beautiful than the cherry blossoms was the frail elderly man … living until he died.

I woke up with tears in my eyes.

October 26

Last day of school. Everything feels like it's changing … shedding leaves. I so hope … blossoms begin to flower real soon. Little buds … that open up to pink and white beauty.

I so hope … that I open up to pink and white beauty. That I become truly beautiful like the frail dying elderly man. Crochet blanket on his lap; pink and white and blue and yellow and orange and red and purple and … Like Mr Reiding … tired lined eyes, smiling, tugging at his beard, 'Excellent work Talia, excellent.'

Or Julie, breasts like melons, full figured … full of kindness. Kind words. And how beautiful was Eva; big assed, black, white teeth and Jewish … her don't give a fuck attitude. That was gorgeous. I so want to be more like that.

I have met so many kind and gentle people that perhaps don't look like the women or the men in magazines. They certainly aren't all thin ... perfect ... groomed. But they are kind and have helped me ... helped me to help myself and that diary ... that I have begun to understand is true beauty.

Beautiful.

And I am grateful.

Still lost ... scared ... full of hate and rage ... still don't know how to get my dead father off my tiny little body or out of my tiny little vagina ... I don't. Perhaps hippo girl got it right by becoming bigger than him ... smothering the fucka.

Fat fat hippo girl; I wish I knew her name ... bedraggled and wet ... she was so kind on the bus that day. Beauty queen ... yes.

Becoming so small I disappear ... that doesn't work ... two hospital admissions later ... I get that.

Diary ... I am scared. Scared of sitting my exams in six days. Scared I'll fail. Scared of never being good enough ... never being truly loved. Scared of going home ... hearing those chirping cold birds. Tweet tweet. Afraid. At least Maggie and Anna will be home in less than a week. I'll have them to hang out with. And Grace, white dreadlocks, colorful woven headband ... she'll be there ... listening ... lovely ... graceful ... listening to me weep.

You know ... I love you my dearest friend. But ... with only two pages left in this journal ... I want to sign off. I want to shed my anorexic past ... like leaves ... want to blossom ... pink and white ... want to find that beautiful me.

October 27

beautiful

it was
the ochre leaf that fell
soon to unfold the cherry blossom smell
you ... I ... I traced the dying leaf against my face
woven silk and delicate lace
leaves shed brown weeping bark
bloom pink and white blossoms
bloom away dark

I love you. Wish me luck.

Bibliography

Burchfield, Robert. *The New Zealand Pocket Oxford Dictionary*. Auckland: Oxford University Press, 1994.

Costin, Carolyn. Grabb Schbert, Gwen. *Keys to Recovering from an Eating Disorder*. New York: W.W. Norton & Company, 2012.

Shapiro, Deb. *Your Body Speaks Your Mind*. Canada: Sounds True, Inc, 2006.

Acknowledgements

Thank you to Mr Reid, my English teacher for many years at Mana College, your praise and positive comments have stayed with me always. You were my Mr Reiding.

And thank you to my guiding lights ... Lesley, Dianne, Anita and Verona.